"So what do you think, Warren?"

Sara glared at him. "Are you afraid that I'm going to go around seducing every man who crosses my path from now on?"

"I think you're a beautiful, sexy woman who's just learned what sex feels like. I'm real sure you're going to want that feeling again," he told Sara quietly. "And I think you're obviously so innocent about the ways of the world, even though you're thirty-four years old, that you need to be warned to be careful."

Sara watched him, searching for some kind of response as he turned the door handle and started outside. Again, he paused and looked back at her.

"Sara? Don't go back to him, even if he begs you. Find yourself a better man. Find someone who can love you properly, and hold on to him."

Then he was gone. Sara moved over to the window and drew the curtains aside a few inches to watch as he strode across the motel square toward the parking lot.

"I don't want another man," she whispered at his retreating figure, blinking back hot tears of misery. "I want you. And I don't even know who you are."

Margot Dalton is acknowledged as the author of this work.

Special thanks and acknowledgment to Sutton Press Inc.
for its contribution to the concept for the Crystal Creek series.

ISBN 0-373-82525-0

MUSTANG HEART

Margot Dalton

MUSTANG HEART

Harlequin Books

TORONTO • NEW YORK • LONDON
AMSTERDAM • PARIS • SYDNEY • HAMBURG
STOCKHOLM • ATHENS • TOKYO • MILAN
MADRID • WARSAW • BUDAPEST • AUCKLAND

Dear Reader,

Here's what the critics have had to say about some of the Crystal Creek books so far...

DEEP IN THE HEART by Barbara Kaye
"Harlequin's new special series called Crystal Creek wonderfully evokes the hot days and steamy nights of a small Texas community... impossible to put down until the last page is turned." —*Romantic Times*

COWBOYS AND CABERNET by Margot Dalton
"You'll never know what will happen next, and the combination of romance and suspense is a real winner...." —*Affaire de Coeur*

THE THUNDER ROLLS by Bethany Campbell
"... Campbell, one of the instigators of this fine series, takes the reader into the minds of her characters so surely... one of the best so far... it will be hard to top...." —*Rendezvous*

With reviews like these, the writing was on the wall! Our readers were thirsting for more Crystal Creek stories, and we're delighted our romance with Crystal Creek continues! Margot Dalton and Bethany Campbell will be contributing several more books to the series, and they'll be joined by Barbara Kaye, Penny Richards and Sandy Steen, who've already planned lots of surprises for you—including a touching and funny glimpse at J.T. McKinney's first marriage, the scandal-packed past of the Reverend and Mrs. Blake, and some insights into the life and times of the irrepressible Hank Travis.

In *Mustang Heart*, you'll be moved and astounded at the remarkable way in which Sara Gibson, Bubba's little princess, turns her life around. And the uncompromising stranger who initiates this change? A man we've not yet met, but one we all know well....

And next month, in Penny Richards's *Passionate Kisses*, Cynthia learns more than she thought possible about the legendary Pauline McKinney, J.T.'s first wife. So stick around in Crystal Creek—home of sultry Texas drawls, smooth Texas charm and tall, sexy Texans!

Marsha Zinberg
Coordinator, Crystal Creek

A Note from the Author

I've always been interested in the way our lives are shaped by the things that have happened to us. That's why I found the main characters in this book so fascinating. There's Sara, who's left behind an unhappy marriage, but is afraid to start over again on her own. Warren has been so badly scarred by events in his youth that he can't seem to leave them behind, no matter how he tries. And Sara's father, Bubba Gibson, wants to forget the past, but is afraid that others won't allow him to. When these three people came together in my mind, the result was instant magic. Not only was I fully absorbed in the story, I was caught up all over again in the enchantment of Crystal Creek—the second time around!

Margot Dalton

Who's Who in Crystal Creek

Have you missed the story of one of your favorite Crystal Creek characters? Here's a quick guide to help you easily locate the titles and story lines:

Available at your local bookseller, or see the Crystal Creek back-page ad for reorder information.

CHAPTER ONE

SARA STIRRED and opened her eyes, feeling the heavy, queasy sensation that often follows daytime sleep, especially in a moving vehicle. She blinked and shifted on the hot vinyl seat, gazing blankly out at the scenery that flashed past the big side windows of the bus.

Suddenly alert, she sat up and looked more closely.

There was a sweet familiarity about the landscape, the character of the green, rolling hills and the gentleness of the light, the gnarled masses of scrub oak and mesquite. Wildflowers starred the ditches and the open fields, a wondrous array of bluebonnets and primroses, of buttercups and poppies and Indian paintbrush.

Unexpectedly, Sara felt tears gather in her eyes and begin to trickle slowly down her cheeks. She dashed a hand at her face and gripped her handbag, comforted by the feeling of the worn leather and the knowledge of the document that it carried.

She was briefly tempted to open the bag and peek inside again, but there was no need. She knew every word by heart.

"This court doth decree and adjudge that the Petitioner, Sara Elizabeth Milne, whose marriage to the

Respondent, Steven Conrad Milne, was solemnized at Hartford, Connecticut, on the 13th day of September, 1980, be divorced from the Respondent...."

Beside her, David wriggled and muttered in his sleep, moving heavily against his mother and crowding her toward the window. His small, grimy hands cradled a shoe box on his lap, but he was sleeping deeply enough that his grip had loosened, and the cardboard carton was threatening to slip to the floor. Sara took the box gently from his hands and bent to stow it under the seat in front of them, careful not to wake her son.

As she leaned past him, her cheek brushed his silky fair head. She felt a quick flood of love that left her weak with tenderness.

How much easier, she thought, looking with gentle irony at his small freckled face, to love a seven-year-old when he was asleep.

Sara glanced over at Laurie, who sat alone in the seat opposite her mother and brother. She was gazing stolidly out the window, showing no emotion. Sara studied her daughter's profile, a little startled, as she often was these days, by Laurie's new maturity.

The girl had her mother's curly auburn hair, though Sara's was cut short in a boyish tumble, while Laurie's was shoulder length and neatly groomed. She also had Sara's dark, hazel eyes and delicate bone structure, her slim, agile body and the same dusting of freckles on her dainty nose that had caused her mother such anguish in her early teen years.

But there was something about Laurie that was different from Sara, a kind of coolness and precision that her mother lacked. Sara's life was usually in a jumble, no matter how hard she tried to keep things neatly organized. Confusion and disorder tended to creep in, and a penchant for bizarre happenings that, in better times, used to make her laugh at the delightful absurdity of life. *Not anymore,* Sara thought sadly, still gazing at Laurie's averted profile. *My life is a complete mess and I feel as if I haven't laughed for a hundred years. And I'm so tired. So terribly, awfully tired...*

Laurie had to be just as exhausted as the rest of them. Still, the girl looked fresh and alert as she gazed calmly out the window, measuring the landscape with detachment. She was only eleven, but Sara sometimes felt that her daughter was the older of the two of them. It must be something Laurie had inherited from Steven, this cool self-assurance, this ability to deal with any situation as it came along without getting all hot and bothered.

Laurie turned to meet her mother's gaze. "We're almost there," she announced. "The last sign said fourteen miles to Crystal Creek."

Sara's stomach churned with sudden excitement. "Fourteen miles!" she echoed. "Oh, my goodness. David, wake up, sweetie. We're almost there. Look, that's the old Mueller place! Grandma said they were tearing the house down and building a new one. And look, see that bridge over the river? That's exactly the place where your grandpa..."

But David was still sleeping, frowning and muttering to himself as his mother moved beside him. And Laurie had returned to private contemplation of the landscape. Sara was alone with her flood of thoughts and memories, with the bittersweet joy of coming home to Texas after fifteen long years in the North.

DROOPING with fatigue, Sara stood in line, waiting to retrieve their luggage from the big rack next to the bus. She was laden with shoulder bags and carryons, boxes and toys and children's knapsacks, and she was so weary that she could hardly keep her eyes open. She kept having brief, hallucinatory flashes of hot baths, of quiet rooms and deep utter stillness....

Oh, God, please help me, Sara thought desperately. *I truly don't think I'm going to make it. I wish I'd told Mama earlier when we were coming so she could have been here to meet us. I wish I still had the car. Damn you, Steven. I wish just once in your life you could have been a tiny bit decent about something....*

"Mom!" Laurie hissed, interrupting her gloomy thoughts. "I have to *go!*"

Sara pulled herself back to reality with an effort, shifted one of the rucksacks higher on her shoulder and gazed blearily at her daughter's outraged face. "What's the matter, dear? Is it locked?"

"No, but it's *gross!*" Laurie muttered. "I can't go in there, Mom. It's awful."

Sara looked down at the girl, feeling helpless. "Laurie, I don't..."

"Mom!" David shouted, stiffening and tugging with frantic urgency at his mother's hand. "Mom, Flipper's still on the bus!"

Simultaneously, Sara remembered stowing the cardboard box under the seat, and saw a dull flash of silver as the big vehicle pulled slowly away from the unloading zone, heading back out into the street.

"Mom!" David screamed in anguish.

A man in front of them at the luggage rack was examining a big wooden carton covered with packing stickers. He turned around, clearly startled by the uproar. Sara had a confused impression of a dark, unsmiling face, a tousled head of black hair heavily frosted with gray at the temples, a soiled denim shirt and jeans and a battered leather jacket.

"It's his turtle," she said in apology as David continued to shout beside her. She tried to smile, though her mouth was trembling and she felt dangerously close to tears. "I guess I...I shoved it under the seat and forgot it."

The child's freckled face was now scarlet with outrage, his eyes squeezed shut as he bellowed.

Sara shifted uneasily on her feet and looked down at her son with a familiar combination of exasperation and sympathy. Considering his age, David had really been quite well behaved for most of this dreadful, interminable journey. And it was so hard for him, she thought with an aching heart. How could a little boy be expected to understand that his mother and father didn't love each other anymore, that because they didn't want to live together, he had to be uprooted, turtle and all, and moved halfway across the country?

Guilt washed over her, and a wave of sadness so deep and dark that it threatened to drown her where she stood. She bent swiftly and gathered the little boy tightly in her arms.

"Flipper will be okay, David," she whispered, lying shamelessly. "The bus driver will find him and take him home, and he'll live out in their nice backyard and catch flies and..."

"I want Flipper!" David sobbed, rolling his head against her shoulder, smearing her jacket messily with his tears.

Sara patted his back and stood up, watching in miserable silence as Laurie marched toward the door of the women's washroom with a fastidious look of desperation.

"Look, lady!" A woman's voice came harshly over her shoulder. "Are you fixin' to get your luggage, or not? Some of us don't have all day, you know."

Sara gulped and swayed on her feet, gazing helplessly at the mass of impatient faces behind her.

Maybe it wouldn't be such a bad idea to drown in that wave of misery. Maybe I should just let go, faint dead away and fall down, down, into a soft dark sea of weariness. Then somebody else would have to take charge and look after things for a while, and I could have a rest.... Just drift and rest and do nothing at all, ever again....

"Here's the turtle." She heard an expressionless voice at her elbow. "Now, which bags are yours, ma'am?" Sara stared, openmouthed, at the disreputable-looking man in the leather jacket, who held the shoe box in his brown, callused hands.

David reached for the box, brushing furtively at his tears as he did so and assuming an expression of manly nonchalance. "Thanks," he said to the dark-haired man with gruff casualness.

"Your bags?" the man repeated patiently to Sara, then paused to glare at the indignant woman behind them, who was now muttering to her companions.

"The...the black ones with the red straps," Sara murmured, feeling dazed. "How did you manage to stop the bus?"

"He wasn't leaving yet." Their rescuer heaved the luggage off the rack and stashed it neatly by the door. "He was just going over to fill up with gas. I flagged him down in the alley."

"Oh." Sara followed David and the man back into the terminal, still feeling confused and disoriented. "That was...that was very nice of you."

But the stranger ignored her, and squatted on one knee to peer inside the box as David lifted the lid.

"He's okay," David announced with a shining smile, looking up at his mother.

Sara smiled back at him and ruffled his hair.

"His name's Flipper," David told the silent man in the leather jacket.

"Why?" the man asked.

"Because he flips over onto his back sometimes and then he has to try real hard to get back on his feet. It's funny."

"What makes him flip over?" the man asked, looking intently at the small boy.

David shifted nervously. "Sometimes he falls off the rock onto his back," he said. "But," he added, compelled to honesty, "most of the time I do it."

The man grinned suddenly, a startling, unexpected smile that lit up his hard features like the sun beaming through clouds. Sara glanced at him in surprise, but the smile vanished so quickly that she was left wondering if she'd imagined that rare glimpse of warmth.

"Is somebody meeting you?" he asked, getting to his feet and looking at Sara with detached courtesy.

She nodded. "My mother's coming to get us."

"Yeah, like in another *hour,*" Laurie muttered bitterly, startling Sara, who hadn't known the girl was behind them. "Mom called her when we got off the bus but she has to wait for the guy who looks after the horses. One of them's *sick,*" she added, rolling her eyes.

"You're planning to wait here for a whole hour?" the stranger asked, glancing around at the shabby terminal with its single bank of molded vinyl chairs.

Sara flushed, stung by his tone and the general implication that she was handling things badly. "Of course not," she said with dignity. "We're going down to the Longhorn Coffee Shop for something to eat, and she'll meet us there."

He cocked an inquiring eyebrow at their small mountain of luggage. "Y'all must be a whole lot stronger than you look," he observed dryly, "if you're planning to lug all that stuff over to the Longhorn."

Sara glared at him wearily, forgetting his recent helpfulness in the matter of the turtle.

"We can manage," she said, bending to lift the largest duffel bag.

Again the man ignored her. He took the bag from Sara and hoisted it effortlessly to his shoulder, then picked up the pullman case in one hand and a couple of duffel bags in the other.

"You kids take the rest of this stuff," he told Laurie and David. "Your mother can carry the turtle."

To Sara's surprise, the children obeyed him without question, hurrying to pick up their knapsacks and suitcases and hauling them out the door behind his tall, erect form. She brought up the rear, carrying the shoe box and feeling foolish. Still, she was tired enough to appreciate the fact that somebody was helping, no matter how brusque he seemed.

"Look," she murmured, falling into step next to the man as he stood aside to let the children walk in front, "this is very nice of you. My name is Sara Gibson," she added, feeling a little unexpected thrill as she reclaimed her maiden name for the first time here in the town where she'd spent her childhood. "And this is Laurie, and David."

"Hi, Laurie. Hi David," the man said, his hard features lightening briefly as he addressed the children. "You kids ever been to Texas before?"

"We were here just last summer," Laurie said. "My grandparents live here."

"They have a ranch," David announced. "We came all the way from Connecticut," he added proudly, "in five days."

"On the bus?" the man asked in disbelief.

David shook his head and paused to shift the knapsack to his other hand. "The first four days we had our car," he said. "All the way to Tulsa. But then Mom had to leave the car in Tulsa with my other grandma because my dad wouldn't let her keep it anymore, and then we had to ride the last part on the bus. My dad said—"

"Shut up, stupid," Laurie muttered, giving her brother a little shove. "You don't have to tell everybody *everything.*"

Sara felt a flicker of gratitude for her daughter's loyalty, and a surge of uneasiness at the amount of detail this hard-faced stranger was learning about them. She noticed, through a vague fog of weariness, that he was asking questions, but volunteering no information at all about himself. He hadn't even given his name when she introduced her family.

David glared at his sister. "My dad said my mom couldn't keep the car because he already had to give her too much money," he continued importantly. "They just got divorced," he added. "But my dad's been living with his girlfriend for—"

"Look, David," Sara interrupted, feeling a growing desperation. "This is the town square. It's hardly changed at all since I was a little girl."

David squinted into the broad leafy square, briefly distracted from his preoccupation with family matters. "What's that big stone thing?"

"It's a memorial," Sara said. "It's for all the men from the county who died in the two world wars."

"Why does it look so weird? What are all those marks and stuff on it?"

Sara frowned at the big memorial as they passed. "That was a terrible thing," she said. "A long time ago, when I was just about Laurie's age, one of the local boys vandalized the memorial. He came out here one night and shot at it with a rifle, chipped it and damaged it really badly."

David paused, fascinated, and gazed up at the granite structure. "How did they fix the holes?"

"I don't know," Sara said helplessly, shifting the shoe box to her other arm and lifting the lid to check on Flipper's welfare. The small painted turtle glared up at her balefully from within his nest of damp grass. "I guess they dug out the bullets and sanded it down and . . . and filled it with plaster or something, then carved the names over again. I don't know how they did it."

"Did he shoot at the statue thing, too?" David asked, peering up at the tall soldier on the top of the monument.

"I think so. I think the soldier's helmet was damaged, and one of his arms. Yes, see? The left arm's been replaced."

"Cool," David breathed, gazing with shining eyes at the statue, although Sara suspected that he was much more impressed by the destruction than by the restoration part of the story.

"Why did he do it?" Laurie asked, pausing beside her brother to contemplate the damaged statue.

Sara frowned, recalling those long-ago days and the fearful anger of the whole county. "*I* don't know," she said impatiently. "He was just a terrible boy, that's all. He was wild and bad, and he was always doing awful things like that."

"What was his name?"

"Warren Trent," Sara said. "There were two brothers, Vernon and Warren. Their father ran the drugstore. David, don't put that bag down in the dirt. Set it on the grass."

"Did you know him?" Laurie asked, still gazing at the scarred monument with rapt interest.

"Of course I did. He was just a few years older than I was. I hated him, though. All of us did."

"Why?" the children asked in unison.

"Because he did so much damage to our town. He didn't just destroy the monument, he went on a kind of rampage that same night and burned down the gazebo that used to be here in the town square, shot at the courthouse, broke a lot of windows . . . it was just terrible. I don't think anybody's ever forgiven him. Vandalism is a very, very bad thing," she added, with a severe glance at her children. "It hurts the whole community."

"How did he shoot all those bullets without people stopping him?" Laurie asked, clearly skeptical.

"It was during a thunderstorm," Sara said wearily. "It was dark outside, thundering and pouring rain, and nobody knew till morning what he'd done. Let's stop talking about it, all right?"

She exchanged a pleading glance with the stranger, who shouldered his bags and nodded curtly to the children, then moved off down the street again with a lithe, swinging stride.

"Did he go to jail?" David persisted, trotting at the man's heels.

"I think so," Sara said after a moment's thought. "I can't remember exactly, but I know they sent him away somewhere after that night. Warren Trent certainly wasn't in school anymore, and as far as I know he never came back."

"My granddad's in jail," David told the man proudly. "He cheated the insurance company."

"I know," the man said.

"My granddad was—" Laurie punched her brother on the shoulder and he yelled in outrage. "Mom! She hit me for no reason at all! My granddad was—"

"David, look over there," Sara said, trying frantically to distract him.

David squinted in the direction of his mother's outstretched hand. "What? I don't see anything."

"See that..." Sara floundered for a moment, grasping at straws. "See that big circle of shrubbery in the far corner, over by the church?" she said at last.

"Yeah? What about it?"

"Do you know what used to be there?"

David frowned suspiciously, examining the big, rounded area that his mother indicated, a circle about fifty feet in diameter planted with tall shrubs and flowers. Laurie and the dark-haired stranger both paused as well, and they all looked at Sara with curiosity.

"What?" David asked. "What used to be there?"

"A beautiful, wonderful carousel," Sara said, her tired face softening with emotion. "The most wonderful carousel in the world. My grandmother used to tell me about it."

David looked unimpressed. "What's a carousel?"

"It's a merry-go-round, you dummy," Laurie told him scornfully.

David looked at his mother in disbelief. "A *merry-go-round?* What's so great about that?"

"It was such a beautiful one," Sara murmured, hardly aware of the others as she gazed at the neat, planted circle. "It was all hand-carved by a man from Germany, and it had fifty-four horses, all different colors. Their saddles were inlaid with gold and jewels. There was a tiger, too, and a giraffe, and two dragon seats made of Chinese elm, and an organ with more than three hundred pipes."

"Did you get to ride on it?" David asked with somewhat more interest.

"Goodness, no," Sara said. "It was gone long before I was born. The county bought it and set it up on the town square about eighty years ago, when my grandmother was just a little girl. People came from all over Texas to look at the carousel, it was so wonderful. Then, when the Depression came in the 1930s, nobody could afford carousel rides anymore, and they broke it up and sold the horses to collectors from up North. It was... it must have been so sad to lose it," she concluded, flushing with embarrassment as she realized that the shabby man and the two children were staring at her in astonished silence.

Even worse, she was certain that she detected a hint of mocking amusement in the stranger's dark eyes.

Sara squared her shoulders and moved on behind the others toward the restaurant, thinking that her momentary foolishness over the old carousel had at least managed to deflect David from his relentless accounting of family business.

But she reckoned without the persistence of childhood.

"Guess what?" David said to the stranger. "My grandma Gibson doesn't have any money since Grandpa went to jail, so she has to grow ostriches!"

Before the man could reply to this stunning announcement, they reached the door of the Longhorn and trooped inside. Sara sagged with relief as they piled their bags near the door. "You two wait here and look at the menu," she said to the children, who were crowding into a booth, "and I'll just go to the washroom for a minute."

Suddenly she remembered their rescuer and turned to thank him, but he had already strolled to the rear of the coffee shop, where he seated himself with his back to them, studying the menu and accepting a cup of coffee from the waitress.

"Thanks very much for your help," Sara called shyly, as she passed him on her way to the washroom.

He waved a dismissive hand and turned back to his menu.

Sara stood in the washroom, studying her tired face in the mirror, and feeling a dizzying sense of confusion, as if she were a time traveler suddenly transported into the distant past. It seemed that nothing at all had changed inside the Longhorn Coffee Shop since she was a little girl, not even the tablecloths or the napkin holders. She wondered how often she'd stood in this exact spot, gazing into this same chipped mirror. How many times had a younger Sara looked back at her from the mirror with wide, thoughtful eyes? A small timid Sara, sick with excitement over the upcoming horse show, in which she was entered in the Pony Class. A taller, prettier Sara, frowning at a blemish on her cheek and wondering if it was visible to the other teenagers at her table. A dreamy, starry-eyed Sara, preparing to graduate from high school and leave Crystal Creek behind forever, heading off to the wondrous romance and excitement of college in the North...

She smiled sadly, recalling those long-ago days when dreams were in the air and anything was possible. Now her life seemed broken beyond repair, and she felt at least a hundred years old. She shivered and turned away from the pale face and unhappy eyes of the woman in the mirror, washed her hands with abrupt, nervous motions and hurried back out into the restaurant.

When Sara returned to their table, a woman in a waitress uniform was standing and talking with the children. The waitress was slender and delicate, with wavy, brown hair, gentle blue eyes and an air of fragile strength. Sara hesitated, remembering details from her mother's letters.

This was Nora Jones, who had still been a young girl when Sara left Crystal Creek to go to college in Pennsylvania. Sara looked at the woman's quiet face and recalled that Nora Jones, too, had certainly known her share of misfortune over the past few years.

"How are you, Nora?" Sara asked, smiling. "It's nice to see you again."

The younger woman smiled back, her shy face lighting with sudden warmth. "Your mama told us you were coming home. Look at Mary's grandbabies! Aren't they growing up fast?"

"That's for sure. Not babies anymore," Sara added ruefully. "No matter what my mother tells you."

"To their grandmas, they're always babies," Nora said, a look of sadness in her eyes.

"I was really sorry to hear about Dottie," Sara murmured. "She was such a wonderful person."

"She sure was," Nora said quietly. "I'll miss her as long as I live." She paused, and turned to the boy. "Do you play baseball, David?" she asked.

"I *love* baseball," David said with enthusiasm. "I'm really good, too. I was second base on my team last year, but Mom said I couldn't play this year because we had to move away."

"Well, my boy, Rory, is just about your age, remember?"

David nodded.

"And," Nora went on, "I'll bet there's a spot on his team for you, David. Would you like me to check with the coach?"

David's face brightened. He glanced hopefully at his mother. "Can I, Mom?"

Sara looked up from her study of the menu. She hesitated, feeling awkward and embarrassed. "I don't know if that's such a good idea. I mean . . . David, I don't know how long we're going to be staying with your grandma." Then she added, with a cautious glance at Nora," I just thought ... just until I can get things a little better organized ..."

The other woman nodded in understanding. "It's probably a real good idea, staying with your mama for a while," she said. "I think Mary can use the help and company."

Sara smiled at her again, grateful for her tact. "Do you ... Nora, would you happen to know if there are any jobs around here?" she asked.

"For you?" Nora looked at her in surprise. "You've got a college degree, haven't you?"

Sara nodded. "For all the good it's likely to do me. I realize there aren't many people in Crystal Creek looking for somebody with a fine arts degree," she added with a bleak smile. "But that doesn't matter. I'll work at anything, just to earn some money."

"Anything?" Nora asked, hesitating.

"I want to play baseball," David interrupted with a dangerous glint in his eye. "And," he added firmly, "I want a cheeseburger. With a chocolate shake and double fries."

Sara turned to her son. "I don't know if ... David, it's almost three o'clock in the afternoon. Don't you think you should just have a bowl of soup or something, so you don't spoil your supper?"

"But I'm *starved!*" David shouted. "We didn't eat anything on that dumb bus since *morning!*"

Sara and the waitress exchanged an eloquent glance. "I'll do anything," Sara assured her in answer to her earlier question. "Anything at all."

"Well, there's a job out at the Lonely Bull, but it's just waitressing and chambermaid. That's the only thing I know of just now. Maybe over in Wimberley..."

"What's the Lonely Bull?" Sara asked. "I don't remember anything like that in town."

"It's fairly new. Some people from Austin built it maybe five, six years ago. It's kind of a truck stop and motel operation out on the east side of town along the highway."

Sara tried to picture herself waiting on tables and cleaning motel bathrooms. "Thanks, Nora," she said at last.

"I want a grilled cheese sandwich and a salad," Laurie announced, frowning at the menu. "I'm a vegetarian," she added for Nora's benefit, sounding very grown-up.

"Good for you," Nora said mildly. "That sure saves a lot on the grocery bill."

The children departed simultaneously for the washrooms, arguing as they went. Sara looked up at Nora's sympathetic face, thinking about the younger woman's comment regarding the grocery bill, and wondering just how much everybody in the region knew about the Gibson family's problems.

Sara's father had always been such a pillar of the community. Good ol' Bubba Gibson with his booming laugh, his good-hearted wife, clever daughter and big spread of land. But now Bubba was in jail for insurance fraud, and Mary Gibson was reduced to an improbable, ridiculous occupation like raising ostriches, all in an attempt to make ends meet and save the ranch.

"It was good of you to be nice to him," Nora whispered, leaning close to Sara and nodding in the direction of the dark-haired stranger in his soiled shirt and jeans. He still sat quietly at the back of the room, well apart from the noisy crowd of coffee-time regulars, reading a newspaper and eating a bowl of soup. "Most folks around here won't even talk to him," Nora added softly.

"He was at the bus depot," Sara whispered back. "He was really quite nice. He helped us carry our things over here."

"Nice!" Nora murmured. "There's not many who'd agree with you on that. Most of them just hate the man, seems to me. Not that it bothers him much," she added, tucking her order pad into an apron pocket.

"Why?" Sara asked, bewildered. "Who is he, Nora? I don't recognize him at all."

"Don't you? I recognized him the minute I laid eyes on him, even though he's been gone all these years."

Sara looked at the back of the man's graying head, his broad muscular shoulders and the hard outline of his tanned cheek. She felt a distant glimmer of mem-

ory, accompanied by cold prickles of uneasiness up
and down her spine.

"Oh, God," she breathed. "It can't be...."

"It's Warren Trent, big as life," Nora murmured.
"Don't you remember what he did?"

CHAPTER TWO

A COLD, SPRING RAIN began to whisper in the trees as night drew closer, filling the gathering darkness with shadows and streams of gentle silver.

Mary Gibson stood by the window of her bedroom and gazed out at the April evening. The rolling landscape of the ranch was a misty, smoke blue and gray, fading into charcoal in the distance as the sky darkened and the rain fell with greater force. Trees bowed and swayed in the wind while the ostriches huddled within their expensive pens, sheltered and warm as the rainwater flowed across their paddock.

The world seemed expectant somehow, waiting for renewal, for life and hope to blossom again. Mary felt a quick lift of her spirits. She thought about her husband, who would be coming home soon, about the miraculous productivity of the big, ungainly birds down in the paddock, and the bank balance that still teetered on the brink of disaster; but was starting to edge almost imperceptibly in the right direction.

"It's all going to work out, Al," she whispered to her absent husband. "Just a few more weeks and you'll be home, and things will get better."

She smiled faintly, still gazing across the rain-washed landscape into the future. Then, abruptly, she recalled the weary, bickering family she'd fetched home from town that afternoon. *Poor Sara,* Mary thought, drawing her bathrobe tighter around her waist and crossing the room to sit at her dressing table.

She recalled Sara's pale face and trembling hands, her transparent attempts to be cheerful and her insistence that nothing was wrong with her, nothing at all, she was just tired.

With the deep, sure instinct of all mothers, Mary knew that Sara wasn't telling everything. Something terrible had happened to her daughter, something beyond the normal trauma of separation and divorce. *If that kind of pain can ever be considered normal,* Mary thought.

She gazed at her reflection as she rubbed cream into her face, remembering her own pain over the past dreadful year, and wondering if Sara suspected any of the truth about her parents' situation, or if she was too miserable and weary to care.

Mary reached for a tissue, then turned as a timid knock sounded at the door.

"Mama? May I come in?"

"Of course, honey." Mary smiled as Sara peeked inside, then came hesitantly into the room, wearing a pink cartoon-print pullover, navy jogging pants and fleecy pink socks.

She looked more comfortable now, Mary thought, watching with keen, loving eyes as her daughter settled herself cross-legged on the bed and hugged one of the pillows. But she was still limp with fatigue, and so pale that her freckles stood out in sharp relief on her cheeks and the bridge of her nose.

"You know, I'm getting to look more like you all the time," Sara observed, trying to smile as she met her mother's eyes in the mirror.

"Well, I hope that's not too disappointing for you," Mary said dryly, picking up another tissue to remove the rest of the excess cream.

"Of course not. You're just beautiful, Mama. Ever since I was a little girl I always wanted to be just like you."

"Bless you, dear." Mary's voice softened as she turned to smile at her daughter. "Those are sweet words to hear."

Sara's face twisted unexpectedly at her mother's gentleness, but she fought visibly to control herself. "Sorry," she said, choking, and buried her face in the pillow. "I'm just so tired."

"I know you are. You all will feel a whole lot better after a good night's sleep."

"I'm sorry about the kids, too, Mama. They're not usually so cranky and terrible. You must wonder what you've gotten yourself into, letting monsters like us into your house."

"I love you, every one of you. And I know how hard this is on the little ones. We have to be patient with them, dear. It takes them a while to adjust."

"I think it's been hardest on David," Sara said, frowning in concern. "He doesn't say much, you know, about Steven or anything, but sometimes he..."

She was silent a moment, while Mary watched her face in the mirror and waited.

"He sure wasn't quiet this afternoon, though," Sara added with a bleak smile. "You should have heard him, Mama, trying to tell that man every single thing about our family history. I thought Laurie was going to kill him."

"What man? You mean Warren Trent?"

Sara nodded. "It was so embarrassing! We were passing the town square and David kept talking about the divorce and why we'd come here. I tried to distract him by telling him how the memorial got vandalized, you know, about the awful boy who did all this damage, and the man was standing right there the whole time! I practically died of mortification when Nora Jones told me who he was. I still get cold shivers just thinking about it."

"I wouldn't be too concerned," Mary said briskly, turning around on her chair to give her daughter a comforting smile. "Warren Trent must be used to that kind of thing by now. He's got to have pretty thick skin or he'd never have come back here in the first place after twenty years or more."

"Why did he come back?" Sara asked. "I meant to ask you, but I didn't want to talk about him anymore in front of the kids."

"Probably a good idea," Mary said, her smile fading. "David seems too impressed altogether with Mr. Warren Trent. Nobody knows why he's here," she added. "Not even Vern and Carolyn, and Vern's his own brother. He just turned up one day a couple of weeks ago, took a room in a cheap motel and moved in, and he hasn't left."

"What does he do?"

"Well, folks say he's up to no good," Mary said thoughtfully. "You know I've never liked to listen to gossip, but there's sure lots of it floating around these days. He obviously doesn't have two pennies to rub together, but he keeps getting all those shipping boxes coming in on trucks and buses, and he's renting the old barn on the Swanson place, remember? Out there neighboring our property to the west?"

"What for?"

Mary shrugged. "Nobody knows that, either. He boarded up the windows and put locks all over the place. There's not a soul knows what he's doing in there, but he spends most of his time in that old barn and wanders around town all shabby and covered with grease.... It's sure a mystery. Pretty soon they'll have the FBI down here checking him out. Folks are real suspicious about what's in those packing crates."

"Why? Mama, what's he doing in that old barn?"

Mary shrugged. "Like I said, I don't like repeating gossip. Just don't bother your head about what happened this afternoon, sweetie. Warren Trent's used to hearing things like that. There's not a soul in this town who's forgotten all the things he did when he was a boy. It wasn't just the damage to the town square, either. He used to steal and vandalize and scare folks half out of their wits all the time. There's not much of a welcome here for that man, Sara. I sure hope he'll realize it pretty soon and move on before some real trouble starts brewing."

Sara nodded, looking thoughtful and unhappy. "It was so awful," she confessed with a little twisted smile, clearly still brooding about the embarrassment of that incident. "When David gets talking, he's just like a...a fountain or something. I was trying to think of everything I could to distract him. I even told them all about the old carousel."

Mary's face softened as she looked at her daughter. "You always loved the idea of that old carousel, didn't you, honey?"

Sara nodded wistfully. "I loved hearing Grandma talk about it. And old Hank Travis," she added, her tired face brightening as she smiled at her mother. "Hank used to brag about that carousel like it was one of the seven wonders of the world."

"Hank's real poorly these days," Mary said with a faraway look. "We all know he has to go sometime, but it still seems like a part of the town is dying along with him."

"And Dottie," Sara added, hugging her pillow again with a gloomy expression. "The Longhorn's not the same without Dottie. Nothing's the same anymore."

Mary looked at the curve of her daughter's pale cheek, her drooping shoulders and the tumble of auburn curls. "Are you sorry you came home, honey? Do you wish you'd stayed up North with the kids?"

Sara jerked her head up and stared at the other woman, her eyes wide and dark with emotion. "No!" she burst out. "We couldn't stay there! Mama, it was awful...."

She began to cry in earnest, burying her face in the pillow. Mary crossed the room to sit on the bed and gather her daughter's trembling body tightly in her arms.

"There, there," she murmured soothingly, as if Sara were about six years old again. "Don't cry, darling. It's all right. You're home now."

Sara burrowed gratefully into her mother's soft dressing gown, her shoulders shaking and quivering as she fought to control herself. Finally she managed to pull away and groped for a tissue on the bedside stand, coughing and sniffling.

"Sorry," she began, her voice muffled by wads of tissue. "Sorry to be such a baby, Mama. It's just so comforting to be with you. It makes me feel like a little kid again."

"You'll always be my baby," Mary said with such tenderness that Sara showed signs of being inundated once more.

"Tell me about it, Sara-Bear," Mary said gently, unconsciously using Bubba Gibson's old pet name for his daughter. "Tell me what was so awful."

"Oh, Mama..."

Mary leaned back and nestled against the broad, carved headboard, drawing her daughter into her arms and cuddling her warmly. "Was he mean to you?"

Sara shook her head, keeping her face lowered as she plucked at the colorful, stitched design on the patchwork quilt. "It was...it just didn't work out," she mumbled. "We were growing apart, that's all."

Mary nodded and patted her daughter's back with gentle sympathy, but her calm, weathered face was skeptical as she gazed over Sara's bent head at the darkening window.

"We wanted different things out of life," Sara went on. "But it's so... Mama, it's so hard for the kids. And I'm scared."

"Of what?"

"Just of being alone. Having to look after the kids all by myself. I don't know if I can manage a responsibility like that."

Mary gave her daughter a dry little grin. "You know, it's always astounding what we can manage, sweetie, if we're forced to."

"I know," Sara whispered. "I know what you're doing, Mama. And at first I thought it was ridicu-

lous. But now I can see that it isn't. Your plans are just
great. But at least you have some . . . some resources,
and a place to start. I don't have anything at all."

"You have your daddy and me," Mary said calmly.

"I know, but it's not the same." Sara moved restlessly on the bed, turning to gaze at her mother with
bleak, red-rimmed eyes. "I can't stay here and live off
you and Daddy. The ranch is barely surviving as it is,
and you have the hired couple to pay as well. I have to
find some way to earn a living and look after my kids
by myself."

"Sara, you don't have to tell me anything you don't
want, but I'd just like to understand a little better.
Didn't you get anything out of this divorce settlement? Nothing at all, even to tide you over?"

"Four thousand dollars," Sara said bitterly.
"That's all I have in the world, and most of it has to
go for Laurie's braces. And he's supposed to pay four
hundred a month for child support, but he's already
told me he won't do it."

"But you can go to court and make him pay, can't
you?"

Sara shook her head. "Not Steven. See, the whole
problem for me is that he owns this business, the
computer shop he's invested in. That's where all the
family assets are, even the second mortgage on the
house, and Steven managed to convince the judge that
if he had to liquidate those assets it would bankrupt
the business and he wouldn't be able to support the

kids at all. So the judge allowed him to retain the shop."

Mary frowned. "I never did have much of a head for business, Sara," she confessed, "but that sounds real unfair."

"Oh, it gets better," Sara continued sarcastically. "The only liquid cash was six thousand dollars in a savings bond. So Steven really dazzled the judge by agreeing to take just two thousand of that and give me the balance. Four thousand dollars. He didn't bother to point out that I wasn't getting another single thing."

"What about the house?"

"It's mortgaged to the hilt. There's no point in selling it, so Steven gets to live in it and keep the furniture, in order to make it easier for him to keep running his business."

"And the cars?"

"Another of Steven's tricks. We only had one car during the divorce proceedings because his Mustang was conveniently out of commission, and he convinced the judge he couldn't work without a car. So I didn't even get to keep the station wagon."

"That's why you arrived on the bus? My Lord, Sara. What a trip with two kids and all your luggage!"

"We had the station wagon most of the way. Steven said I could drive it as far as Tulsa and leave it with his mother, and he'd pick it up next month when he comes down to see the kids."

"Is she still in the condo in Tulsa?"

Sara nodded miserably. "I loaded up the wagon, fully expecting that she'd tell me to just keep it and bring the kids the rest of the way, and that Steven would come here to get the car. After all, his mother has no use for an old station wagon. She goes everywhere by cab. But she was so awful, Mama! She looked at us like we were strangers wanting a handout, and hardly let the kids into her house to use the bathroom."

"Her own grandchildren?" Mary breathed.

"Divorce does strange things to people. Apparently she believes that any woman crazy enough to divorce her wonderful Steven must be just poor white trash, not good enough to be allowed inside the house."

"I never liked that woman," Mary said firmly. "But I didn't say so, you know, because she was Steven's mother and it's important to keep peace in the family."

"Peace in the family!" Sara murmured with rancor, her face averted.

Mary studied her daughter's delicate, freckle-dusted profile.

"What about all the money we gave you, sweetheart?" she asked gently. "All those bonds for the kids' college education? Who controls them now?"

"All the money went into the business," Sara repeated tonelessly. "I probably shouldn't have allowed it, but Steven always argued that the best security for the kids was a healthy, thriving business, and it was worth making sacrifices now to achieve that in the future.''

Mary shivered and rubbed her arms beneath the heavy fabric of her dressing gown. ''So,'' she said briskly, ''what it boils down to is that you have four thousand dollars and the possibility of some child support from time to time.''

''And our clothes and the kids' toys, a B.A. in fine arts and a turtle,'' Sara concluded with a small, awkward laugh that turned suddenly into a sob. ''Oh, Mama . . .''

Mary gathered her daughter into her arms again and patted her shoulders. ''Sara . . .'' she began hesitantly.

''Mmm?'' Sara murmured, rummaging for more tissues.

''Sara, he didn't always seem like such a monster. Steven, I mean. That first time you brought him down to the ranch to meet us, and later when Laurie was just a baby, I thought you all were real happy together. Even these past years when your daddy and I visited you up in Connecticut, things didn't seem so bad.''

''I think we were happy in the beginning,'' Sara said, frowning as she tried to remember. ''It seems so long ago now. And it was tough, too. I was still in school, and Laurie was coming before we knew it. We had to work so hard to finish our degrees and hold down jobs once we had the baby, but we did it together. It was even fun. We used to laugh all the time. But,'' she added grimly, ''not lately. Seems like we haven't laughed for years.''

"Did he find somebody else?" Mary asked quietly.

Sara jerked her head erect and stared at her mother, her hazel eyes wide and dark with pain. "Mama! What would make you say such a thing?"

"These things happen," Mary said philosophically, keeping her eyes fixed on the darkened square of window. "They happen, baby."

She could sense her daughter's sudden tension, the anguish in her eyes as she gazed at her mother. "Mama," Sara whispered, "I know about Daddy and... and that..."

"Everybody knows," Mary said, trying to smile through the familiar wave of pain.

She turned to face her daughter, who was still staring at her with a stricken expression.

"Your daddy got to that age, honey," Mary said matter-of-factly. "Life was passing him by and he tried to grab a little more of it for himself. I hate to talk about it, Sara," Mary went on, chilled by her daughter's expression, "but it's better that you hear it from me."

"But she was so young! How could you stand it?"

"It's amazing what you can stand," Mary said dryly, "when you have no choice, sweetheart."

"I still think it's just awful. How could you ever look at him again?"

"I love him," Mary said quietly. "Al Gibson's a good man who made some real bad mistakes, and he's paying for them. I thought about throwing everything away, Sara. You'll never know how close I came last fall to selling the ranch and moving up to Connecticut. But I didn't do it, and when he comes home, we can still build a real good life together. And we aim to do it."

Sara gave her mother a bleak, wintry smile. "If you'd moved up North to be close to us, you'd have seen a lot of things you never expected."

"I suppose I would. I truly thought you were happy, Sara. Though I did wonder why you never came down to the ranch together for holidays after that one time when Laurie was a baby."

"Steven hates Texas. He says he wants to be up North where the action is."

"Your daddy misses you and the kids real bad," Mary went on. "He was so disappointed when he got that pass to come home for Christmas and you all weren't here."

"I really wanted to come home for Christmas this year like we'd planned, but by then we were in the middle of lawyers and divorce proceedings. There was just no way."

"We know that now, dear."

Misery darkened Sara's eyes again. "Mama," she whispered, "should we—the kids and I—should we drive up and visit him in jail?"

Mary shook her head and patted her daughter's cheek. "No, baby, you don't have to. Your daddy and I talked about that last week. He's coming home in just a couple of months, and he thinks it's better if the kids see him here on his ranch where he belongs. He wants to teach them to ride and fish..."

Sara tried to smile. "That'd be...that'd be so nice," she murmured, her voice trailing off into silence.

"What is it, dear?"

Sara looked up and met her mother's eyes directly. "Can anything ever be the same again? Us, and the ranch, and you and Daddy...is all of it spoiled forever?"

Mary shook her head. "I don't think so. Life changes all the time, and I think it'll certainly be different, but I wouldn't be a bit surprised to find that things are even better after a while. Just you wait and see."

"But does everybody know about..."

Mary looked at her daughter. "Everybody knows about everything. That's always mattered a whole lot to you, hasn't it, Sara?"

Sara nodded, her face troubled. "I was real conscious of my position, I guess, especially when Daddy always made me feel so special. I was the little princess of the Flying Horse Ranch, and it meant so much to me that people knew and respected that position. Now everything's just such a mess."

"Messes can be good sometimes, you know," Mary said comfortably. "When something gets all mussed and jumbled up, then you have a chance to put it back together better than it was before. Wait and see," she repeated, hugging Sara.

"I'm going to get a job, Mama," Sara said, crawling off the bed and standing erect to face her mother. "My kids and I won't be a drain on your finances. I intend to start paying our way and looking for a place of our own just as soon as I can."

"Don't you even think about it."

"Of course I'll think about it," Sara repeated quietly. "I've already heard about a job. It might not be exactly appropriate for the princess of the Flying Horse," she added with a wry little smile, "but it's honest work for an honest wage."

"Sara..." Mary began helplessly.

But her daughter was already leaving, walking toward the door with a little more purpose to her step, a slightly more confident lift to her chin.

"Sleep well, honey," Mary said softly as the door closed.

Alone in her room, she moved silently to the window, then took off her dressing gown and hugged her elbows in her ruffled flannelette nightgown as she gazed out at the cold spring rain, wondering about Sara's marriage. The phrases she'd used, like "grew apart" and "didn't work out," were the common parlance, but they didn't satisfy Mary. There had to be something else to explain the profound despair in her daughter's eyes, and the sadness that clouded Sara's face when she thought nobody was watching her.

As if to confirm this suspicion, Mary heard a distant choking sound when she climbed into bed, and knew that it came from Sara's room. Mary lay quietly, staring at the ceiling, listening to the hiss and patter of rain on the windows and the muffled, heart-broken sobbing of her only child.

MARY WAS ABOUT TO PUT her bookmark in place and switch off her reading lamp when she heard another tentative knock at the door.

"Who's there?"

"It's me, Grandma. Can I come in?"

Mary smiled at her grandson, who stood in the doorway in his bare feet, wearing a pair of ragged polo pajamas with a Hartford Whalers logo on the front. His golden hair stood up in damp tufts, and his eyes were shadowed with fatigue.

"What's that you've got, Davey?"

"It's Flipper, Grandma. Do you have something we can put him in so he can see out?"

Mary frowned and leaned up on one elbow, peering into the shoe box that her grandson set on the edge of her bed. The turtle glared back at her from the depths of a small bowl, partially filled with water, that was jammed in one end of the box.

"Let me see, honey," Mary said thoughtfully. "You know, I think there's an old aquarium of your mama's down in the storage cupboard. It's a good-size one, too. Wouldn't that be perfect for him?"

David brightened. "Could we put grass and stuff in it? And some rocks and water?"

"Sure we could. You know Maria?"

"Bobby's mother? The lady who helps you with the ostriches?"

"That's right. Well, she works in the library in town. So tomorrow we'll ask her to bring home some books about turtles, and we'll learn all about how to make a nice place for Flipper to live. How's that?"

David smiled gratefully and turned to leave, still cradling the box in his arms. Near the door he paused and looked back at his grandmother.

"My mom's crying," he announced, trying to sound offhand and casual. "I heard her from my room."

Mary's heart twisted with sorrow as she looked at the anxious, freckled face that belied the child's nonchalant tone.

Except for the freckles, David didn't look at all like the Gibsons, she thought. He was much more like his father. Still, Mary suspected that this child was probably quite similar in nature to his mother. At his age, timid, sensitive Sara couldn't endure pain for herself or others, not even animals. The preoccupations of her shy, thoughtful daughter had always seemed far removed from those of other young people.

When most children got wildly excited about holidays, Sara brooded over the little chicks held captive in cages at Easter time, or the gruesome monsters that roamed the streets at Halloween. She even disliked Santa Claus, Mary recalled with a brief grin, because she was troubled by the thought of that fat stranger wandering around their house in the darkness when everybody was asleep.

And her father had always sheltered Sara so fiercely from the harsh realities of life, surrounding her with a cloak of love and tenderness that he thought would keep the world from ever hurting her.

But you couldn't keep the world from hurting your loved ones, Mary thought sadly, listening to her daughter's muffled sobs and looking into the worried, unhappy eyes of her grandson.

"Come here, son," Mary said gently to the little boy. "Come and snuggle with me a bit. I'm real cold."

David obeyed gratefully, setting his box on the edge of the dresser and climbing into bed beside his grandmother.

Mary drew him close and smoothed the covers over him, her heart aching with love as she hugged his thin body and smelled the damp cleanliness of his hair, the warm little-boy fragrance of his skin.

"Your mama's just tired, dear," she whispered against his cheek. "She's traveled such a long way, and had you and your sister to look after, too. Sometimes when women get tired, they just cry a bit and then they feel better. That's all."

"Do you, Grandma?" David asked, twisting to look at her. "Do you cry like that?"

"Oh, lots of times," Mary said cheerfully. "There's nothing like a good cry to make the world look a whole lot better."

David thought this over, looking somewhat relieved, then frowned again. "My mom cries lots of
times," he reported. "She fights with my dad and then
she cries."

Mary hugged him in silence, her eyes fixed on the
darkened square of window.

"Once my mom took Laurie and me to the circus," David went on, "and Laurie got sick so we had
to come home, and my dad was upstairs in our house
with his girlfriend and they didn't have any clothes
on."

"In your house?" Mary asked in disbelief, trying to
keep the shock out of her voice.

David nodded. "In my mom and dad's room. My
mom yelled real loud and locked herself in the bathroom until they went away."

Well, the goddamn bastard, Mary thought in an
unaccustomed burst of profanity. *Bringing his fancy
lady right into Sara's own bedroom, for God's sake!
My poor baby...*

"And I heard them yelling at each other that
night," David went on tonelessly, "and the next day
my mom was crying almost all day. She said she had a
bad stomachache."

"Well, that can sure happen," Mary said in a deliberately casual voice, though her heart was pounding and her throat was tight with emotion. "You
know, when your stomach hurts real bad like that, it
just makes you feel like crying."

"My mom used to cry a lot of times," David repeated. His voice was still noncommittal but Mary, holding him close to her, could feel the terrible tension in his little body. "She told me she was always a crybaby when she was a little girl, but she was trying to get over it."

Mary stared at her grandson's tousled head, thinking about poor Nora Jones, who'd also gone through this kind of nightmare. Maybe Sara hadn't been physically knocked around as Nora had been, Mary thought grimly, but there were different kinds of brutality.

"Was she, Grandma?"

"What?"

"Was my mom a crybaby?"

Mary again remembered their intense young daughter, with her passionate causes and deep convictions about life.

"Sara wouldn't cry," Bubba used to say proudly, "if you tied her up and whipped her with a stick."

And it was true. Though she was a shy and sensitive child, Sara Gibson had always been fiercely private about her emotions, and even her parents seldom saw her in tears.

That was what made this story of David's so disturbing....

"Well, to tell you the truth, I don't remember her crying much when she was little," Mary told the child with forced cheerfulness. "Only when she hurt herself, and couldn't help crying."

"How did she hurt herself?"

"When she was a little girl, your mama was real accident prone. Her daddy used to say it was because she spent her whole life daydreaming and never noticed what was happening around her."

"I do that sometimes," David said eagerly. "Once I walked right into a lamppost and cut my cheek because I was looking at the skateboards in the store window."

Mary laughed and cuddled him. "Well, now, that was a pretty silly thing to do," she teased. "Walking into a lamppost! Davey Milne, you just better pay attention around here or you'll go bumping into one of my ostriches, and then we'll all be in trouble."

"Can we stay here, Grandma?" David asked shyly. "Mom says we're just going to be here a little while and then we have to go live in an apartment or something."

Mary hesitated, her mind whirling with images of troubled children, of shaky bank accounts and stormy relationships and an uncertain future. But all she could really see clearly was her daughter's face.

Poor Sara, with her wrecked life, her bruises that went far deeper than surface trauma and her gallant refusal to burden her mother with the worst of her problems.

"Do you want to stay here, Davey?"

"I like it here," David said. "I like the ranch and the ostriches, and Bobby, too. He's neat."

Mary smiled, thinking about the little family who lived out in the bunkhouse and helped her with the ostriches. Maria also worked in the library in Crystal Creek, and Joel was attending college full-time in Austin. Their son, Bobby, aged four, stayed with Mary while his parents were away.

"Bobby's a real nice little fellow," she agreed. "You could teach him lots of things."

"I know," David said, sounding manly and capable. "He doesn't even know how to play baseball. I'm going to play on Rory's team this year," he added, looking up at his grandmother.

"Are you? Your grandpa will sure be happy to hear that. He loves baseball."

"When's Grandpa coming home?"

"In just two months," Mary said with a dreamy smile. "At first it was July, and now it's been moved up to June. The fifteenth of June."

"Are you mad at Grandpa for being in jail?"

"Of course not." Mary looked into the little boy's anxious blue eyes. "See, Davey," she said at last, gathering him close again, "it's kind of complicated, being a grown-up. Big people can have fights and problems, and even do all kinds of bad things to each other, but if they love each other, they can forgive and put all that behind them. That's what your grandpa and I are doing. We're putting the past behind us and making the best of life."

"Why can't my mom and dad do that?"

"I don't know," Mary said gently. "Maybe they just don't feel the same about each other anymore, Davey, so they don't want to try."

"Maybe it's because of me," David whispered, his voice muffled as he looked down at his hands. "I get the house dirty all the time, and once I . . . I started a fire in the garage and they were both really mad at me."

Mary's throat tightened with sorrow again. "That's nothing to do with it, sweetie. Your parents aren't getting divorced because of you. They both love you very, very much, but they just don't want to live together anymore, that's all."

"Will they always be mad at each other?"

"Of course not. People get real upset sometimes, but they don't stay mad forever. After a while they forgive and forget."

"Nobody forgives that man for what he did."

"What man?" Mary asked, bewildered by the swift leaps of her grandson's mind.

"Warren Trent. The man who saved Flipper. He wrecked the memorial, and everybody's still mad."

"That's not all he did, Davey. He was a very wild boy. He did lots of bad things in this town."

"Yes, but nobody forgives him."

"I swear, David Milne," Mary said with a weary sigh, gazing down at the little boy, "if you're going to argue all night, I'll be too tuckered out to feed my ostriches in the morning."

"What do ostriches eat, Grandma?"

"Mostly they eat pellets and grain. Davey..."

"Yes?" David leaned back against the pillows, raising his knees high in the air to make a tent out of the blankets.

"It might be a good idea," Mary said, trying to sound casual, "if you didn't tell your grandpa or anybody about all those times your mother used to cry. All right?"

The child gazed up at her solemnly. "Why not, Grandma?"

"Well," Mary said briskly, "we don't want everybody thinking your mother's still a crybaby, do we, now? So let's just make it our secret, okay? And then you and I, we'll both watch her real close to make sure she doesn't...get stomachaches or get so tired anymore, or anything like that."

"Okay," David said. "We won't even tell Laurie, right?"

"Not even Laurie. It's our secret."

"Grandma, can I have a pellet gun?"

"Well...you're still pretty young, David. Wait till your grandpa comes home, all right? He knows all about guns and things."

"Okay." David climbed out of bed, looking greatly cheered by their conversation. He picked up the box containing his turtle and headed for the door.

"Grandma?"

"Yes, dear?"

"Would a pellet gun make a pretty big hole in rock?"

"Rock?" Mary asked blankly. "What kind of rock?"

"Like, say, what that old statue's made of?"

"David Lewis Gibson Milne," Mary said with mock fierceness, glaring at her grandson, "whatever thought is in that little pointed head of yours, you just forget it this instant, you hear? This very instant!"

The child chuckled, a warm boyish sound in the darkness of the night, and vanished down the hallway. Mary watched him go, smiling sadly, then reached over and switched off her light.

CHAPTER THREE

CAROLYN TRENT OPENED her kitchen door and breathed deeply, smiling with pleasure. Traces of last night's rain still lingered on the morning air, along with the crisp fragrance of damp sagebrush and mesquite. The sky was pearl gray and opaque, swirling with diffused light in the east, where the sun struggled to break through masses of cloud.

"What are you thinking?" her husband asked, coming up behind her and putting his arms around her, resting his chin against her soft golden hair.

Carolyn stirred and smiled, linking her hands over his. "That I'm never going away again. I missed you so much, Vern."

"It's been a long two weeks," Vern agreed. "Aunt Rachel may have needed you in Houston, but I need you more right here."

Carolyn nodded. "I was also thinking it's been a whole year since you came up the drive with that pitiful little mop dog in your car."

"A lot of things started happening that day," Vern said, nuzzling her ear.

"They sure did. Turned my whole life upside down."

"Are you sorry, Caro? Do you wish I'd just driven right past your gate and taken that dog into town for Manny to fix up?"

"Oh, Vern," Carolyn murmured softly, turning to put her arms around her husband's neck and kiss him thoroughly.

"She still loves me," Vern said with a soulful grin, when he was able to speak again. "I'm the luckiest man in the world."

"You're just an old silly," Carolyn told him sternly, though her mouth twitched with amusement. "A married man like you, carrying on like a teenager. Come and eat your breakfast."

They seated themselves at the table in companionable silence, eating dishes of fruit salad along with their buttered toast. "Come on, fill me in on the rest of the news. I've been away almost two weeks, you know," Carolyn said.

"What do you want to know?"

"Well, about Warren, for instance. You mean to say he never told you a single word about what he's doing here?"

Vern shook his head and gazed wistfully at the toaster. "I'd sure like another slice, Caro. I'm still hungry."

"Go ahead. You're the one who's so strict about this diet of yours."

"I just want to stay healthy and enjoy living with you for another hundred years or so."

Carolyn grinned at him fondly. "Let's split one," she suggested.

"Okay. You know, Warren didn't say much of anything, actually. It was a real awkward conversation. Everyone in the coffee shop was watching us, and he kept looking at his watch like he had a train to catch."

Carolyn frowned as she dropped a fresh slice of rye bread into the toaster. "I wish he'd come out here for a meal or something. Does he even know we're married, Vern?"

Vern nodded. "I told him."

"What did he say?"

"He said it was about time, considering he figured I'd been in love with you for thirty years or more."

"But he wouldn't tell you what he's doing, or why he came back?"

"Not a thing."

"What do you think he's been doing all these years, Vern? Where's he been?"

Vern frowned, watching as his wife took the slice of toast and buttered it with quick, graceful motions. "I don't have the slightest idea. Probably wildcatting on the oil rigs, following the rodeo circuit, doing time in prison... Whatever it was, he looks like he's had a pretty hard life. Poor little Warren," he added softly.

Carolyn sliced the toast in two and handed a piece to her husband, looking troubled. "He's your brother, Vern," she said finally. "It just doesn't seem right, somehow, that he won't come out and visit us, or at least spend some time with you. Your own brother."

"We were seven years apart, Caro. Warren was just thirteen when I left for Vietnam, and I never saw him again until now."

Carolyn nodded. "It was...how long? Three years after you left when he went on his big rampage? They sent him away right after that, didn't they?"

"I guess so. He went to a juvenile detention center somewhere in Arkansas, but he ran away before he'd been there a month. My folks never knew where he was after that. He sent some letters to them before they died, but there was no return address on any of them."

"Poor Warren," Carolyn said softly. "It's so sad."

Vern looked at her curiously. "You don't hold all that old stuff against him, Caro? You don't want to ride him out of town on a rail?"

Carolyn shook her head. "I don't think anybody does, Vern, not really. People aren't that cold and unforgiving. Most of the problem right now is probably his own fault."

"How do you mean?"

"I mean," Carolyn said, "if he'd come back to town and apologized, or even been halfway decent to folks, they'd mostly be willing to let bygones be bygones. But you say that he just walks around town with this huge chip on his shoulder, this damn-you attitude. That gets people riled, Vern."

"I know." Vern paused to chew and swallow a healthy mouthful of toast. "But he's not really like that, you know. At least he wasn't when he was a boy.

Warren was one of those kids with all kinds of feelings that he kept bottled up, hidden under a kind of cold, smart-aleck surface."

"I never really knew him," Carolyn said thoughtfully. "He was so much younger than us. I always wondered what made him go on a rampage like that."

"I've never said this to anyone before, but I think it was the war," Vern said, after a moment's silence. "I think it was because I was over there fighting and he just hated it. My folks said the real bad problems with Warren all started after they got the MIA notice about me."

Carolyn shivered. "Lord, that was an awful time. I remember how we felt, all of us, until we finally heard you were safe." She looked up at her husband, her blue eyes widening. "Vern . . . you think that's why he shot up the memorial? It was some kind of protest?"

"I think it might have been. Like I said, Warren was always a real strange kid."

"Well, in that case, why doesn't he just apologize and make it right? Why come back here and march around town like he hates everybody?"

Vern shrugged, his pleasant face looking worried and unhappy. "I don't know, honey. Maybe he feels their anger and he's just giving it back to them. Maybe the life he's lived has turned him into a real hard man. I just don't know."

"Vern, tell me the truth. Why do you think he's here?" Carolyn asked bluntly. "Why did he come back to Crystal Creek? What's he really doing out in that old barn on the Swanson place?"

Vern shook his head. "There's a new story every time I go into the Longhorn. Wayne says somebody called the sheriff's office the other day and tipped them off that Warren's smuggling machine guns into some Central American country. This caller swore he'd seen gun parts through a hole in one of those packing crates."

Carolyn grinned briefly. "I bumped into Mary, and she heard it was drugs coming in from Colombia. Two of the women at the church bazaar told her they heard a helicopter landing at the barn in the middle of the night."

Vern looked skeptical. "I heard that one, too. Seems to me if a helicopter landed out there, *everybody* would know about it, wouldn't they? Not just a few people? Besides," he added, "if Warren wanted to do something illegal, why come back here and base his operations in a place where he's so damned conspicuous? It just doesn't make sense."

Carolyn shook her head. "I don't know what to think anymore. It makes me real sad, that's all. I wish he'd either soften up a bit or else move on and leave us all in peace."

They were silent a moment, sipping their coffee.

"So what else did Mary have to say?" Vern asked finally.

Carolyn brightened and smiled at him. "Oh, lots of news. Sara and the kids arrived yesterday. They're just getting settled in."

"Is Mary happy about that?"

"She seems happy. But a little...cautious, you know?"

Vern grinned. "We'd be cautious, too, if Beverly came home with two kids and said she was planning to live with us."

"We sure would. But I don't think this is permanent. Just till Sara can get back on her feet. Mary says she's already talking about looking for work and finding them a place of their own."

"Around here?" Vern shook his head. "Not much work in town for a girl like Sara."

"I know. Sara was always so..."

Carolyn's voice trailed into silence as she searched for the words to describe her friend's daughter.

"Above it all," Vern suggested.

Carolyn nodded. "I guess that's it," she agreed. "Bubba always called her his little princess, remember? She grew up believing she was really special."

"Bubba sure spoiled her, that's for sure. He thought the sun just rose and set in that girl. Is she still like that?"

"I don't think so. Life has a nasty way of bringing princesses down to earth, you know. Mary never said it in so many words," Carolyn added, "but I think Sara's had a pretty rough time. It probably took some real courage for her to come back home and face everybody after a failed marriage and all.''

"So, why did she?''

Carolyn shrugged and sipped her coffee. "No choice, I guess. She really got cheated in the divorce settlement. Now the poor girl's got two kids and no money to speak of. Mary told me that in confidence, of course,'' she added.

"Of course,'' Vern agreed. "So she and the kids are living with Mary because they're broke?'' he added. "Can Mary afford that?''

"Mary says another of her female ostriches just started laying. She sounds real optimistic.''

Vern smiled at his wife. "Should we start raising ostriches, Caro?''

She smiled back at him. "I don't know, dear. Tell you what. Let's just keep breeding cattle till the money's all gone, then decide what to do next.''

Vern chuckled, got to his feet and leaned across the table to kiss his wife. "See you later, love,'' he said, grabbing his briefcase as he headed for the door. "There's real estate out there to sell, and I'm the man to sell it.''

"You sure are.'' Carolyn watched him go, her face soft with affection. "Vern!'' she called.

"Hmm?'' He popped his head back in through the door.

"If you see Warren again, try to talk him into coming out on Sunday for dinner.''

"Right,'' Vern said without conviction. "I'll try.''

Carolyn nodded, still smiling as his jaunty silver sports car pulled out of the garage and made a wide turn in front of the house.

THE MOST IMPRESSIVE THING about the Lonely Bull was the huge sign at the edge of the parking lot. A massive black bull, easily thirty feet high, stood on his hind legs with his front hooves leaning casually over a rail fence. The bull looked fierce, with long, wicked horns and a glittering gold ring in his nose, but he carried a bouquet of Texas wildflowers between his teeth in a flirtatious manner.

"Our rooms are the cheapest in town!" the bull proclaimed in bright neon lettering. "And real clean," he added as an afterthought.

Sara parked a cautious distance from the big glass-and-plastic bull, then hesitated behind the wheel of her mother's truck and looked around nervously. The Lonely Bull was not at its best in the dull, midmorning light. The strip motel consisted of about fifteen units, each joined firmly at the hip and forming a U-shape with the lobby, tavern and café at the lower end. The whole structure was modern and glossy, but on closer inspection, the units looked cheap and hastily built. A cold spring wind sent scraps of paper and weeds skittering across the asphalt square in front of the lobby, many of them spilling from the black trash bags that lined the sidewalk by the motel rooms.

Sara gripped the wheel and fought down a rising panic. More than anything, she wanted to turn and drive away from this place, back to her mother's big cozy home. But her children were in that house at this very moment, shouting and running up and down the stairs, washing their clothes in the basement laundry, gobbling up all the food in the cupboards.

Sara's mouth set in a firm line. She squared her shoulders, drew a deep breath and took a quick look at her face in the rearview mirror, catching a blurred impression of freckled skin, of frightened hazel eyes and auburn curls glistening with little droplets of rain.

As she often did in moments of extreme stress, Sara paused to run a timid finger along the bridge of her nose. She had such a lovely nose. It had always been a comfort to her in troubled times, just to know that one small thing, one feature in the midst of confusion, fear and general inadequacy, was absolutely perfect.

Then she pulled her jacket up tighter around her chin, grabbed her handbag and stepped out of the truck, sprinting across the asphalt toward the motel's reception area.

The lobby was empty, and so was the office opening behind the front desk. Sara stood uncertainly, reading posters on the walls that advertised upcoming attractions in the tavern. Mama and the Pumpkins, The Line-Dancing Cowgirls and Earl, King of the Elvis Impersonators were all apparently booked to play the Lonely Bull in the near future.

The rest of the wall was given over to stern injunctions concerning the behavior of guests. Residents were warned about the consequences of spitting tobacco on the rugs, smuggling in "extras," removing the venetian blinds, cooking in their rooms or making holes in the walls for any purpose.

Sara felt once more an urgent desire to be somewhere else, doing anything at all except standing in this empty room preparing to apply for a job as a chambermaid and cook's helper.

The job, she noticed suddenly, was also advertised. It was right next to a poster with the picture of a fearsome, wild-haired individual that read Have You Seen This Man? Help Your Police!

Sara avoided the man's glaring eyes and concentrated on the ad, her vision blurring with apprehension.

"Yeah?" a voice called suddenly through the screen door.

Sara looked up in alarm as a blond woman entered the room, bringing a gust of cool damp air. The woman, who topped Sara by a good six inches, wore faded jeans and an old blue sweatshirt under a man's denim jacket with a matted sheepskin collar. Besides her height, the most striking thing about her was her hair. Pale ash gold, rich, thick and lovely, it was swept carelessly back from her face and tied with a bit of blue wool at the nape of her neck. Heavy earrings, a much brighter gold than her hair, glittered in her ears as she moved.

"Lookin' for someone?" the blonde inquired, dumping an armful of soiled towels onto the counter.

"Don't move them," she warned Sara. "I want him to see what kinda pigs some people are. I want them towels right under his nose the minute he gets here."

Sara glanced nervously at the towels, which certainly appeared to be in a disgusting state. "What... what time will he be here?" she ventured, hoping they were both discussing the proprietor, who could be assumed to be in charge of job interviews.

"His Lordship? Soon as he gets done feedin' his skinny face," the woman said with vast contempt. "You wanna talk to him now?"

Sara gulped and nodded. "If I... if I could. I was hoping to apply for the job," she added impulsively, waving her hand at the small notice tacked on the wall.

"You?" The big woman paused with her hands on her hips and appraised Sara with a disbelieving smile. "Well, I never," she commented, shaking her head so that her big earrings, shaped like tangles of golden crescent moons, flashed dangerously in the fluorescent light. "Kinda like Princess Diana comin' to clean out the toilets, ain't it?"

Sara's cheeks warmed. "I know how to work hard," she said defensively. "In fact, I waited on tables when I was in college."

"When I was in college," the big woman mimicked, not unkindly. "Well, c'mon, might as well give Louie a good laugh, too."

Sara trotted behind her new friend as they went out into the dirty courtyard and headed for the tavern. "My name's Sara Gibson," she ventured timidly.

"I know your name," the blonde said calmly. "I know all about you."

Sara stopped and studied the golden hair and tall sturdy body in front of her.

"June Pollock," the other woman said in that same detached voice. "Remember me? I sat at the back of the room from the seventh grade on because I was too big to fit in them little desks at the front."

"June Pollock," Sara breathed, pleased to discover a hint of familiarity in these alien surroundings even though, if truth be known, she had gone through childhood terrified of June and her noisy friends. "I remember you, too. You . . . grew up very early," she added, flushing crimson at her unfortunate choice of words.

But June was apparently unoffended. "I sure did," she agreed placidly. "And the boys all noticed, even if you and your snotty little friends hated me."

Sara paused, stung by the words. "June, I never..."

June waved a heavy, callused hand. "Hell, forget it. You was never as bad as the others, anyhow. You was always a real little lady, mind you, but you seemed to be off in the clouds most of the time. You never even noticed when your pretty little friends was fixin' to do something awful to poor old June."

Sara recognized gratefully that these words were probably true. Much of her childhood had passed in that same kind of misty dream. She'd often been dimly aware of her classmates doing and saying things that were terribly important to the group, but Sara could never quite grasp what was going on.

Part of that old miasma of uncertainty and unreality began to settle over her again as June ushered her into the tavern, a big square room so full of stale blue smoke that the air seemed almost palpable. Through the haze Sara could make out various ornaments on the rough wooden walls, including displays of cowboy memorabilia and a huge mural featuring another lonely bull frolicking in a field of daisies.

Some ragged musical instruments and amplifiers leaned against one wall, looking wretched and abandoned, and the wooden floor was sticky with spilled beer. The room was empty, except for a waitress in one corner who stared gloomily out the window, with a tray balanced on her pert blue-jeaned hip, and a small man eating at a table near the bar.

"Louie, this here's Sara Gibson," the blonde announced, hauling Sara forward. "She wants the chambermaid job."

"She does?" The man looked up at Sara, his mouth full, a forkload of bacon and runny eggs suspended in midair.

"Swallow, Louie," June told him firmly. "Chew and swallow, and say hello."

The man obeyed, giving Sara time to look at him. Louie was a thin-faced man in his early thirties, wearing crisp new jeans, a white cowboy shirt with flowered yoke and cuffs, and gray alligator boots. His dark eyes were furtive and his hair was so heavily slicked with grease that it looked black and shiny. Louie wore it combed back carefully, with long sideburns.

"You want the job?" he inquired, wiping his mouth on a paper napkin from the bar. "What qualifications do you got?"

Sara shifted from one foot to the other, somewhat inhibited by the fact that June still leaned on a chair nearby, listening with calm interest.

"Go away, June. You ain't finished your work," Louie said sharply. "You ever chambered?" he asked Sara, watching as June turned away, unruffled, and strolled out of the room.

"Chambered?" Sara echoed blankly.

"Chambered," Louie repeated with a gusty sigh. "We're lookin' for someone who's chambered before."

"Yes," Sara said recklessly. "For five years, while I was in college and just after I graduated."

"Yeah?" Louie's eyes didn't actually brighten, but they opened a fraction wider. "What kinda place? A big place?"

Sara frowned thoughtfully. "Not too big. It was a . . . kind of a supper club."

"You chambered at a *supper club?*"

Sara nodded, trying not to smile. "I played the cello."

He lifted his head and stared at her suspiciously.

"Chamber music," Sara murmured, avoiding his gaze. "It was . . . we played chamber music in the dining room. Just a . . . I'm making sort of a joke," she confessed lamely.

Louie gave her a reproving glance. "What I want here, I want a girl with experience."

"Oh, come on," Sara pleaded, her anxiety giving her courage. "How hard can it be? Scrubbing and cleaning . . . I've done that at home for years. And . . . and waiting on tables, I did that for one whole semester in college, and I've been the cook in my own house for a long time. I can certainly *help* the cook."

"The job starts at seven-thirty in the morning," Louie said, suddenly brisk. "You're expected to be here sharp on time. First you clean the kitchen and the fry grill. Eight till eleven you clean the units. Then you go over to the coffee shop and wait on the lunch crowd, and then you do the salad and vegetable prep for the cook. You leave at three-thirty. It's a seven-hour day for forty dollars, half-hour lunch break, two coffee breaks, maximum fifteen minutes each."

Sara was a little shaken by this bald recital of facts, but she lifted her chin proudly and gazed at the man in the cowboy shirt. "I can do that."

"You think so? You figger you can clean all them units in three hours?"

"There's about fifteen units, right?" Sara asked.

"Fifteen," Louie agreed. "Plus the café, the office and the tavern."

"And there's three hours to clean them in. That's five per hour, less the coffee break and time to move the equipment, which gives me about ten minutes a unit. I think I can clean and vacuum a motel unit in ten minutes.''

Louie's caution turned to disapproval again. "You keep acting so smart, girl," he warned, "ain't nobody gonna like you around here. Just try to forget you went to college, okay?''

Stung by his words, Sara nodded in subdued fashion and turned to leave.

"You start tomorrow," Louie called behind her. "Seven-thirty sharp. June's gonna be helping you out at first. Once you learn the job, she'll move up to cooking full-time.''

Sara pushed through the swinging doors of the tavern and caught a cool, enigmatic glance from the big blonde woman, who was running a noisy vacuum inside a motel unit next door.

Sara paused by the room and leaned through the door, waiting for June to switch off the vacuum. "I start tomorrow," she said shyly. "Louie said you'd be helping me at first.''

June nodded abruptly, then flipped the vacuum on with a dismissive air and returned to her work, running the nozzle listlessly along the grimy baseboards.

Somewhat deflated, Sara turned away and wandered down the bank of rooms, heading for the parking lot. She felt herself buffeted by one of those dark waves of despair that attack everybody from time to time, those wells of sadness so deep and terrible that hope seems impossibly far away.

It would have been easy to blame all this on Steven, the whole dreadful mess her life was in. But something deeply stubborn within her wouldn't allow Sara to do that. She truly believed that women needed to stop blaming men for all their unhappiness. Until women took charge of their own lives, including the need to make intelligent decisions and be in control of their personal destinies, they'd continue to be helpless victims, not powerful successful people.

Sara's mother had certainly reinforced that view when they'd had an early breakfast together. In fact, Mary had surprised Sara with her clearheaded, independent thinking. There was no doubt that Mary Gibson had grappled with many of the unpleasant realities of life, come to terms with them and triumphed over them. Sara was stunned with admiration for her mother, whose most significant accomplishments during Sara's growing-up years had been a prize-winning apple pie recipe and the best garden in the region.

But it was *hard,* Sara thought, lapsing briefly into self-pity once more. It was so hard when you were all alone, and had the fearsome responsibility of two young children to care for, and hardly enough money to pay the next orthodontist bill, and no prospect of earning any...

Deep in her gloomy thoughts, Sara neared the end of the strip just as a tall man emerged from one of the rooms and almost collided with her.

She stepped back abruptly, then turned crimson with embarrassment when she recognized the dark, sardonic features of Warren Trent.

"Well, Miss Gibson," he said courteously, although Sara caught that familiar glint of mockery in his dark eyes. "How's the turtle this morning?"

"He's...he seems fine, thank you," Sara murmured uneasily, longing to disappear. "My mother's fixing up an old aquarium for him to live in. David's real happy about that."

The stranger smiled, affording a rare glimpse of the shining boyish grin that could transform his hard face. But, as before, the warmth vanished so quickly that Sara wondered if she'd imagined it.

"Look..." she began awkwardly, drawing a nervous ragged breath and thrusting her fists deep into her jacket pockets. "Look, Mr. Trent, I'm really sorry about what I...about the things I said yesterday to the children. I didn't know you..."

"Were that awful boy?" he finished calmly, his lip curling with amusement. "The one that all the other kids hated, including you?"

He looked a little better this morning, Sara noticed. At least his jeans and shirt were clean, though he wore the same scuffed, badly worn boots and leather jacket.

"I said some really stupid things," Sara murmured. "And I'd like to apologize. It wasn't true that I hated you. I didn't even know you. Now, if you'll excuse me..."

"Why are you here?" Warren Trent asked abruptly. "What's Bubba Gibson's precious little girl doing, wandering around a dive like this so early in the morning? Did you spend the night out here with some old boyfriend?"

Sara's cheeks drained of color and her body tensed. "Why do you have to be so rude?"

He shrugged. "I don't know. Habit, I guess. Well, see you," he added, turning to leave.

"Since you ask," Sara called after him, stung both by his implication and by his apparent indifference to any answer she might give, "I came to apply for a job."

That stopped him briefly. He turned and looked back at her, cocking one eyebrow in surprise, his weathered face alight with interest.

"A job? You?"

"Yes, me. I'm..." Sara lifted her chin proudly, summoning all her courage to fight a sudden and completely irrational urge to turn and run. "I'm going to be the new chambermaid."

"Well, well," Warren Trent murmured softly, gazing down at her with that same look of sardonic humor. "Who'd have ever thought it? The little princess of the Flying Horse is going to be cleaning up after Warren Trent. What a world."

Sara stared at him, appalled. "You...you *live* here? In the motel, I mean?"

He waved a hand at the room he'd just exited. "My humble abode," he said. "Though a man's home is his castle, isn't it, Miss Sara Gibson? Be it ever so humble?''

Sara gazed at the wooden door with a kind of horrified fascination.

"I've already mentioned to the other chambermaid," Warren went on, his face hardening, "that the things in my room are to remain absolutely private. If anything is touched or disturbed, believe me, I'll know. And I take a very dim view of people messing with my belongings."

There was something sinister and threatening in his tone, a warning note that hadn't been there before. Sara trembled, touched by a sudden chill of fear. This was a side to the man that she hadn't seen before, a dangerous ambience like a knife edge glittering in the darkness. Again, summoning all her courage, she forced herself to square her shoulders and look directly into his piercing eyes. "I can't imagine anything less interesting than poking through other people's little souvenirs, Mr. Trent," she said lightly. "I assure you, your privacy is safe with me."

He held her glance for a moment, while Sara concentrated on not being defeated by that brilliant gaze, not flushing or turning away.

Worst of all, she was becoming aware of something terribly upsetting, something she'd only perceived dimly the day before through her waves of fatigue. Today Sara was sharply conscious of the man's raw physical appeal, of a forceful male sexuality that drew her in spite of her own horrified reluctance.

Even as she longed to turn and flee from his presence, a part of her was wondering how it would feel to kiss that firm mouth, to feel the strength of his rangy, hard-muscled body pressing and thrusting harshly against her own....

Sara's heart thundered in her chest, so loud that she was afraid he might be able to hear its crazy, hammering beat. She swayed on her feet and began to feel dizzy, but her eyes didn't waver.

"I'm a dangerous man, Miss Sara Gibson," Warren murmured softly, staring directly at her. "Everybody in this town knows it, and you'd be real smart to remember it, too."

Before she could answer, he was gone, turning on his booted heel and striding off toward the parking lot without a backward glance, his jacket collar turned up against the cold, rainy wind. Sara watched his broad shoulders, his lean hips and long lithe stride, the dark graying hair that stirred in the cool morning breeze. She clenched and unclenched her fists within the depths of her jacket pockets, still shaken by his parting words.

Why had he found it so necessary to let her know he was dangerous? Was that just some kind of obscure masculine boast... or a genuine threat?

CHAPTER FOUR

SARA SOON LEARNED that she had seriously underestimated the amount of time necessary to clean the motel units, even when only half of them were occupied.

By the time she finished scrubbing the big, grease-splattered grill each morning, her hands were raw and scraped and her back ached. Afterward, even with June's grudging assistance, she was barely able to complete the cleaning of the rooms before it was time to present herself in the restaurant, pad in hand, ready to take the lunch orders and run heavy trays of burgers and fries out to the tables.

The promised seven-hour day never seemed to materialize. She always had to stay late to finish her work, with no extra pay, and ended up dragging herself home in a fog of weariness so intense that she was barely aware of Mary and the children peeking at her anxiously across the supper table.

At the end of the first week, Sara was almost defeated. In fact, the only thing that kept her going was the skeptical amusement in June's blue eyes, and the sardonic grin on Warren Trent's face when he occasionally came into the restaurant for lunch. For some reason the attitudes of those two people angered Sara bitterly, and she clung to that warm fury like a talisman, a private charm that helped her to struggle on through blinding waves of pain and exhaustion.

On Friday morning, after an entire week of this misery, her spirits gradually began to lighten a bit. She felt herself growing stronger, a little more competent with the work she had to do, better able to cope with the grinding physical demands. Best of all, she had a two-day holiday coming up, and the prospect of a rest had never seemed more blissful.

Sara vacuumed the stained rug in one of the motel rooms, thinking about what she'd do with those two precious days. She'd sleep in, for sure, spend a leisurely time showering and washing her hair, probably sit out on the porch and mend a few of the kids' clothes, and then, if the weather was nice, maybe she'd saddle old Misty and go for a ride along the creekbed. . . .

She sighed, lost in wistful dreams, and wrapped the hose around the vacuum's plump body. With a last, satisfied look at the dingy room, Sara gathered up the cleaning equipment and backed onto the sidewalk, locking the door behind her.

Outside, she breathed deeply of the fresh springtime air, brushed back her hair with a chapped hand and glanced at her watch.

Nine-thirty, and just six units to go! She was actually ahead of time this morning, Sara realized in gratified amazement. Wonder of wonders, she might even have enough time for a cup of coffee before the noon-hour rush.

With a fresh surge of energy, she burst into the next unit, unwound the cord and plugged in the vacuum. She hurried across the room to strip the rumpled bedclothes and pile them in the middle of the mattress, then grabbed a couple of pails and a bottle of liquid cleaner and rushed into the bathroom. Just inside the door, she stopped short in alarm, staring at a partially clothed man who seemed to fill the little room, and a dark face, smeared liberally with shaving cream, that looked at her from the mirror.

Warren Trent grinned through the shaving cream and put a finger to his cheek, leaning toward the mirror to run a careful blade down the curve of his jaw.

"Sweetheart," he murmured from the other side of his mouth, "we've got to stop meeting like this."

Sara gaped at his reflection, mesmerized, her arms still laden with cleaning supplies.

"I'm—I—look, I'm sorry," she stammered. "I just thought... I mean, the room's always empty by this time, and I never..."

"Guess I slept in," Warren told her, taking another swipe at his jaw. "I had company last night."

Sara flushed scarlet at his words, and the vivid images they evoked in her mind. She remembered the pile of rumpled bedclothes and felt a reluctant heat creeping though her body.

"Well, I'm sure your social life is no business of mine," she said stiffly, still addressing his mirrored image. "But I'm sorry to have burst in on you like this. I'll just go next door and—"

"Be quiet," Warren said curtly, taking the pails from her and setting them on the floor.

Sara gaped at him again, too surprised to be angry.

"Give me your hands, Sara."

Sara looked at him blankly. Warren Trent wore a white, sleeveless undershirt that showed off a pair of broad, flat shoulders and arms rippling with corded muscles. His chest was covered with hair, dusted with gray, that curled densely around the edges of the white cotton fabric. He was so close to her that she could feel the warmth of his body and smell the rich menthol of the shaving cream he was using.

Once again, she was overcome by a hot flood of intense sexual desire. This emotion was something she hadn't experienced for years, certainly not to this degree, at least. And considering what Sara knew about the man who aroused her, it was so irrational and distressing that she was hardly able to cope with her feelings.

She backed awkwardly toward the door, still not looking at the man in the steamy little bathroom.

Warren reached out and grasped her arm. "I told you to give me your hands. Put the rest of that stuff down," he said sharply.

Sara set the rags and cleaning compounds silently on the floor, then held out her hands with frightened obedience.

She felt him moving closer to her as he took her hands and held them, studying them with close attention, but there was no tenderness in the action.

After a long moment, Warren swore harshly under his breath, dropped her hands and turned aside to finish shaving. Sara gazed in astonishment at his broad, half-naked back, then bent nervously to gather up her rags and pails.

"Your fingers are bleeding around the knuckles," he said, with his back still turned. "They're practically worn to the bone."

"It's...it's the cleaning compounds," Sara whispered, still so frightened that she was close to tears. "They're really harsh."

"Then why the hell don't you wear rubber gloves?"

She stiffened at the contemptuous tone of his question.

"I can't."

"Why not? Any idiot can learn to put on a pair of rubber gloves, can't they? I mean, it's not a really difficult procedure."

He finished shaving and splashed water on his face. Sara watched him. Both her random sexual urges and her fear were replaced by a surge of anger so intense that it made her briefly dizzy. She drew a deep breath and struggled to keep her emotions in check. Finally, she gathered the last of her supplies and started for the door.

"Why can't you?" Warren repeated, grasping her arm again to hold her in the little room.

Sara looked down at his brown fingers against the sleeve of her shirt.

"If I wore rubber gloves," she said at last, "I'd be taking them on and off every five minutes as I switched from one job to another. It would be so clumsy that I'd never get my work finished, and then I'd probably be fired. Maybe you don't know a lot about getting and holding a job, Mr. Trent, but it happens to be important to me."

He looked at her, his gaze so intent that it took all Sara's strength of will not to cower before it.

"Well, then, Miss Sara Gibson," he murmured at last, toweling his clean-shaven face and gazing at her thoughtfully, "I think I'd get a different job if I were you."

"Oh, would you?" Sara muttered scornfully. "And what kind of job would you get if you were me?"

He shrugged. "Something that makes more use of your unique abilities."

"What unique abilities? What are you talking about?"

Warren moved past her into the hallway, reached for a clean plaid shirt hanging in the closet and buttoned it as he looked at her. "Come on, sweetheart. You've got a college degree, they tell me. You've always been a talented little artist and musician. So why the hell are you working at a job that makes your hands bleed? What's wrong with you?"

He buttoned the cuffs and unzipped his jeans to tuck the shirt inside, as calmly and unselfconsciousnessly as if he were alone in the room. Sara stared in horrified fascination at a brief glimpse of well-filled navy blue undershorts. She felt another hot, prickly flush creeping up her throat and neck, and looked away hastily.

"There's nothing wrong with me!" she said, outraged by his words and his careless behavior, feeling another unsettling tide of emotion that she was afraid to analyze. "Just because I choose to do an honest job for honest pay to support my children instead of taking handouts, people like...people like *you* think there's something wrong with me. Well, let me tell you, Warren Trent, *I'm* not the one with the problem!"

She paused, breathing heavily, unable to talk anymore because she was in real danger of bursting into tears.

Warren sat on the bare mattress to pull on his socks and boots, then shrugged into his leather jacket and stood by the door, smiling back at her with maddening calm.

"You want to know what I think, Princess?"

"I don't give a damn what you think," Sara muttered, flipping the switch on the noisy vacuum and plying the nozzle with more energy than skill.

Warren crossed the room and calmly switched off the machine. "I've been watching you," he said, "ever since you took it on yourself to tell your kids my life story in front of me. I decided to learn what I could about *your* story. And you know what?"

Sara glanced at him sharply, her cheeks draining of color. "What?"

"I think you've made a few bad choices here and there, Princess. I think you probably got married far too young, to some shifty little bastard who didn't know much about being a man, and he never taught you much about being a woman. I think you're so scared to spread your wings and fly that you think *this*..."

He moved back to the door and opened it, waving his hand to indicate the shabby motel, the garish neon sign, drifts of weeds blowing across the dusty parking lot. Sara gripped the vacuum hose and stared at him in tense silence.

"You really think this is the best you can do," he concluded.

"I see," Sara said grimly. "Well, since we're comparing histories and personal performance, Warren Trent, let me tell you what I think about *your* record to date. I think you've behaved in destructive, cowardly ways all your life. Wreck and run, that seems to be your motto. And you really haven't changed much, have you? If you had, you wouldn't be living all alone in a seedy motel when you're forty years old, and still going out of your way to antagonize a whole lot of people who'd probably be ready to forgive and forget if you'd just show a bit of human decency!"

Sara paused, breathless from her outburst, and noted with satisfaction that her shots had apparently struck some sensitive chord in the man. His eyes flashed and his jaw tightened but he said nothing, just watched her with a steady, cold gaze.

Again Sara had that powerful sense of Warren Trent's dangerous edge, a feeling of simmering violence that was barely controlled. After a strained moment, he turned on his heel and strode outside, allowing the flimsy door to slam behind him and bounce hollowly a couple of times.

Sara looked at the closed door, her hands shaking, still barely able to believe she'd said all those things to him. Except for a few bitter fights with her ex-husband, Sara Gibson had never in her life spoken to anybody like that.

She switched on the vacuum and began to work again, more slowly this time, brooding about Warren Trent. Gradually her feeling of heated triumph began to fade, replaced by a growing uneasiness.

The man had clearly taken time to research the major details of her life, not a very difficult thing to do in a town as full of gossip as this one. And he already knew, of course, where she was living and who her family was. Sara shivered, thinking about those eyes, the sardonic grin, the man's menacing edge. Was she being a fool, allowing herself to become involved in open conflict with a person like Warren Trent? Could she be creating a genuine threat to herself?

Sara stopped short, her hand to her mouth, eyes wide with fear.

Could she be creating a threat to her children?

"Oh, God," she whispered, as she carried one of her pails into the bathroom and sprayed cleaning fluid into the running water. "What a fool I am...."

She edged slowly out of the bathroom and looked at the pile of suitcases stacked in the bottom of the closet, the plaid shirts and faded jeans on hangers, the neat shaving kit in the bathroom.

Sara reached out a nervous hand and touched one of the cotton shirtsleeves, then dropped it as if the fabric burned her fingers.

She looked down at the battered suitcases again, and saw that the hasp was open on one of the smaller ones. Holding her breath, Sara hurried across the room, drew the curtain aside cautiously and watched as Warren Trent's pickup truck pulled out of the parking lot, heading down the highway toward Crystal Creek.

Long after the truck was just a speck in the distance, Sara stood leaning her forehead against the cool glass, thinking about their angry exchange of words and the ominous expression on his face just before he walked out.

Finally, she strode back through the room, knelt by the suitcases and opened the smaller bag, her heart thundering so noisily that she was sure it must be audible in the next unit.

She lifted the lid and gazed at a stack of folded men's underclothes. There were singlets like the one he'd been wearing this morning, plain white T-shirts, blue cotton undershorts and rolled socks.

Sara touched the soft garments with a tentative hand, then forced herself to rummage beneath the underwear where she could feel a series of hard, square edges. She pushed the socks to one side and drew in her breath sharply.

The bottom of the little case was partially lined with money, bundles of bills in large denominations, piled neatly together and secured with rubber bands. Next to the bills were a stack of faded books and a bulky object wrapped in stained deerhide that Sara recognized even before she drew the covering away to expose polished woodgrain and gleaming blue steel.

Warren Trent, a probable criminal and known sociopath, who'd expressed an interest in learning a great deal about Sara Gibson's life and history, kept a suitcase full of money and a well-used revolver hidden in his motel room. And she had just insulted him with cruel accuracy.

And he knew who her children were, and where they were....

Sara bit her lip and stifled a soft moan of panic.

She wrapped the folds of leather over the gun again, trying to make it look exactly as she'd found it, then turned her attention to the books placed next to those neat stacks of bills. One of them seemed to be an address book, but at first glance its contents were puzzling to Sara. After a brief examination, she recognized what was strange about the book. Very few of the addresses seemed to be for individuals. They were almost all business addresses, some underlined and marked with stars and cryptic notations, others crossed out with a heavy blue fountain pen.

Sara shivered again, a long uncontrollable spasm that crept along her spine and into her stomach, gripping her whole body with little chills. She replaced the address book and picked up one of the others, then gazed in stunned amazement at the opened pages.

The book was an illustrated volume about children's toys, a rare old first edition with brightly colored plates.

"He must have stolen it," Sara whispered aloud, partly for the comfort of hearing her own voice in the silent room. "It has to be worth a fortune."

She turned the brittle, gold-edged pages reverently, awed by the beauty and freshness of the colored illustrations. Wicker doll carriages, painted trains, wooden rocking horses...

Sara set the book aside and reached for another. It, too, was an illustrated history of toys, almost as rare and lovely as the first one. She crouched in front of the little open closet, gazing blankly at the smiling face of a porcelain doll in a Victorian lace wedding gown.

"I don't understand," Sara murmured, setting the book carefully back with the others. "I just don't understand...."

She picked up a larger book, then stared at it with shocked recognition. This expensive volume was a copy of one of the reference books she'd used in her senior year of college, a scholarly work on methods and procedures employed in the restoration of old paintings and other artworks. Sara leafed through the book and paused at a series of familiar illustrations. They showed a crew of students high on a scaffolding, doing the arduous work of cleaning and repainting the Sistine Chapel.

This book was one that she'd always dreamed of owning herself. It was a rare edition, difficult to obtain, and would have been extremely valuable, except that it was quite badly worn.

Sara's bewilderment grew as she realized that passages of the book were heavily annotated and underscored. The markings on the text were made with the same blue fountain pen that had written those addresses in the other book.

Sara replaced the big, leather-bound volume with shaking hands and rearranged the piles of underwear, trying desperately to make some kind of sense out of what she'd just seen.

He must have held somebody up and stolen those things. Maybe some poor man who was a dealer in rare books, a traveler who'd just sold a lot of his stock and received the money for it, and then Warren Trent had come along with his gun and...

But even as she developed this scene in her mind, Sara knew that it wasn't true. With some deep, sure instinct that she couldn't possibly explain, she knew that the writing in that impersonal, businesslike address book and the notations in the volume on art restoration had both been done by the same hand.

By the hand of Warren Trent.

But who *was* the man? Why was he carefully hiding a whole suitcase full of old art books? What kind of man carried stacks of bills and a concealed weapon, and yet read about the restoration of an Italian chapel at night in the loneliness of his motel room?

"Well, well," a voice drawled at her elbow, frightening Sara so much that she almost fainted. "Doing a little snooping, are we?"

She dropped the lid on the suitcase and looked up, flushing to the roots of her hair.

June Pollock stood in the room with her hands on her hips, gazing down at her colleague with mild interest. "He'd kill you if he caught you doing that, you know," she commented. "I wouldn't be in your shoes for anything, kid."

"I was just...it fell down when I was vacuuming," Sara said, floundering, and waving her hand nervously at the suitcase, "and some of the things came out, and I was just putting them back. It's just...underwear and socks, stuff like that."

"Yeah, sure," June said, her knowing blue eyes fixed steadily on Sara's face. "Sure it is, Princess. And you're all bright red like that because you got allergies, right? Maybe you're allergic to scrubbing other folks' toilets."

"Look, give me a break, all right?" Sara said wearily, getting to her feet and facing the other woman. "I don't know why you're always so hard on me. I'm doing my best."

"But you're sure not liking it much, are you, Princess?"

"No," Sara told her bluntly. "I'm not. I'm worn out, and I'm underpaid, and I'm sick of people hammering at me and criticizing me. So just go away and leave me alone. And I wish you'd quit calling me Princess," she added, remembering Warren Trent. "I *hate* being called that."

"You got a little spunk left, anyway," June said with grudging approval. "It didn't all get knocked out of you, I guess, all them years up in the North."

"I don't see how it's any of your business." Sara crossed the room to flip the switch on the vacuum. "What happened to me anywhere, I mean. I just work here, that's all. It doesn't give you any right to pass judgment on my life."

"Okay, okay," June said mildly. "Don't get so huffy. I just came by to see if you wanted a little help. You got six units left counting this one, you know, and it's almost ten o'clock."

"I know what time it is!" Sara shouted, though she was actually shocked to learn how much time had slipped by while she was in Warren Trent's room. "I don't need you to tell me what I have to do."

June continued to gaze at the smaller woman with calm interest. "Lordy, you *are* cranky today, ain't you?" she commented. "How come you got such a bee in your bonnet? Hey," she added with a shrewd look, "you got the hots for Mr. High-and-Mighty Trent? Because you're a real fool if you do. That man wouldn't give nobody the time of day, you know. I think he's probably hiding from the law out here.''

"I don't care what he's doing," Sara muttered, slamming the vacuum off again and marching past June to rattle buckets in the bathroom. "And I'd thank you to stay out of my business, please."

"Actually, I was just wondering if you wanted to come over here tonight," June said after a moment's hesitation. "They got an Elvis impersonator in the bar this weekend who's real good. He's just a scream. I thought you might like to have a few drinks and watch the show."

Sara came out of the bathroom, cleaning rag in hand, and stared at the tall blond woman in disbelief.

June Pollock had not been unkind during Sara's first week of employment, but she had been a rigid taskmaster, and had certainly shown no inclination toward any kind of friendliness. In fact, Sara still smarted from some of the other woman's rude teasing and the bluntness of her comments.

"You've got to be joking," she said flatly. "You think I'd come *here* on my free time? I'd rather die than spend an evening here if I didn't have to."

"Warren Trent will likely be here," June commented with a significant grin. "Sitting in a corner of the bar, staring off into space and looking mean, just like he does most every night. Ignores everybody, even the pretty little cowgirls. Maybe you could get him to dance."

Sara pictured Warren Trent sitting all alone in the noisy bar, a drink in his hand, watching the dancers in brooding silence.

She gripped the neck of a spray bottle, holding it so tightly that her fingers ached. "Look, June," she said coldly, "I have to work here because I need the money, and you happen to be a co-worker. I don't have any desire for the relationship to go any further than that, all right? I'll look after my own social life, and it certainly won't include evenings with you and your friends in the bar at the Lonely Bull!"

The big woman nodded and turned away, but not before Sara was surprised by a sudden look of hurt in those deep-set blue eyes.

She opened her mouth to say something more, then paused and watched unhappily as June strode out the door, hunching her broad, denim-clad shoulders against the cool morning breeze.

"I'm sorry," Sara whispered to the empty air. "I'm really sorry. I didn't mean to hurt your feelings. I'm just so..."

But June was already moving with grim silence down the row of motel units toward the restaurant kitchen.

LATER THAT DAY, David Milne ran down the steps of the school bus, his canvas pack bouncing on his shoulder, and hurried across the road to a pickup truck waiting on the other side.

"Hi, Grandma," he said breathlessly, clambering into the truck. "Hi, Bobby."

Four-year-old Bobby sat solemnly beside David's grandmother in the front of the truck, holding a clean glass mayonnaise jar in his lap. David punched the dark-haired child lightly on the shoulder and smiled at him with gruff affection.

"Hi, Davey," Mary said, leaning over to kiss her grandson. "Where's Laurie?"

"She went to Stacey's house after school. She said she'll phone."

"Good," Mary said, shifting the truck into gear and moving off down the road. "It's real nice to see she's making some friends already."

"Yeah," David said without interest. "What you got there, Bobby?"

"It's a bug," Bobby said, with a proud glance down at the jar in his lap.

David leaned over for a closer look. Bobby's jar had a number of air holes punched in the lid. A shiny black beetle crouched on the glass floor, lifting and folding its iridescent wings as it glared bitterly at the outside world.

"Cool," David said with admiration. "What are you going to do with him?"

"I'm going to make him a house," Bobby said. "With a garage and a swimming pool and everything."

David bounced with excitement on the truck seat. "I'll help you, okay?"

"Okay," Bobby said, giving the older boy a shy smile.

"It's Friday," David went on with growing enthusiasm, "so we can work on it all day tomorrow. Hey, Bobby, what should we make the house out of?"

The two boys were soon immersed in construction plans, and it was a moment before David noticed where they were going.

"Hey, Grandma," he said, sitting up to peer out the window. "How come we're turning down this road? This isn't the way to the ranch."

"Brock called me this morning and said one of my mares out in the west pasture looked to be in foal. I thought I'd just run down here and check."

David sighed in bliss. After a week at his grandmother's home, he was growing to love everything about this new life. It was fun living with his grandmother and playing with Bobby, and the animals on the ranch were an endless source of interest. Best of all, his mother didn't cry anymore, although she was always really tired when she came home from her job at night.

David still missed his father a great deal, and felt sorrowful and deeply troubled in the scary dark hours at night when he couldn't sleep. But in the morning, when the sun washed over the rolling green hills outside his window, there were so many things to do and see that he forgot his night terrors.

"What's that place, Grandma?" he asked, pointing at a weathered old building with fresh boards nailed across the doors and windows.

"It's all that's left of the old Swanson place. It used to be a barn."

"What is it now?"

"God knows," Mary said briefly, parking the truck and turning to the two little boys. "I'm going to walk down the fence a little ways and see if I can get a look at those horses. You boys coming with me?"

Bobby shook his head, climbing out behind her and squatting by the side of the road with the glass jar in his hands. "I want to put some grass and stuff in the jar for my bug."

"I'll help," David volunteered.

Mary hesitated, peering through the trees at a half-dozen mares grazing quietly in the adjoining field.

"Look after Bobby, then, Davey," she said, starting off along the fence. "Make sure he doesn't wander off anywhere."

"I will, Grandma," David promised. He watched as his grandmother's small body, clad in jeans and yellow cotton shirt, moved briskly along the trail toward the fenced pasture.

"Davey, do bugs like flowers?" Bobby asked, glancing over his shoulder at the other boy.

David considered, enjoying the grown-up feeling that he always had when he was alone with Bobby, taking care of him. "Sure they do," he said. "I think they even eat them."

"Yellow ones, like this?"

"I think they like red ones the best," David said, after serious consideration. "There's some red ones over there by the barn. Let's go pick them, Bobby." The two little boys started across the flower-starred field next to the barn, pausing along the way to examine bits of vegetation and insect life that they thought might interest the captive beetle.

"We should give him a name," David said. "If he's going to have a house and everything."

"I want to call him Maria," Bobby said.

David stared at the smaller child. "You can't call him that, dummy. It's your mother's name."

"It's a nice name," Bobby argued. "I like it."

"Yeah, but..." David tried another approach. "It's a girl's name, Bobby. He should have a boy's name, like George or something."

"I want to call him Maria," Bobby said, with a stubborn set to his gentle mouth.

"That's stupid!" David began with some heat. "For one thing..."

"Hey!" a voice said above them. "What's all this?"

The two little boys stiffened and looked up in terror at a man who had just come looming up on them from behind the old barn.

He seemed huge with the light shining over his shoulders, dark and menacing in the quiet afternoon. David squinted up at him in growing alarm and drew closer to Bobby.

"What's the fight about?" the man asked mildly.

David gave a sigh of relief when he recognized the man. It was the stranger who'd rescued his turtle when they arrived at the bus station. David squared his shoulders and looked at the newcomer with lively interest. Warren Trent was just the way David remembered him, tall and strong-looking, with a tanned face and graying hair. His shoulders were wide, and he moved like a tiger or some other powerful scary animal.

"It's this bug," David said with scorn, indicating the glass jar in Bobby's shaking hands. "He wants to call it *Maria.*"

Warren Trent squatted beside the smaller boy and examined the jar. "I think that's a real pretty name," he said, smiling at Bobby.

Bobby, who was on the verge of tears, brightened and smiled back cautiously.

David watched them, wondering why all the grownups thought Warren Trent was such a terrible man. When he smiled like that, he looked so nice that David wanted to draw closer to him, lean against him like he used to with his father....

"It's a girl's name," he told the man.

"Well, sure. This is a girl bug," Warren said solemnly.

David cast him a skeptical glance. "Yeah? How can you tell?"

"Oh, she just has that confident look," Warren said with a grin, getting to his feet and looking over at the pickup truck. "Who brought you guys here?"

"My grandma," David said. "She's looking at her horses. Why are you here?"

The man indicated the old barn behind him. "I work here."

David looked at the weathered building in surprise. "Doing what? Can I go inside?"

Warren Trent's face darkened. "No, you can't," he said curtly. "In fact, if I ever catch you snooping around here, you'll be in big trouble."

Bobby looked terrified again and gripped his jar in shaking hands, but David stared up at the man with cheerful interest. "Why?" he asked.

"Don't ask so many questions," Warren said, taking a set of keys from his pocket and starting toward his truck, which David could now see parked behind the old barn. "Doesn't your mother ever tell you not to talk to strangers?"

"Yes, but you're not a stranger. You lived here when you were little, just like my mom," David persisted, trotting behind the man as he strode off toward the truck.

"Is that so?" Warren paused and squinted down at the child. "And what does your mother say about me, David?"

"She says you're a bad man," David replied promptly. "But I don't think so."

Warren's dark eyes narrowed thoughtfully as he opened the door of his pickup. "Is that what she said? Did she tell you I was a bad man?"

David frowned, leaning against the truck, trying to remember just what his mother had told him about Warren Trent.

"Davey!" a voice called, interrupting his thoughts. "What are you doing?"

"We're over here, Grandma," David said, watching as his grandmother hurried around the corner of the barn, then stopped short when she saw Warren Trent standing at the door of the truck with her grandson. She took Bobby's hand and drew him close to her, staring at Warren and David.

"Hello, Mrs. Gibson," Warren said quietly.

"Hello," Mary said after a tense silence, then turned to David. "Come on, Davey. We have to get home."

David started toward her reluctantly, turning to watch as Warren Trent climbed into his truck and backed it around in a swirl of dust. It pulled out onto the highway and headed off toward town.

"David Milne!" his grandmother said sternly. "Don't you know any better than to go around talking to people like that? We don't know a blessed thing about that man!"

"I like him," David said placidly, following his grandmother as she gripped Bobby's hand in an agitated way and rushed across the field to her truck. "I think he's nice."

"Well, you're probably the only one in the whole county who thinks so," Mary said grimly, opening the door and bundling the two little boys inside. "I don't want you talking to him anymore, Davey, you hear?"

David nodded obediently.

But when they drove back out onto the highway, he turned around on the seat and watched the old sagging barn until it faded from his sight.

CHAPTER FIVE

"IT'S LAURIE," Sara said, putting a hand over the telephone and turning to her mother at the kitchen table. "She says she wants to sleep over at Stacey's house tonight, then go with Stacey's parents to a basketball game in Austin tomorrow."

Mary nodded thoughtfully. "Sounds fine to me, Sara. The Algers are both real nice people. Maggie's a nurse here in town, and Don works for a real estate company in Austin."

Sara gazed at her mother, still holding the phone uncertainly, then spoke into the receiver. "Well . . . all right, Laurie. Do you need anything?"

She grinned at her mother and covered the receiver again. "She says she took all her overnight stuff to school in her backpack this morning, just in case."

Mary chuckled. "Kids," she said eloquently, glancing at David, who was eating his way industriously through a huge wedge of apple pie with cheddar cheese. "They're always one step ahead of you."

Sara said goodbye to her daughter, returned to the table and caught a strange look passing between David and his grandmother.

"What's up?" she asked.

David looked furtive and gulped hastily at his milk. "Nothing," he said, scrambling from his chair and grabbing a jacket by the door. "Gotta go. Bye, Mom. Bye, Grandma. See you later."

"Hey, mister, not so fast!" Sara said. "First, sit down and excuse yourself properly."

David hunched in the chair again, looking rebellious. "Please may I be excused?" he muttered.

"Yes, you may. Now, where are you going?"

"To Bobby's place. We're starting the house tonight."

"House?" Sara asked, giving her mother a questioning glance.

"It's for a big old bug that they've got in a mayonnaise jar," Mary said. "They're all excited about it."

"It's going to be a really neat house," David said with enthusiasm, pausing halfway through the kitchen door. "Wait'll you see it, Mom!"

"I'm certainly looking forward to it," Sara told him solemnly. "Have fun, dear."

But she was speaking to empty air, because David was already running across the ranch yard in the mellow spring twilight, heading for the bunkhouse.

Sara went over to the window and watched him, her tired face gentle with love. "He's happy here, Mama," she said. "Both of them are."

"They seem to be," Mary said, pouring herself a fresh cup of coffee.

Sara turned, caught by a troubling nuance in her mother's voice. "Mama?" she asked, coming back to the table and accepting a refill of her own cup. "Is anything the matter?"

"Well, now, baby, I don't know," Mary said. She smiled at Sara, her cheerful, tanned face looking half amused and half despairing. "I just don't know how much of this damn gossip to believe, Sara. A person hears so many things, you hardly know what to believe these days."

Sara sipped her coffee, looking bewildered. "What are you talking about, Mama?"

"Well . . . this afternoon after I picked up Davey at the school bus, I stopped off beside the west field to look at the mares, because Brock says one of them is in foal, even though I didn't think any of those mares were bred last year."

Sara nodded, gripping her coffee mug, her eyes fixed on her mother's face.

"The west horse pasture is right beside that old Swanson barn," Mary went on.

Sara felt a sudden little chill of alarm. She tensed and waited silently.

"You know the place, Sara? Where that man Warren Trent is supposed to be doing all his dark, mysterious deeds?"

"I know the place," Sara said with growing concern. "What happened, Mama? Did it have something to with David?"

"Well, partly," Mary said uncomfortably. "I was just real stupid, dear. I left David and Bobby by the truck and climbed through the barbed wire to get closer to those mares. When I got back, the boys were nowhere to be seen. I found them around behind the old barn, talking to Warren Trent.''

"Talking to Warren Trent!'' Sara echoed, her throat tightening with fear. ''David was actually talking to him, Mama?''

Mary nodded again. ''And Warren was opening his truck door, almost like he was inviting David to get in. Now, Sara, I truly don't know. It could have been completely innocent. He certainly spoke to me polite enough when he saw me. But it gave me a start, that's all, what with all the things folks are saying.''

"I know. I don't know what to think, either, Mama.'' Sara hesitated, longing to tell her mother about the bewildering contents of Warren Trent's suitcase...the gun and bundles of money and antique books. But she was ashamed to tell anybody about her outright invasion of another's privacy, or of the harsh things she'd said to anger the man.

Still, he'd been talking to David just a little while later, possibly inviting the child into a vehicle. . . .

"There's something puzzling about that man,'' Mary went on thoughtfully. ''He looks scary, and he acts rude and mean sometimes, but way down deep in my heart I think he's all right. Maybe,'' she added with a wry smile, ''that's just because David keeps saying so, and I tend to trust kids. Their intuition is pretty good.''

"Sometimes," Sara said coldly, "children's intuition is terribly wrong, and it leads them into situations that can be tragic."

"That's true." Mary sipped her coffee, brooding. "Still, I wish I hadn't been quite so rude to the man. After all..."

Sara was barely listening. "I wish I knew what was in that barn," she said. "If we knew what he was actually doing here, it would solve a lot of the mysteries, wouldn't it?"

Mary nodded, still looking gloomy. Sara glanced at her mother in sudden surprise. "Mama? You're honestly wishing you hadn't been so rude to him? I don't understand why it should bother you. He's always rude to everybody. He might have been about to abduct my son, for God's sake!"

"I don't think so," Mary said mildly. "You know, I never did feel as harsh toward that boy as a lot of folks did. I could see something behind Warren's eyes back when he was a little fellow, a sort of sad, lonely look, even when he was doing those awful things, and it made me just want to give him a big hug."

"Oh, Mama." Sara got up and briskly began to clear the table. "You were always softhearted about children. But this isn't a sad little boy anymore, you know. He's a grown man who's been twisted and embittered by his childhood experiences, and he could easily be dangerous."

But as she spoke the words that sounded so plausible, Sara wondered again if they were true. She stacked plates by the dishwasher and gathered up the place mats.

"Well, we'll maybe know a little more about the mystery man next week," Mary said cheerfully, joining her daughter at the counter.

"Really? Why?"

"Carolyn finally talked him into coming out to the Circle T for a meal with her and Vern. He's coming to Sunday dinner this weekend, she says."

Sara smiled. "That's hard to picture. Warren Trent sitting down to Sunday dinner with Carolyn's good china and crystal."

"Carolyn will get him to talk if anybody can. Damn, I wish I'd at least said how are you, or something," Mary went on, rinsing dried gravy from the plates. "I was startled because David was so close to him, but still, it wasn't a real neighborly way to behave."

"Actually, I'm feeling a bit the same way tonight," Sara confessed, giving her mother a troubled smile. "But not about Warren Trent," she added hastily.

"No? What's bothering you, then?"

"It's my holiday, two blessed days off, and I should be feeling wonderful, but I don't, because I was rude to somebody today without meaning to be."

"You, too?" Mary grinned faintly. "These Gibson women, they're a real mean bunch, aren't they? And who were *you* rude to, Sara-Bear?"

"To June."

"June Pollock? The girl you work with?"

Sara nodded. "She asked me if I wanted to go to the bar with her tonight and watch the entertainer, and I just sort of brushed her off. I was...upset about something when I did it," she added awkwardly. "I didn't mean to hurt her feelings. But she hasn't exactly gone out of her way to be nice to me, either."

Mary gripped a plate in her hands and glanced out the window. "Poor June," she said quietly. "That girl's had a lot to deal with."

"She has?" Sara looked at her mother. "You never said anything before about June having problems, Mama."

Mary smiled dryly. "It's not easy to catch you up on fifteen years' gossip in a few days, Sara. Especially when you're usually too tired to see straight."

Sara nodded ruefully, looking down at her hands. "It's a hard job," she said, spreading out her fingers for her mother to see. "Look, Mama. My hands are scraped raw. Almost bleeding. They've never done this kind of work before."

Mary touched her daughter's reddened fingers tenderly with her own small, callused hand. "I'll give you some salve to put on them tonight," she said. "You should wear rubber gloves while you're using that cleaning stuff, dear."

Sara smiled without humor. "That's exactly what Warren Trent told me this morning."

"Warren Trent? How did he come to be talking about your hands?"

Sara remembered his naked shoulders, those glittering, dark eyes, the smell of his shaving cream.

"Never mind," she said hastily. "Tell me about June. Is she married, Mama?"

"I don't think she ever was. She ran off with that boy in high school, remember?"

Sara nodded. "It was in the tenth grade. She never graduated."

"That's right. Well, they lived all over the place, and finally split up. When June came home about ten years ago, she was broke and pregnant, and he never even came back to see the baby."

"Oh, my," Sara said thoughtfully, stacking plates in the dishwasher. "Where does she live now?"

"In that same big old house the Pollocks have always lived in. Down along the river just past Main Street."

Sara nodded. "Her mother went away when the kids were little, didn't she? Is June's daddy there with her?"

"No, he died not long after June came back home. Finally drank himself to death, folks say. But her grandmother lives with her in the house."

"Old Granny Pollock? Is she still alive?" Sara asked in surprise.

"She sure is. Has to be close to ninety now, and she's not quite right in the head anymore."

"She was an educated woman, wasn't she?"

"Yes, she was," Mary said. "Ellen Pollock had a college degree back in the days when not many women

went to college. Nowadays she only remembers folks'
names on her good days.''

''And June looks after her at home?''

''She sure does. And the little girl, too.''

''Oh, yes, you said she was pregnant when she came
home. Come to think of it, I remember June saying
something about her daughter,'' Sara added, frowning.

''She has a little girl about nine or ten years old.
Sweet and pretty as a little golden angel,'' Mary said,
smiling. ''Her name's Carlie, and she was born with a
clubfoot. Poor June, she's spent a lot of money on
medical bills for that child. At least three operations,
and then therapy, and special shoes to help her
walk...''

Sara closed the door of the dishwasher and stood
gaping at her mother. ''I didn't know,'' she whispered. ''I didn't know any of this, Mama.''

Mary patted the younger woman's cheek. ''How
could you be expected to know? Still,'' she added,
turning away and gazing out the window again with a
faraway look, ''it's good to remember that everybody
has problems, dear. We all have tough patches in our
lives, and it's real important for folks to be kind to one
another. That's why I wish I'd been a little more
neighborly to Warren Trent this afternoon. He's...''

But Sara was already leaving, hurrying out of the
kitchen toward the stairs.

THE POLLOCK HOUSE loomed dark against the vivid sunset sky, its faded clapboards gleaming dull silver in the waning light. Wooden trim, like ragged bits of lace, still clung to some of the eaves, and the sagging, pillared veranda hinted at better days, long-ago gracious times of lawn parties and ice tea overlooking the rose garden.

Now, though, the rose garden was only a dim memory. The yard was dusty and overgrown with weeds, littered with torn food wrappers and old advertising fliers carried on the wind from the center of town.

Sara parked her mother's truck at the curb and got out to look up at the house, rubbing her arms in the evening coolness. She let herself through a sagging gate in the picket fence, hurried up the walk and stepped onto a porch that groaned hollowly beneath her feet.

The doorbell hung loose on a single wire, looking as if it hadn't been used for years. Sara hesitated, then knocked on the peeling front door.

"Hi," a voice said when the door opened. "Who are you?"

Sara looked down at the child and realized how apt Mary's description had been. This little girl was truly angelic, so fair that her skin was almost transparent. She was small and delicate, with wide-set blue eyes and her mother's beautiful flaxen hair. She wore a faded cotton dress, and her right foot was encased in a clumsy black boot that looked massive on her thin little leg.

"Carlie?" someone called from within the house. "Who's there?"

"It's...it's Sara Gibson," Sara called back into the dimness.

"Who?" A woman appeared in the doorway behind the little girl, wiping her hands on an apron. She was about forty, small and brisk, with curly graying hair and a blunt, pleasant face.

"I'm Sara Gibson. I work with June at the...over at the motel." Sara faltered. "I just wanted to talk with her for a minute, if I may."

"She's not home. She went back over to the motel to watch the show tonight."

"I see." Sara hesitated, wondering what to say.

"I'm Millie Klein," the woman went on. "From next door. I watch them for June when she's out. Not that the poor girl goes out much," she added. "Just when she's working, and then on Friday night for a couple of hours, that's all."

"Do you know my mama?" the girl asked, smiling up at Sara.

Sara smiled back at her, touched by the child's sweetness and the eager glow in her flower blue eyes. "Yes, I do. I went to school with her when I was no bigger than you."

"Would you like to step inside?" Millie Klein offered, holding the door wide.

Sara hesitated. "Really, I just wanted to talk with June. I should be going."

"Come and say hello to my granny," Carlie said. "She likes meeting people."

Sara looked helplessly into the child's earnest face. She was reluctant to go inside the house, but she also didn't want to seem standoffish and risk offending anybody else in this family. "Well," she said finally, "maybe just for a minute, then."

She stepped through the door and looked around cautiously.

The Pollock house had at one time been one of the splendid residences of Crystal Creek, but those days were long gone. Now the wallpaper was faded, the floors sagged, and the rugs and furnishings were worn and threadbare.

"This way," Carlie said, gripping Sara's arm and limping rapidly toward a doorway on the left. "She's sitting in the parlor."

Sara followed the child through the door, then blinked in the dimness of a musty little room lit only by the fading, twilight glow from outside.

Near the window, an old lady sat in a rocking chair, a white fluffy cat in her lap. Her veined hands stroked the cat with a slow, rhythmic motion that made her rings glitter faintly in the waning light.

Sara moved closer to her, drawn by the little girl, who pulled her forward eagerly.

"Granny, here's a lady," Carlie said loudly. "She went to school with Mama. Her name is..."

"Sara Gibson," Sara supplied, when the child cast her an inquiring look.

The old woman hunched in her shawl and stilled her hands for a moment. Her eyes, deep-set and glistening, shifted to glance up at Sara. "Gibson? Elvira Gibson, did you say?"

"That was my grandmother, Mrs. Pollock."

"Elvira Gibson is a real hellion. She rides in race meets all over the county, dressed like a boy in cap and trousers."

Sara smiled hesitantly. "I came to see June, Mrs. Pollock, but she's not at home."

"Who? Who did you come to see?"

"June. Your granddaughter."

"June doesn't read poetry," the old woman said unexpectedly. "Young people get no education to speak of these days. In my day, we read poetry. We memorized it by the yard."

"Yes," Sara murmured. "I know."

" 'Tiger, Tiger, burning bright,' " the old woman crooned, stroking the fluffy cat. " 'In the forests of the night,' " she added, glancing slyly up at Sara again.

"That's by William Blake," Sara murmured in surprise. "It's always been one of my favorite poems, Mrs. Pollock."

"So you read poetry?"

"Yes, sometimes I do."

"Have you seen the tiger?" the old lady asked.

Sara shook her head, feeling numb and disoriented.

"I've seen the tiger," Ellen Pollock said with a mysterious smile on her lined, ancient face. "I went into the depths and I saw him. His eyes were red as fire and he shone gold like the sun. And his teeth were sharp and white, so cruel...so cruel..." Her voice trailed off and her withered chin dropped to her chest.

Sara looked down at the thin child beside her.

"She'll sleep awhile now," Carlie murmured, drawing her great-grandmother's shawl closer around her shoulders and then heading for the door. "We might as well go, because she won't talk anymore."

"What did she mean, all that about the tiger?" Sara asked Carlie in a half whisper as they tiptoed out into the hall.

Carlie shrugged. "I don't know. She always talks about poetry. Mostly I don't understand any of it, but it's fun to listen to her. Are you going over to the motel to see my mama?"

Sara, who was longing only to go home and soak in a hot bath, looked uncertainly at the front door.

"It'd be real nice if you was to go there and see her," Carlie went on shyly. "My mama doesn't have hardly any friends to talk to. I think she gets lonesome sometimes."

"Isn't she with friends tonight?"

The little girl shook her head. "She always just goes over there all by herself. She likes to listen to the music."

In spite of herself, Sara had a sudden, vivid memory of her careless words and the look of hurt and sadness in June's eyes. She thought of the big woman working all day to support a disabled child and a senile grandmother, and going back to her place of employment on Friday evening for a few hours of pleasure, the only bright spot in her week. And sitting there all alone . . .

Sara sighed, then forced herself to smile at the little girl. "Well," she said, "just for a little while."

THE LONELY BULL was certainly a different place after nightfall. The dusty parking lot was a black pool of mystery, filled with shadows and whispers, while the motel bar and restaurant cast a golden, welcoming glow into the night.

The place rocked with a powerful country beat that drifted on the evening air, reverberating through the shabby buildings and down the rows of parked pickup trucks. Even the bull in the big neon sign had a garish kind of appeal at night, looming bright and rich with color against the starry sky. He seemed to promise fun, excitement, an end to the daily cares of life, perhaps even the chance to find a new love.

Sara, who knew the bull was lying, trudged reluctantly beneath his smiling face and paused by the entrance to the bar. A young couple spilled out, laughing, and jostled past her. With them came a deafening blast of music, a wave of laughter, loud talk and a warm, smoky wind.

Sara looked down at herself, wondering if she was dressed all right. She wore a long denim skirt, leather flats and a soft chambray shirt.

No sequins, fringes or turquoise, she thought dryly. *No snake-hide cowboy boots or feather-trimmed Stetson. Maybe they won't even let me in.* But when she finally pushed open the heavy plank doors and ventured inside, she realized that it couldn't possibly matter what she wore. The people here ranged from eighteen to eighty, and their wardrobes spanned the whole spectrum from working cowboy to city glamour, with many odd variations in between.

People were crowded everywhere, on stools around the bar, on chairs at the sticky tables, jamming the hardwood dance floor and clustering around the walls. The noise level was deafening, made up partly from the huge amplifiers belonging to the band on the little stage, and partly from the patrons' earnest attempts to make themselves heard over the music.

Sara wrinkled her nose delicately at the smell, a rich combination of tobacco smoke, spilled beer, clean wood shavings, human warmth and a hundred different brands of perfume and shaving lotion.

She edged her way through the crowd, relieved at least to find that she wasn't at all conspicuous. A circus elephant probably wouldn't have been conspicuous in this place.

At the end of the bar, she caught sight of June sitting alone on a stool, nursing a drink as she watched the young man who was performing on the stage behind a mike. He swung into a moody, Elvis-like rendition of "Love Me Tender." Sara noticed her co-worker wipe a furtive tear from her eye as she sipped from her glass.

June had apparently dressed up for her Friday evening on the town. She wore a yellow cotton dress that brightened her blond hair and creamy complexion, and made her tall body look statuesque and luscious. Men glanced at her from time to time, but June was oblivious to all of them, Sara observed. She sat alone with her drink and listened to the music, eyes half-closed in pleasure.

"Hi, June," Sara shouted, edging closer and taking the empty stool next to the big blonde. "Is this seat taken?"

June's eyes widened briefly in surprise, then turned deliberately cool. She shrugged. "Doesn't look like it."

"He's really good, isn't he?" Sara ventured after a moment's awkward hesitation. "The singer, I mean. He sounds just like..."

Sara paused, interrupted by the bartender, who was watching her with pointed inquiry.

"I'll..." Sara floundered, wondering how long it had been since she'd sat at a bar and ordered a drink. "I'll have a rum and coke, I guess," she told the bartender. "Light rum," she added.

"Sure thing." He moved away to take down a glass.

Sara turned back to June. "Has he been singing long? Tonight, I mean."

"Long enough," June said abruptly. "Matter of fact, I'm about ready to go home and check on things."

"Your granny and Carlie are both fine. I was at your house just now, before I came over here."

June's eyes narrowed. She stared at the other woman through a blue cloud of smoke that came drifting along the bar. "Oh, is that so? What were you doing at my place?"

"I...I went to see you," Sara shouted, wishing desperately that they could have this conversation somewhere else, some quiet place where a person could speak in a normal voice.

"Yeah? Why?"

"I felt badly about...about being rude to you!" Sara shouted helplessly, leaning close to June's swinging golden earrings. "I just wanted to tell you how sorry I am!"

"I see." June settled back and looked coldly at Sara for a moment, then bent forward to speak again. Her voice was taut with emotion, so low and penetrating that it carried well despite the noise. "So that's it, hey? You went to my place and saw that I got some problems and your little conscience was all upset, so you decided to come over here and make nice. Is that it, Princess? Well, you can just forget it."

Sara looked at the big woman's glacial expression, feeling a little bewildered. "Why are you so angry at me, June? I said I was sorry. I honestly didn't mean to hurt your feelings."

"But you didn't mean to be my friend, neither, did you, Princess?" June said, with heavy emphasis on the final word. "Because princesses, they don't make friends with commoners, do they? And you'll never, ever forget you're a princess, no matter how many toilets you scrub."

She got up, tossed a few bills on the surface of the bar with a contemptuous gesture and strode away into the crowd, her golden head high.

Sara watched her go, feeling miserable. Alone in the swirl of noise and heat, she sat sipping her drink and pondering June's accusations.

Was she really such a despicable snob? Did someone like June actually seem like a lesser person to her, a woman who could be a co-worker and a casual acquaintance but never a friend, just because of her social distance?

Sara looked down at her reddened hands with a rueful smile.

Probably, she decided, June was at least partly right. Sara Gibson had certainly been told often enough by her father that she was a cut above her peers in looks and brains and breeding.

And that sort of thing was so insidious, Sara thought. It took a lot of painful years for life to knock those high-and-mighty notions out of you, and teach you that there really were no princesses or peasants, because every woman's hands bled when she worked too hard at a scrubbing job.

She pondered June's courage and selflessness, spending the rich years of her young womanhood on a disabled child and a confused old grandmother.

"Oh, God," Sara muttered wearily, watching June vanish through the mass of people around the door.

Another face caught her attention as she lost sight of June, that of a man sitting alone in the shadows near the stage.

The man was Warren Trent.

Sara tensed and pretended not to see him, although she'd already taken in every detail of his appearance. He wore a clean white shirt and jeans, and even his boots seemed to have been polished recently. His thick, dark hair was washed and combed into some semblance of order, though it still needed cutting and lay loose and shaggy against his shirt collar. Had he seen her? Sara turned toward the bar and hunched over her drink, hoping that he'd been too absorbed in the crowd and the music to pay her any notice. If she could just slip along the bar and get out the door, she could make her escape without ever catching his attention.

The last thing she wanted tonight was another angry confrontation with Warren Trent....

The young man on the stage leaned into the microphone again, caressed his guitar strings and began a haunting rendition of "Fools Rush In." Sara paused in the act of climbing down from the bar stool, caught by the sensual beauty of the song.

Maybe she'd stay for a couple more songs. Just until her drink was finished. Warren hadn't seen her, and nobody else was bothering her.... She sipped her drink and listened dreamily, letting her mind drift with the music.

Suddenly, she had a confused impression of nearby warmth, of a whispered threat and the scent of danger. She whirled to find Warren Trent seating himself on the stool that June had just vacated.

"What . . . what did you say?" she asked.

"I just said I'm probably rushing in where angels fear to tread. How are you tonight?"

Sara gazed at his dark, sober face, then down at her old denim skirt and faded blouse. She shifted on the bar stool. "I'm . . . I'm all right. I just came in to talk with June for a minute."

"You don't have to apologize for being here," he said, staring at her intently. "Do you?"

Sara stared back, thrilling in spite of herself to the nearness of him, the remembered fragrance of shaving cream and warm, clean cotton, the rough texture of his hair. "I'm sorry," she whispered at last, unable to take her eyes from his.

"Sorry? What for?"

"For . . . for saying those awful things to you this morning. I had no right. I was just so angry because—" Sara fell abruptly silent, and took a hasty sip of her drink. She drained the glass and set it down again without looking at him.

"Because I was right?" Warren prompted her coolly. "Because some of the things I said were a little too close to the bone?"

Sara shrugged her shoulders and focused on the rows of bright glasses lining the back of the bar.

Warren accepted another drink from the bartender, then indicated Sara's empty glass with a silent wave of his hand.

"No!" she said in alarm when she saw what he was doing. "No, please, I don't want another drink. I'm leaving right away. Besides, I'm a terrible drinker. Any more than a couple of ounces and I fall asleep."

Warren and the bartender exchanged a glance. "Give her just one more, Jim. I'll be responsible for her if she starts to tear the place apart," Warren promised.

Sara watched helplessly as another shot of liquor spilled into the glass in front of her. "I really shouldn't be doing this," she murmured.

"Why not?" he asked placidly. "Because you might start having fun? Because there's a slight danger that you could actually enjoy yourself for a minute or two, and that's absolutely forbidden?"

He was smiling. Sara was again drawn to the lines of humor etched into his hard, tanned cheek, the way his hair shone silver at the temples, the flash of his strong white teeth.

The danger in this situation, she knew, had nothing at all to do with alcohol. But how could she explain something like that to Warren Trent without making a complete fool of herself?

They sipped their drinks together for a while, sitting side by side in a silence that was charged with emotion and all kinds of unspoken possibilities.

At last, Warren stepped off his stool and reached for her, drawing her down beside him and leading her to the dance floor. A few people in the crowd watched in mild curiosity as Sara Gibson turned to Warren Trent and slipped into his arms.

I shouldn't be doing this, she thought again in helpless confusion. *I don't know anything at all about the man, except that he carries a lot of money and a gun. He's probably dangerous, and he talks to Davey. I should stay far, far away from him....*

But her body wasn't prepared to heed any of the warnings that her brain was shouting. Her body wanted to nestle close to his, to sway and turn with him in the slow rhythms of the dance, to feel his strong arms around her and his fingers spread firmly in the small of her back, holding her tightly against him.

"I'm sorry," she said softly into his hard, clean-shaven cheek.

"Again?" he murmured, smiling. "What are you sorry about this time, Sara?"

"I'm sorry that my hand is so rough and worn. It mustn't feel very nice to hold."

He looked into her eyes enigmatically, then glanced down at her right hand, nestling in his. Slowly, fixing his eyes on hers once more, he drew her hand toward his lips and kissed her fingers, running his mouth softly over the raw places.

Sara shivered and almost moaned aloud at the feel of his mouth on her skin. Despite the hardness of his big, muscled body, his lips were soft, as cool and gentle as silk against her aching flesh.

Her eyes, wide with alarm, met his. He drew her closer and gave himself to the dance, holding Sara and moving her with him across the floor, as if the two of them were just a drift of feathers, a wisp of thistledown.

"Come on," he murmured when they whirled near the door. "Let's go outside and get a bit of fresh air, shall we?"

Breathing fast, Sara nodded, too lost in the music and the nearness of him to make any response.

They moved outside, where the freshness of the spring evening was as welcome as a cool drink of water. As Warren strolled along the row of motel units, Sara found herself walking tensely at his side.

Was he planning to take her to his room, make some kind of move on her?

Sara remembered the soft tenderness of his lips against her fingers and shivered, wondering how she would respond if he asked her to go inside. But he passed the door of his room in silence and rounded the end of the motel, taking Sara's elbow lightly to steer her across the dusty street.

"Just down to the edge of the road and back, okay?" he said in a noncommittal voice.

"All right," Sara murmured, feeling hot and foolish about her sexual thoughts. "The . . . the fresh air feels so nice," she added awkwardly.

"I hate cigarette smoke," he said, surprising her. "Never did take up the habit myself."

Sara recalled the mysterious books in his suitcase, the bundles of money and that strange, impersonal address book.

And the gun . . .

"Why did your friend leave so soon?" he asked, interrupting her thoughts.

"My friend?"

"The tall blonde who helps you with the cleaning. June Pollock, isn't it?"

Sara felt a brief wave of misery. "She's not my friend."

"Isn't she? I thought you said you came here to talk with her."

"I did, but we're not friends. I was rude to her earlier in the day," Sara said, wondering why she was telling him this, "and I wanted to apologize, that's all."

"Why? What does it matter to you what she thinks?"

Sara considered the question, and realized in surprise that it actually mattered to her quite a lot what June thought. For some reason, she hated having June consider her shallow and snobbish. But she certainly didn't intend to confess all that to Warren Trent.

"Sara?" he asked, looking down at her intently.

Sara shrugged and contemplated the crowded parking lot. "I don't know," she said in a dismissive voice that told Warren none of this was really any of his business.

He was silent a moment, his profile silvered in the dim moonlight when they passed beyond the glare of the parking lot. "How's your daddy?" he asked finally.

"He's fine, I guess." Sara's cheeks warmed with embarrassment, and she felt grateful for the sheltering darkness. "I haven't been to see him at the... where he is. Mama said we might as well wait until he comes home, since it's not long now."

Warren glanced down at her with a hint of his old mocking grin and turned her around, heading back toward the blazing lights of the motel bar. "You'd really hate to visit your daddy in jail, wouldn't you, Princess?" he asked softly. "Not your style at all."

Sara paused and glared at him. "How do you know? What do you know about my style?"

"Not much," he said mildly. "But it's pretty easy to see what makes you mad."

"I get angry when people jump to conclusions," Sara told him stiffly. "I hate that. People should be evaluated on their own merits, not on...on gossip and hearsay."

He cocked a teasing eyebrow at her and she fell nervously silent, recalling all the harsh conclusions she'd formed about this man based on those very things.

Again, he surprised her by commenting wistfully, "You know, I always liked your daddy." He watched the moon as it drifted out from behind a dusky bank of clouds. "Bubba Gibson was real good to me when I was a boy."

"He was?" Sara looked blankly at the man's hard profile.

"Yeah, he was. You were just little in those days," Warren added, glancing down at her with a brief smile and then squinting up at the moon again. "Bubba used to carry you around like you were the crown jewels or something. I never saw a man so proud of a little kid as he was. I used to envy you when I was a boy, even though I was years older."

"Envy me? Why?"

"Because your daddy thought you were so wonderful. I reckoned that must be a pretty good feeling."

Sara stared hard at the row of shabby motel units, her throat tight. "It's not always such a good feeling," she murmured. "Sometimes it's really awful, having someone believe that you're wonderful. It's so hard to live up to."

"Even for you, Princess?" he whispered.

Sara looked up at him quickly, suspecting him of teasing, though his eyes were solemn and his face was still.

"Yes," she said curtly. "Even for me. Let's go back in, shall we? It's getting cool out here."

He looked down at her again for a moment as they stood by the entrance. Then he nodded courteously and held the heavy door open for her.

Sara preceded him into the noisy, smoky room, conscious of his eyes resting thoughtfully on her back, still uneasy about the conversation they'd just had.

In some ways, it was surprisingly easy to talk with Warren Trent. She actually found herself wanting to tell him things she wouldn't normally say to another person. But there was always that mocking edge to him, that dangerous glint that both attracted and repelled her....

"Come on," he whispered in her ear. "Let's dance, Sara."

"I should..." she faltered. "I should be getting home. Really, Warren. I have a lot of things to do tomorrow...."

"Just a couple more dances," he said softly, taking her easily in his arms and moving her out onto the floor.

Again, she was overcome by the feeling of him, appalled at herself for how readily she yielded to his hands and his body. Despite the uneasy tension in their relationship, despite all her suspicions and reservations, and the bitter anger that he often aroused in her, Sara realized in horror that, on a physical basis, she was practically incapable of resisting this man.

They moved slowly around the floor, swaying in time to the country ballad that filled the room with the sobbing sounds of lost love and loneliness. Sara felt his lips at her ear, whispering something she couldn't hear. His mouth lingered on her cheek, then moved slowly over her face as his arms pulled her even closer.

She could feel all of his body, even the thrusting hardness of his arousal. The knowledge of it made her own body respond in a deep and primitive way. She felt herself opening, moistening, yearning and aching with need. Sara pressed and moved against him, hungrily, shamelessly, wanting him more than she'd ever wanted a man in all her life.

If he asks me to go with him to his room, I won't be able to say no, Sara thought.

She was stunned by the knowledge of her own helplessness. The man must have hypnotized her somehow. Sara Gibson had never been the type of woman to get carried away by physical lust. And certainly not with someone so absolutely unsuitable, so dark and dangerous and unstable...

"Sara..." he whispered.

She thrilled with a wild, breathless excitement.

Now he was going to ask. She was going to go with him to his room, watch him strip his clothes from that tall, muscular body, lie naked with him in the shabby room and discover secrets that life had never shown her....

"Don't...do this, girl," he murmured huskily.

Sara pulled back and looked at him in surprise. His face was flushed and taut, his eyes shadowed with pain. They stopped dancing abruptly, hidden together in a darkened alcove near the entrance to the storage rooms.

"Warren..."

"What the hell are you doing to me? Is this your idea of amusement, or is it revenge? Let me tell you, Princess," he went on bitterly, "it's a real dangerous game to play with me. Maybe you should learn to pick your playmates a little more carefully."

Sara watched helplessly, one hand covering her mouth, as he pushed her away and strode off through the colorful throng of dancers.

"Warren!" she called, plunging after him. But by the time she worked her way out of the crowd and reached the door, he was nowhere to be seen. The moonlight spilled coldly onto the littered rectangle of the motel yard, and the only sound came from Warren Trent's pickup, roaring out of the parking lot and down the highway.

CHAPTER SIX

"WHAT'S IN THE OVEN?"

Carolyn Trent looked over her shoulder at her husband, who leaned in the kitchen doorway gazing expectantly at the stove.

"It's sweet-and-sour chicken balls," she said, stripping leaves from a stalk of broccoli.

Vern brightened. "That's Lettie Mae's recipe, with all the ginger?"

Carolyn nodded and moved past him to get some carrots from the fridge. "And we're having wild rice, stir-fried vegetables and some of those small breaded shrimp."

"Sounds great," Vern said, looking blissful. "I wonder if Warren's used to eating like this."

Carolyn paused with the carrot peeler in her hand and stared at her husband. "Come on, Vern. You can't be serious. Chicken balls aren't that exotic."

Vern took one of the carrots from the chopping block and began to gnaw on it thoughtfully, ignoring his wife's glare. "You haven't seen him close up, Caro. He looks like he's spent all his time living in bunkhouses and eating tinned beans."

Carolyn momentarily forgot about the stolen carrot and returned to her task, her face drawn with concern. "Vern, I just don't know what to think about all this. I truly don't.... If you take another of those carrots," she added sternly, "I'll chop your fingers off."

Vern chuckled. "What don't you know about?"

"About Warren. He's your baby brother, Vern. He's coming over here for Sunday dinner and neither of us has the slightest idea where the man's been these past twenty years, or what he's doing now, for that matter. Doesn't it just...bother you a little?"

Vern grinned at her. "Not near as much as it bothers you, Caro."

"Why not?" she asked suspiciously.

Vern shrugged. "Well, because women are just naturally so curious. You and Cynthia and Mary and all those church ladies, you all just can't stand not knowing what's going on with poor ol' Warren."

Carolyn stood, knife in hand, glaring at him for a moment. Finally, she relented and leaned forward to kiss his cheek. "That may be," she admitted cheerfully. "But there's nothing wrong with a little natural curiosity. And let me tell you, Vernon Trent, by the time that man leaves here tonight, I intend to know a whole lot more about him than I do now. You just wait and see."

BUT TWO HOURS LATER, when they'd finished the chicken and rice and demolished all of Carolyn's delectable stir-fried vegetables, she still hadn't learned much of anything about Warren Trent.

Carolyn studied the man sitting across from her, his face quiet and unrevealing in the flickering light of the candles. What was behind those enigmatic eyes, that courteous, withdrawn expression?

"Thank you, Carolyn," he said, looking up at her. "That was a delicious meal."

She nodded, uncomfortably conscious of her husband's eyes resting on her with a bright, teasing sparkle. "Thank you, Warren," she said with dignity. "I'm real glad you enjoyed it."

He stirred cream into his coffee, his callused hands strangely graceful with the tiny silver spoon and Carolyn's best cream pitcher.

Carolyn watched him, aching with curiosity.

Vern was just as obtuse as most men, she thought in mild scorn. He hadn't read his brother correctly at all. It was true that Warren looked hard-edged, and he'd probably led a pretty rough-and-ready kind of life. But his manners were impeccable. You could put Warren Trent in a black tie and tux and take him to dinner at the governor's mansion, and he wouldn't look out of place at all.

This was something she hadn't suspected, the fact that Warren Trent might be something more than the usual roughneck. In fact, the growing mystery of him, as Vernon had observed, was almost driving her wild.

"So, Warren," Carolyn asked with elaborate casualness, passing him a little silver basket filled with mints and fortune cookies, "what have you been working at lately?"

"Lately?" he asked, glancing up at her sharply. Carolyn had a blurred impression of brilliant dark eyes, of a sudden tautness in the man's jaw and around his mouth.

"I mean . . ." Carolyn floundered briefly, watching as Warren broke open a fortune cookie and extracted the little printed message. She took a deep breath and plunged on. "I was just interested in what line of work you took up after you . . . left Crystal Creek," she finished lamely, wondering what it was that made their guest so formidable.

Carolyn Randolph Townsend Trent was not accustomed to feeling intimidated at her own dinner table. But there was definitely something about this man. . . .

"Oh, mostly I just worked here and there," he said courteously in response to her question. "What's your fortune, Vern?"

Vernon grinned at his younger brother, took a pair of glasses from his shirt pocket and slipped them on. "You will enjoy long life and good fortune," he read.

Carolyn patted her husband's hand, relieved that the awkward moment was behind them. "That's a real good fortune, Vern. Mine just says I'm about to have a pleasant outing with friends."

Vern smiled at the silent man next to him. "How about you, Warren? What's your fortune?"

Carolyn looked at the two brothers, struck all at once by the similarity in their faces. They were both masculine and handsome, with finely sculpted, regular features and vivid brown eyes. But Vern had a cheerful, open look, as warm and ingenuous as a big puppy, while Warren's face seemed shuttered and unapproachable, almost menacing in repose.

It was easy to see, Carolyn thought, that Vernon Trent still loved his little brother. There was tenderness in his eyes, a wistfulness and warmth as he looked at the younger man that made her feel a sudden hot surge of protective anger.

Would it hurt Warren Trent to be a little warm in return, to respond just a bit to Vern's overtures of friendliness? If he didn't want to open up to *her,* the least he could do was...

"Your secret passion will be rewarded," Warren read serenely from the slip of paper in his hand.

Vernon and Carolyn both regarded him, momentarily at a loss for words. They watched as he folded the slip of paper with quiet deliberation and tucked it away in his shirt pocket.

"Speaking of work," Warren said, looking up to find both of them observing him, "I wanted to ask you something, Vern."

"You did?" Vern stared at his brother. Carolyn, who knew her husband better than anyone on earth, could see the flare of hope in his eyes.

He thought Warren was going to ask him about a job, find work, settle down and become a productive, peaceful member of the community. And nothing, Carolyn thought, would make Vernon Trent happier.

"I was thinking about your real estate office," Warren went on.

Vern gazed at his brother in surprise. "You want to sell real estate, Warren?"

Warren gave a short, harsh laugh. "Me? God, no!" he said, then grinned to soften his words. "No offense, Vern, but I just can't see myself as a salesman, can you?"

Not bloody likely, Carolyn told herself, unwrapping a chocolate mint and popping it into her mouth.

"Actually, I was thinking about Sara Gibson," Warren went on.

Again, both host and hostess stared at him. "She's working as a chambermaid at the motel I'm staying in," Warren said, stirring sugar into his coffee, "and I don't think she likes it much."

"Is Sara . . . ?" Carolyn began, wondering what to say. "Are the two of you . . . are you friends, or something?"

Warren smiled without humor. "Not so you'd notice. She can't stand me, and she's made her feelings pretty clear."

"So why are you . . . ?" Vern looked at his brother in confusion. "Are you asking me to find Sara Gibson a job, Warren?"

The younger man shrugged. "It's no concern of mine. But her hands are bleeding from the work she's doing," he added, casting a quick glance at Carolyn. "I don't think she's used to hard manual labor, and I know she's qualified to do something better than scrubbing motel rooms. I just wondered if you knew of any jobs around town, that's all.''

"I'll see what I can do," Vern promised. "But there's not much out there, Warren. Not these days."

Warren shrugged, his interest apparently waning, and drained the last of his coffee. "It doesn't matter. It was just a thought," he added, pushing his chair back. "Well, I should be getting on home, I guess."

"So soon?" Vern asked with obvious disappointment. "Why do you have to rush away?"

"I have some business to tend to," Warren said. "I'm driving into Austin to meet with a fellow later on."

"On Sunday night?" Carolyn asked, nervously conscious once again of his raking eyes and tightened jaw.

But Warren's voice was mild when he spoke, and his mouth was smiling, though his eyes remained cautious and withdrawn. "I guess business doesn't stop on the weekends, Carolyn," he said politely. "Thanks again for the meal."

Carolyn and Vernon Trent stood side by side in their doorway, watching as Warren's battered pickup wheeled out of their yard and vanished among the oak trees lining the road.

Vern draped a casual arm around his wife's shoulders and hugged her fondly. "Well, that's sure a relief," he said.

Carolyn turned to him suspiciously.

"What's a relief?"

"That you got all that information out of him," Vern said, carefully avoiding her eyes. "You know, I was a little worried about the boy, but now that he's told you every single thing he's been doing the past twenty years..."

He broke off, choking with laughter, and turned to follow his wife, who had stalked into the dining room and was noisily clearing the table.

LAURIE LEANED on a long wooden counter, gazing raptly into the glass-topped incubator at a thick creamy egg about the size of a flattened softball.

"When will it hatch, Grandma? You told me before, but I forget."

Mary Gibson paused at the doorway with a bucket of pellets in her hand and smiled at the girl's eager face. "They incubate for forty-two days, sweetie. That egg there, it's marked 3-22, right?"

Laurie squinted at the egg. "That's right. 3-22."

"Well, that means it was laid on March twenty-second. So it should hatch..." Mary calculated rapidly. "Right around the first of May," she said after a moment. "Just a few more days."

"That's so cool," Laurie breathed, staring at the egg again. "Can I stay home from school and watch?"

Mary hesitated. It was so hard for her to deny her grandchildren anything, but Sara might have strong objections to Laurie missing school just to witness the hatching of an ostrich egg. Still...

"We'll see," she said finally, moving back to the doorway to peer out. "Carolyn should be here any minute," she said. "Let's get the chicks fed and watered so we can visit, Laurie."

Laurie trotted behind her grandmother into a brooder pen attached to the incubating room, where three leggy ostrich chicks ran around in the warm, enclosed space. The chicks jostled and played with each other, scooting through a small opening and out into the waning sunlight, then ducking back through the little door to snatch pellets from their feeder.

"Just look at them," a cheerful voice said from behind Mary as she measured pellets carefully into the trough. "They're such ugly little suckers, and every one of them's worth thousands of dollars on the hoof. Who'd ever believe it?"

Mary turned, smiling, to greet Carolyn Trent, who had strolled into the pen and was gazing at the fluffy gray ostrich chicks with rueful admiration. Laurie, too, looked up and smiled, then went outside to fetch another pail of fresh water.

Mary took advantage of the girl's absence to lean close to her friend and grasp her arm. "Well?" she asked eagerly.

"Well what?" Carolyn said.

"Did you find out all about Warren Trent? Do you know what he's doing over there in the Swanson barn?"

Carolyn grinned and shook her head. "He's a real tough customer, Mary. It's been three days since we had him over for supper, and Vern's still laughing at me because I was so sure I could get him talking.''

"And you didn't?''

"Mary, I still don't know any more about the man than anybody else in town. He just stonewalled me all night.''

Mary started to speak, then fell abruptly silent when Laurie came back, lugging a heavy pail of water.

"When's Bubba coming home?'' Carolyn asked, watching as the girl tipped the water carefully into a tall glass tank.

Happiness flowed through Mary, warm and tremulous. "The middle of June,'' she said. "Just six more weeks.''

"I wonder what poor Bubba's going to think about riding herd on ostriches,'' Carolyn said, smiling as one of the big chicks ran up to her and pecked happily at her boot.

"Al thinks this is wonderful,'' Mary said. "Every time I visit, I take him the books and show him how the ranch is doing, and he can hardly believe it.''

Carolyn looked at Laurie, who had wandered into the outdoor enclosure. The girl knelt in the trampled dirt playing with the baby ostriches, teasing them with a handful of straw. "Is everything all right, Mary?'' Carolyn asked quietly. "Are you going to be able to manage?''

"What do you mean?''

"Well, you've got a lot on your plate right now, don't you? Sara and the kids, and all this work, and then adjusting to having Bubba back home..." Carolyn's voice trailed off.

"It won't be hard to adjust," Mary said gently, smiling at her friend reassuringly. "He's a different man, Carolyn. Folks around here, they'll hardly recognize Al when he comes home. Jail's been real hard on him, but in some ways it's been good, too."

Carolyn looked briefly uncomfortable. "Vern's visited a couple of times since Christmas. He says Bubba seems a lot quieter," she said, watching Laurie run across the pen, laughing, pursued by the eager chicks.

"He is. Al's done a lot of thinking this past year. He's spent hours sitting in that cell, running things over and over in his mind, and I guess that either drives you crazy or else it makes you see life a whole lot clearer."

Carolyn nodded and turned aside with her friend, walking out of the ostrich brooder and up toward the house. "How about Sara?" she asked. "How's she doing?"

Mary felt a brief tug of worry. "I don't know," she said, frowning. "Sometimes I think she's..."

She fell abruptly silent as Sara came around the corner of the barn and started toward them, waving.

"Hi, you two," Sara called, coming up to greet her mother and their neighbor. "I was just out for a ride. Mama, have you seen David?"

"He and Bobby are down by the creek catching frogs."

Sara smiled. "I used to do that when I was Davey's age, but I could never bear to keep them. I always let them go right away, remember?"

"I remember, dear." Mary turned to her daughter, her smile warm with the memory.

Sara didn't look as desperately weary these days as she had when she'd started her job. And the pinched, haunted expression she'd brought home with her seemed to have vanished as well. But there was still something about the girl that worried Mary, a kind of taut restlessness that was almost palpable.

"Where did you ride, Sara?" Carolyn asked, following Mary and her daughter into the kitchen.

"Up along the creek bed," Sara said, setting coffee mugs on the table. "It's so pretty in the evening, riding up into the hills."

"West?" Carolyn asked, seating herself at the table and smiling as Mary produced a plate of her famous doughnuts.

"Yes, just out to the edge of our property."

"Anywhere near the Swanson barn?" Carolyn asked with a teasing grin.

Sara's delicate face turned pink. "I try to stay away from that place," she said, in a low, strained voice that elicited a thoughtful glance from Mary.

"Have you all heard the latest rumor about that man?" Carolyn asked, taking a healthy bite of doughnut. "Lordy, these are good," she remarked, sighing. "Mary, it's real mean of you not to give me the recipe."

"That recipe's a family secret," Mary said firmly. "I'm teaching it to Laurie one of these days."

"What rumor?" Sara asked, pausing with her coffee mug suspended in midair. "About Warren Trent, you mean?"

Carolyn nodded, swallowing another bite of doughnut. "Millie Klein says he's part of the Witness Protection program. She figures Warren was a big-time gangster who gave information to the police, and now they're hiding him here until they can do all this plastic surgery and ship him off somewhere to spend the rest of his life."

"Well, that's the dumbest story yet," Mary said scornfully. "For one thing, he's not hiding much, is he? And what does Millie think he's doing out in that old barn? Building himself a spaceship so he can fly to the moon?"

"Millie Klein," Sara said, so hastily that Mary suspected her daughter of trying to change the subject. "I met her a while ago."

"Did you? Where?" Carolyn asked, stirring sugar into her coffee.

"At June's place. I went over there after work to talk with June last Friday night, and she wasn't home, but Millie was there baby-sitting."

"Baby-sitting who?" Carolyn asked with a grin. "Carlie, or Granny Pollock?"

"Both of them, I think. I had no idea Ellen Pollock was still alive."

"She was quite a woman in her day, Ellen Pollock was," Carolyn said thoughtfully. "Ellen was a crusader for women's rights way back before it was fashionable."

Sara frowned. "She seems really confused now."

"The Pollocks have fallen on real hard times," Mary said gently. Mary Gibson had learned something about hard times these past couple of years. In fact, her experiences had given her a great deal of sympathy for anyone else who was suffering.

"They sure have," Carolyn agreed. "I can remember when that big old house was a real showplace, can't you, Mary?"

Mary nodded wistfully. "When we were going to school, the parties there used to be the talk of the county."

"And by the time I was in school," Sara contributed, "June's father was already drinking so much, and her mother had run off, and everything was going downhill for them."

"It sure was," Carolyn said. "And now old Ellen hardly knows her own name, and little Carlie's had so many medical problems, and poor June works for peanuts at that pitiful job.... Oh, I'm sorry, Sara," she added hastily, her face reddening with embarrassment. "I'm such a fool."

Sara smiled and patted their neighbor's hand. "Don't worry, Carolyn. Believe me, I know it isn't much of a job. But I've earned a paycheck already, and that's a pretty good feeling."

"You know, Warren mentioned your job when he was at our place," Carolyn said casually, selecting another doughnut. "I shouldn't do this, but they're so good!" she added.

Sara was staring at her in tense silence. "Warren Trent?" she said finally. "What do you mean, Carolyn? What did he say about my job?"

Carolyn chewed and swallowed blissfully, her eyes half-closed, then turned back to Sara. "Nothing much. He just mentioned that you were working so hard, and that you could probably find something easier for better pay. He asked Vern to check around in town and see if there was anything open."

Mary watched in concern as her daughter's face drained of color, and she became so pale that the freckles stood out in stark relief across her cheekbones and the bridge of her nose.

"Now, why would he say that?" Mary asked. "I didn't know you and Warren Trent were on friendly terms, dear."

"We're not," Sara said, pushing back her chair with an abrupt motion. "Not at all. I don't know what on earth the man was talking about. My job is certainly none of his business. I'm going for a drive, Mama," she added. "I'll be back in an hour or so."

She nodded to the two women at the table, set her chair back into place and marched out of the room, slim and erect in her blue jeans and shirt.

In the silence following her departure, Carolyn and Mary exchanged puzzled glances.

"Do you think something's going on there?" Carolyn asked finally.

"I don't know," Mary said. "Actually, I think she's scared of the man for some reason, but I don't believe he's threatened her or anything. He'd better not," she added darkly. "I don't care if he *is* your brother-in-law."

Carolyn grinned. "There's nothing more fierce than a protective mother," she observed cheerfully. "I wouldn't be in Warren Trent's shoes if he made a false move around your family, Mary."

Mary smiled at her friend's teasing. "Did I tell you that Steven's coming to visit next weekend?"

"Sara's Steven?" Carolyn asked, looking at her friend in surprise.

Mary nodded. "He says he's coming down to see his kids and then pick up the station wagon at his mother's place in Tulsa, but just between you and me, I think there's more to it."

"More?" Carolyn eyed the other woman with sudden interest. "Like what?"

"I think he wants her back."

Carolyn watched in silence as Mary got up to fetch the coffeepot and refill their cups.

"When he phones, he always asks where Sara is and how's she's doing, even though he's really supposed to be calling to talk with the kids," Mary went on. "He sounds real lonesome to me."

"I thought he had a girlfriend."

"He told me that was all over. Last time he called, Steven told me he was alone in the house. He talked about how hard it was to manage with cooking and laundry and everything."

"So now he wants his cook and housekeeper back," Carolyn said scornfully, sipping her coffee. "His girlfriend dumps him, so his poor little wife starts looking good again."

"I don't know if that's the way it is," Mary objected mildly. "I know he didn't treat her well, but maybe he's learned his lesson."

Carolyn stared at her friend. "I just can't believe you, Mary," she said finally. "How can you be so forgiving all the time? A man does something that's just purely awful, and the minute he seems to regret it and want to fix things up, you're all set to forgive and forget."

"You don't get anywhere in this world by holding grudges," Mary said quietly. "That never solved anything."

"You don't get anywhere by walking right back into a terrible situation, either," Carolyn said. "Look, I don't mean you and Bubba," she added hastily. "I believe he was always a decent man at heart, and he got sidetracked by a lot of things. And I think you're probably right when you say Bubba's changed during the past year. But that doesn't mean every man is going to change the same way. Some of them just keep right on being rotten, selfish bastards no matter what happens to them."

Mary grinned at this heated speech. "I don't think she should go back to him just because he asks. After all, he hurt Sara real bad, and I can't stand to think of her getting hurt like that again. But I don't think she should hate him for the rest of her life, either. It's not good for the kids, that kind of bad feeling."

"But what if he asks her to come back? What advice will you give her?"

Mary opened her mouth and was about to respond when David and Bobby came tumbling into the room, carrying a plastic bucket full of frogs.

"Grandma!" David shouted. "If I put these frogs in the aquarium with Flipper, will they eat him?"

Startled, Carolyn and Mary turned their attention to the little boys, forgetting for the moment about Sara and the men in her life.

SARA DROVE her mother's truck along the winding country road, tapping her fingers restlessly on the wheel and brooding about the conversation she'd just had with Carolyn Trent. She hated to think about Warren Trent going around discussing her behind her back, making disparaging comments about her job.

What concern was it of his, anyhow? The man was just so...

She gripped the wheel suddenly and slowed to a crawl, staring at the old barn nestled in the trees just off the road.

The graying, weathered sides of the Swanson barn were washed with pink in the sunset glow, and the tips of the overgrown grasses all around the building carried a bright dusting of gold. The twilight air was silent and rich with the scents of spring, while a touch of freshness in the shadows hinted at gathering darkness and nighttime mysteries.

Warren Trent's dusty pickup was partially hidden behind the barn, but there were no other signs of human occupation, no open doors or windows, no movement or sound.

Sara gazed at the derelict building, her heart beating faster. Finally she speeded up, rounded a curve in the road and pulled onto a dusty track winding up through the trees and onto the boundaries of the Gibson property.

When she was a safe distance past the old barn, Sara drove the truck into a sheltering grove of oak trees, locked the doors and started back on foot, working her way through brush and undergrowth toward the barn.

As she walked, her tension gave her a heightened awareness of everything around her. The soft crush of dead leaves and branches underfoot sounded like rifle shots in the twilight stillness, and the mournful hooting of an owl in the trees nearby seemed to shout a warning to the man inside the barn.

Sara took a deep breath, paused to get her emotions under control, and then edged forward once again, wriggling though tangled mesquite and sagebrush and into a dense grove of trees surrounding the clearing where the barn stood.

At last, she reached a vantage point where she was almost directly behind the old building, peering through a screen of shrubbery at Warren's truck parked next to the back door. A small car was parked there as well, hidden behind the barn so it was completely invisible from the road. Sara crouched in the bushes watching the two vehicles, conscious of the gathering shadows in the brush behind her and the insects creeping over her face and inside her shirt collar.

As she waited, she wondered with mild desperation just what was wrong with her. Why did she feel driven to this kind of ridiculous behavior? This was the sort of thing David would do, hiding in the bushes and spying on somebody. What did it matter what Warren Trent was doing in the old barn, who was with him, what he said or did? He was just a no-account drifter, a hard-faced man with a dark past, no part of Sara Gibson's life at all. If she had any sense, she'd leave this place right now and go home to her children.

But she stayed hidden in the trees while the sky darkened from pink to violet, then soft dusty gray, and the shadows deepened all around her. Her legs cramped and her body felt chilly as the breeze freshened. Finally, just when she was about to give up and retreat to the warmth and safety of her parked truck, she saw the small barn door open abruptly. A ray of golden light beamed across the ground from within the building.

Sara tensed, peering anxiously through her screen of leaves at the shadowy area at the back of the old barn. Warren Trent appeared in the lighted opening, turning to say something over his shoulder. A small man approached behind him and the two of them stood in the doorway, conversing earnestly in low tones while they turned to look at something inside the barn.

Sara gazed in surprise at the little man standing next to Warren. This fellow had arrived in town a week ago and was staying at the motel, but Sara had had no idea that he was acquainted with Warren Trent. In fact, she realized that the two of them must have gone to considerable effort to discourage any impression that they knew each other. She thought about the past week, during which both Warren and the stranger had eaten in the motel coffee shop on numerous occasions, sitting at separate tables without ever acknowledging each other's presence.

With intense interest, Sara studied the newcomer. He was very small, barely more than child-size, with an alert manner and a bright, wizened face. His clothes were shabby and loose-fitting, and heavily stained with grease or some other dark substance. The man's sandy hair was thinning on top, but grew in tangled locks almost to his shoulders and was pulled back into a ragged ponytail.

Sara eyed the two men with distaste from her screen of shrubbery, trying to place the little man, to put some kind of label on him. He didn't look like a gangster, somehow, but he certainly didn't appear to be a productive, law-abiding member of society, either.

Was he an aging biker, perhaps, or just a homeless transient involved with Warren Trent in some kind of illicit dealings? Sara recalled the wads of money and the shining revolver in Warren's suitcase, and felt another cold chill in her stomach. She shivered and hugged her arms, wishing she'd brought a jacket from the truck.

As she watched, Warren reached inside the barn and switched the light off, then pulled the door shut behind him and secured the hasp with a heavy padlock. The small, ragged man said something and Warren laughed in response, throwing his shaggy dark head back and chuckling aloud. His laugh was a warm, masculine sound, strangely out of place in this sinister twilight.

Suddenly, Sara's eyes widened and she stared, holding her breath, as Warren took something from his pocket and moved along the wall of the barn to conceal it in a crevice near one of the shuttered windows.

She strained forward, memorizing the hiding place, making a mental note of its exact location. The object must be a key to the padlock, and it was behind the second window covering, about halfway up on the left-hand side. Sara's heart pounded and her chilled body was flooded with a sudden, energizing warmth. She watched as Warren and the strange little man climbed into their separate vehicles and drove off.

At last, when the evening was silent and the sound of their vehicles had long since died away into stillness, she crept back through the undergrowth to her parked truck. As she walked, she hugged the thought of the key to herself, the memory of where it was hidden, and the terrifying, delicious power that knowledge gave to her, anytime she chose to use it.

CHAPTER SEVEN

SARA WALKED with Steven Milne along a narrow path at the edge of the creek bed, watching her children, who were strolling ahead of them through the rustling cedars lining the path. David's thin body was electric with happiness, and even Laurie, normally so reserved, broke into a little spontaneous dance step now and then as she walked.

They both loved this feeling, Sara realized with a hollow ache in her heart. Her children loved the illusion of being a family again, even for a brief time, of walking together with both their parents in the warm, Texas sunshine.

She glanced over at Steven, who looked somehow out of place here on the sprawling ranch where Sara Gibson had spent her childhood. Even in faded jeans, sweatshirt and deck shoes, Steven had a strangely formal air, as if he wasn't entirely suited to such a casual outdoor setting. His fair hair glistened in the sunlight, and his boyish, handsome face was determinedly cheerful.

"Hey, kids," he called heartily. "See this big flat rock here?"

Both children turned and nodded.

"Well," Steven said, "I want to sit here and talk with Mom for a bit in private, okay? You two go on ahead and tell Grandma we'll be back soon."

David's face creased with disappointment. He opened his mouth to object, but Laurie punched him on the shoulder, her usual method of silencing him, and then hauled him firmly off in the direction of the ranch house.

Steven sat on the rock, watching them as they vanished around the bend of the creek. "They're such great kids, Sara," he said wistfully. "I miss them every single day."

"You should have thought of that a long time ago," Sara said coldly, "before you did all those things to destroy our family."

"Don't say that, Sara," he murmured in anguish. "Don't say that our family is destroyed. I can't stand to hear it."

"We've been legally divorced for months, Steven. All the papers are final. We're not a family anymore, so what's the sense in pretending?"

"Sara . . . sit down here beside me. Please, just for a little while."

Sara hesitated. "I really don't want you to touch me, Steven."

"How can you talk that way? I never hurt you, Sara. I never laid a hand on you, not once."

"Oh, Steven," she said wearily. "There are all kinds of ways to hurt someone besides hitting them. Don't you understand that yet, after everything that's happened?''

''I just know that you have no reason to be afraid of me. The least you can do is sit down and talk to me for a minute.''

Sara seated herself gingerly on the big rock, keeping well away from any contact with the man next to her.

''Sara,'' he went on, turning to her with an eloquent, pleading glance, ''I know I was a fool. But can't you forgive a man for making one mistake?''

''One mistake!'' she echoed in disbelief. ''For God's sake, Steven, you brought that woman right into my own bedroom! You made a fool of me in front of all our friends, for months and months. David cried himself to sleep almost every night. And now you're saying it was all just a *mistake?*''

''Your mother is forgiving your father,'' Steven argued stubbornly. ''He's coming home and they're going to make the best of it. She's not throwing everything away because of what he did, and he was a lot worse than I ever was.''

''That's different,'' Sara said.

''How? How is it different?''

Sara hesitated, thinking about her mother's gentle, forgiving spirit, and the surprising strength of character that was restoring health and happiness to a desperately wounded marriage and two ruined lives.

''I don't know,'' she said finally. ''It just is.''

"Sara, look at you," Steven said, trying a different tack. "You're working yourself to death, and there's no need for it. I can take care of you and the kids. I *want* to take care of you."

"Terrific," Sara said grimly. "Send us the money you're supposed to, and then I won't have to work so hard."

Steven flushed. "You know what I mean. I want you to come home. I want the kids to live in their own house and be with their friends again. I want to have my family back and I don't see why I shouldn't, when I've learned my lesson."

"And do you intend to have her, too? Or somebody like her? A newer, younger model, maybe?"

"Never again," Steven said fervently. "Believe me, Sara, that sort of thing is all over. Forever."

"I see," Sara said with a brief, mirthless smile. "So you're telling me everything will really be different from now on, right?"

"Yes," Steven said eagerly. "Yes, it will. I promise, Sara."

He gripped her arm and she flinched automatically, pulling away from his grasp.

"Sara," he went on, "just think about it. Think how nice it would be not to have to work like this all the time, to live in comfort in your own home again and have a real family for the kids."

Despite herself, Sara felt a surge of wistful longing as she pictured what he described.

Her own home and garden, the kitchen she'd always loved, leisure time to read, to do crafts and volunteer work at the hospital, to feel like part of a familiar unit once again, instead of a lonely, isolated misfit in a terrifying world . . .

Seeing her expression, Steven leaned forward to press his advantage. "Look, I won't make you give me an answer right away. I know there's a lot for you to think about. I'm leaving my rental car in Austin tonight and flying back up to Tulsa in the morning, then driving the station wagon home from there. I'll call you next weekend after I get back, and you can tell me what you've decided."

"All right," Sara said, anxious to put an end to the conversation.

She got off the rock and stood up, brushing awkwardly at her jeans to keep from meeting his eyes.

But as they walked back to the ranch house she could sense a new confidence in Steven's step, a certain lightness and buoyancy in his manner.

He thinks he's won, she told herself. *He thinks he's convinced me, and I'm really coming back.*

Sara gazed bleakly at the tidy sprawl of ranch buildings, warm and tranquil in the midday sunlight, and wondered if he was right.

FOR MOST of the following week, Sara thought constantly about Steven's offer. She was surprised and even a little appalled at herself for being so strongly tempted. After all, Steven had rejected her, publicly humiliated her, soiled the whole fabric of their marriage by his selfish behavior.

Each day, Sara went grimly about her work at the motel, and as she scrubbed and cleaned and carried trays, the debate raged in her mind. She forced herself to remember the worst times in her marriage. She thought about Steven's infidelity, the casual cruelty of his put-downs, his deliberate refusal to understand and sympathize with her problems, his general lack of consideration.

But, a part of her argued, weren't all men like that in some ways? What woman wasn't annoyed with her husband's selfishness at least part of the time? And there was no denying that Steven was a good father. Both children still loved him in spite of everything that had happened. And perhaps a lot of the problems had been Sara's fault, too. She hadn't always been as warm and spontaneous as he would have liked, as sexually responsive and willing to experiment. . . .

Sara gave a small grimace of distaste as she wound the vacuum cleaner cord, thinking about some of the bedroom experiments that Steven had proposed in recent years.

But he had promised that everything would be different now. Maybe, like her mother, Sara should believe him and give him a chance. If she did, she could quit this grueling job, leave behind all the townspeople with their shrewd, appraising eyes, and worse, their occasional looks of pity. She could go back home and live in dignity in her own house instead of sleeping in the same bedroom where she'd grown up, a room that still had wallpaper with pink ballerinas on it.

There was no denying, either, that Steven's offer was deeply flattering to Sara's bruised and suffering ego. It meant that she'd actually won out over the glamorous girlfriend, over all the other women available to a man like Steven. He wanted her, not them, and Sara was almost prepared to forgive him anything just because of that one fact.

She ached to talk with someone about the problem, but she couldn't discuss her decision with Mary. It wasn't fair to her mother, who had her own problems to deal with and shouldn't be made to feel responsible for Sara's life as well. It would be better to talk things over with someone absolutely detached and impartial. In fact, irrational as it seemed, there were two people whom Sara hungered to talk with, to explain the whole situation to and ask for advice. One was June Pollock, and the other was Warren Trent.

She thought of June's level blue eyes with their calm, no-nonsense appraisal of the world. Nothing would shock or offend June. She'd just listen and think it over and then say something bluntly accurate that would summarize the whole situation in a nutshell.

But Sara couldn't take her troubles to June. Since that unfortunate day when Sara had snubbed the big woman's tentative offer of friendship, and their awkward meeting later in the bar, June had scrupulously avoided her co-worker, exchanging no more than the cursory words necessary to allocate their separate duties throughout the day. Sometimes Sara's heart actually ached with the longing to be friends with June, to make her smile and joke and be friendly with Sara, as she occasionally was with the cook and even with little Louie, the motel owner, on the days when June was in an unusually tolerant mood.

It was funny, Sara thought, bundling her cleaning things out of the motel room and onto the wheeled cart, how life worked out. She had started out by looking down on June, comfortably feeling herself quite a few cuts above this big, rough-spoken woman. And then, over the weeks, she'd grown to admire June's strength, her quiet fortitude and selflessness. Now Sara actually craved June's company, entirely for its own sake. But it was too late for them to be friends. June's curt silence made that bitterly clear.

Sara hauled her cart down the walk in front of the motel units, still thinking about the huge problem that faced her, and the other person whom she wanted, for some unfathomable reason, to talk with about her decision.

The image of Warren Trent haunted her all the time, sleeping and waking, working and eating, no matter what she did. Memories of him were always there at the back of her mind, especially the intensity of his eyes and the gentleness of his hands when they'd been dancing. Sometimes Sara would remember that night so vividly that she could actually feel his lips moving across her bruised fingers, softly caressing her cheek....

Every time the memory intruded, she felt a deep, visceral shiver that stabbed all the way down into the most private core of her, making her feel moist and vulnerable, full of yearning and confusion.

She understood in some muddled way that this yearning had an important bearing on the decision she was struggling to make. Unless she could sort out the issue of Warren Trent in her mind, learn who he was and why he affected her so powerfully, she could never decide whether to accept Steven's offer.

Sara paused outside Warren's room in the early-morning sunlight. Automatically, she glanced down at her watch, then out to the lot where his truck was still parked. She looked away, pretending she hadn't seen the truck, and unlocked the door of his room. Then she hauled the cart inside, closed the door carefully behind her and unloaded the cleaning supplies with a noisy clatter of pails.

"Hey," Warren said mildly, coming out of the bathroom with a razor in one hand and a towel in the other. "What's all this racket?"

"Sorry," she muttered, not yet able to look at him. She busied herself with the cleaning rags, folding and stacking them back on the cart, and then selecting a couple to use in the bathroom.

When Sara had herself sufficiently under control, she looked up and was almost overcome once again. Warren Trent wore only his blue jeans. His broad, naked chest, dusted with that springy, graying hair, showed the warm beginnings of a tan, and the muscles rippled as he moved aside to lift the vacuum cleaner into position.

Sara smiled awkwardly. "Thanks," she murmured. "Will it bother you if I start in here? I want to get done early today because Mama's going to visit Daddy this afternoon, and I need to get home to babysit so Maria can go to work after lunch. They both..."

She subsided, recognizing that she was babbling like an idiot, and felt a flush creep over her cheeks. Abruptly, she plugged in the vacuum and began to make noisy swipes across the floor near the window.

Warren ducked back into his bathroom and returned after a few moments, carrying a navy blue T-shirt, which he pulled casually over his head and tucked into his jeans. He stood watching her in silence.

"Sara," he said at last, bending to switch the vacuum off, "is something the matter?"

"What do you mean?"

"You've been edgy and jumpy as a cat all week. I just wondered what was wrong, that's all."

Sara toyed with the fastening on the vacuum hose, avoiding his eyes. "How do you know how I've been? You've only seen me a couple of times all week. Are you a mind reader now, too?"

"Look, let's not get into another sparring match, all right? I know we tend to set each other off a bit, and I think I know why, but that's not the issue. I'd just like to know if you've got a problem, that's all.''

Again, Sara ached to confide in Warren, to tell him all about Steven's offer and ask what he thought. Yet even while she entertained the thought, she recognized how unsuitable he was as a confidant. There was nothing between Sara and him at all but some kind of bizarre, inexplicable sexual attraction.

Still, she wanted to talk to him, longed to tell him all about her muddled, confusing life and hear his opinions. In fact, the urge was almost more than she could bear.

"I've just got...some things on my mind," she said with more shortness than she intended. "Are you almost finished in the bathroom?"

"It's all yours."

He followed her to the door of the little bathroom, watching over her shoulder as she filled a pail with water and added the liquid cleanser.

"Your hands are getting tougher," he observed with a sudden grin that Sara could see in the mirror above the sink.

She met his eyes in the mirror and smiled shyly back at him. "I'm getting tougher all over," she said. "I'm really learning a lot."

"Good for you." He hesitated, leaning in the doorway while she knelt to scrub out the bathtub. "So why do you look so worried all the time?"

"My ex-husband wants me to come back to him," Sara said, as calmly as if she were discussing the weather. Her hands trembled a little, but she kept scrubbing, her shoulders turned well away from him.

"I see." Warren seated himself on the edge of the tub and took the cleaning rag gently from her hand. "Sara, come here. Talk to me for a minute."

She felt a brief flood of panic. "But I can't. I have to..."

"Just for a minute."

She nodded and felt him drawing her up beside him, holding her arm as she settled herself on the edge of the tub and stared down at the toes of her grimy sneakers.

"Now, is that what this is all about? He's asked you to go back and you're trying to decide?"

Sara nodded, still gazing at the floor. "He came down for a visit last weekend," she whispered. "I have to make my decision before tomorrow when he calls."

"Do you still love him?"

Startled, Sara pondered the question. She realized that love had never really been a part of her considerations. She'd been thinking more about finances, security, familiarity, social position, what was best for the children....

"Sara?" he prompted gently.

"I don't know," she responded at last in a low, strained voice. "I used to, I think, but he did some really cruel things, and I got to feel..."

"Why would you even think of going back to a man who was cruel?"

"Life is cruel!" Sara burst out in sudden anger. "This job is cruel. It's cruel for David and Laurie not to live with their father. Who am I to decide which kind of cruelty is worst? How can I ever make such an impossible decision?"

Warren looked at her, his dark eyes unreadable in the small, brightly lit room. "God knows," he said at last, "I'm sure not the man to be lecturing anybody about marriage, Sara. But it seems to me that if there's no love there, the whole situation is impossible."

"Those are just empty platitudes. Love isn't all that important," Sara muttered scornfully, staring at her feet again. "It's never been important to me. Not that kind of love, anyway."

"What do you mean? What kind of love isn't important to you?"

"That kind," Sara repeated helplessly. "Physical love. *Sex!*" she flared in anger, stung by his look of silent appraisal. "Is that what you want me to say? All right, I'll say it. Sex isn't really all that important to me. The fact is, I've never been very good at it, and I don't like it much, either."

He was silent for a long time, and Sara was afraid to look at him. When she glanced up timidly, he was staring down at her, his face taut, his dark eyes blazing. Without a word, he gathered her into his arms, lifted her like a child and carried her out into the other room. He kissed her with searching tenderness, then set her down on the rumpled bed.

"Warren..." she protested. But even in her own ears her voice seemed small and faraway, lost in a rising storm of emotion.

He lay next to her, unbuttoning her shirt, kissing her face and throat. Sara gasped as his hands moved over her bare skin, unsnapped the fastening on her bra and tossed it aside. Then he was stroking her breasts with a slow, loving touch, palming them and caressing them with quiet reverence, gazing down at her body as if he had never before seen anything so exquisite.

She felt herself drowning in confusion, lost in wondering sensation. Her last feeble reserves of caution and inhibition were swept away as his dark head bent low and his mouth began to move across her breasts.

"So beautiful," he whispered, pulling away to kiss her mouth again. "Sara, you're so beautiful. Look at you."

He unzipped her jeans and tugged them down over her ankles, then began to caress her body with long gentle strokes, outlining the curve of hip and thigh.

"Skin like silk," he murmured. "So lovely. I always knew you would be lovely."

Sara gave herself up to the pleasure of his touch. She had never known a feeling like this, a sense that she was being utterly cherished, loved with a strong, male tenderness bordering on worship. She understood that there was nothing she had to do, nothing to remember, nothing in all the world to think about. He was doing everything. All that was required of her was to give herself up to this emotion, drift with it, fall and spin and float in rapture.

Her body was completely naked and Warren was touching her again, stroking the intimate parts of her with fingers so sure and lingering that she almost sobbed with pleasure. He seemed to understand the rhythms that surged at the very core of her, and his hands both soothed and aroused.

She was no longer aware of time or place. She had only a hazy sense of who lay with her or even who she was. All she knew was pleasure, a surging, pounding, thrusting kind of pleasure that seemed to go on forever, and threatened to carry her into a place she'd never known.

"Please," she whimpered blindly, arching against his touch, moving her head on the pillow. "Please..."

"It's all right, Sara," he whispered in her ear. "It's all right. I'm looking after you, and you don't have to be afraid of anything you're feeling. It's all right."

She sensed movement beside her, the distant rocking of the bed as he pulled off his shirt and jeans and settled himself beside her again. He drew her into his arms, cuddling her tenderly, kissing the tears that ran down her face. "It's all right," he told her again. "It's all right, sweetheart."

"I want... Please, I want..." She panted, breathless and aching with need.

"Shh. Don't worry," Warren hushed her gently. "Don't worry. I know what you want." Sara tensed as he moved above her, rocked against her, entered her with a slow gentleness that seemed to fill every empty part of her body.

"Just move now, Sara," he whispered, his mouth warm against her face. "Relax and move. Do whatever you want. I won't hurt you."

Tentatively, cautiously, she began to respond, to let her body take over and seek its own release. Her pleasure mounted, throbbed and surged, grew almost unbearable.

"I'm afraid!" she gasped into the storm that raged all around her. "I'm so afraid...."

"Don't be afraid, Sara. There's nothing to be afraid of. Just go with it. Go with your feelings. You're so beautiful, Sara...."

And then, suddenly she was there. The world shivered and trembled, split into a thousand shimmering fragments that rained down all around her. Sara lay panting on the bed, washed over with slow, rippling tides of delight that began at the very center of her body and warmed her like molten sunshine.

"Oh, God," she murmured, incoherent with amazement. "Oh, my God."

She rolled her head cautiously and studied the silent, dark face of the man who lay beside her.

"Did you finish?" she asked with childlike concern.

He chuckled. "Would I have stopped otherwise?"

"I don't know." Sara gazed at him, still too amazed to be cautious about what she said. "That was the very first time for me," she told him.

He grinned and bent to kiss the tip of her nose. "Oh, sure," he teased. "And those two kids were immaculate conceptions, right?"

Sara watched his face, her eyes wide and serious. "No," she said earnestly. "I mean, I never felt that before."

"Oh, Sara," he whispered.

"Steven was the only man I ever slept with," she went on, turning away to stare at the ceiling. "I was nineteen the first time we slept together. I had no idea what it was like with somebody else."

"And he never satisfied you in bed?"

"He said it was my fault." Sara rolled her head to look again at the man beside her. "He said I was frigid, and it would be impossible for any man to get me to respond. He said it was my fault that he was driven to be unfaithful, because I wasn't able to fulfill him properly."

Warren's face darkened. "My God," he said finally, sitting up and pulling the blanket over her naked body. "How could any man say that about you? If ever a woman was made and designed to pleasure a man, Sara Gibson, it was you."

"Me?"

"Yes," he said, swinging himself off the bed and reaching for his clothes. "You. You're a beautiful, sexy, desirable, responsive woman. From now on, don't ever let anybody tell you different, all right?"

Sara watched him, drowsily pleased by the lines of his big hard body, the muscular legs and lean hips and long powerful torso.

But gradually, as he dressed, reality began to creep back into her consciousness. She felt a sharp awareness of the shabby little motel room, the glare of morning sunshine beyond the ill-fitting drapes and especially of the barefoot man by the bed who was still a virtual stranger to her, even though he had just explored the most intimate parts of her body.

Sara got out of bed, snatched her clothes and bolted for the bathroom, dressing hastily with nervous, shaking hands. At last, she buttoned her shirt and gazed at herself in the mirror. The flushed face that looked back at her seemed familiar, yet there was a subtle difference. Despite her growing anxiety, she saw a satisfied languor in the eyes, a new lift of confidence in the chin.

I'm thirty-four years old, and I've just experienced sexual fulfillment for the first time in my life, Sara thought in wonder. *I guess it's natural that I'd look a little different after something like that.*

She edged her way back out into the main room, feeling suddenly cold and taut with apprehension. Warren Trent stood by the door, fully dressed and wearing his battered leather jacket, truck keys already in his hand.

"Are you all right?" he asked.

Sara gave him a jerky nod and bent aimlessly to pick up the vacuum cleaner hose. "I guess..." she began in a low voice, then choked and couldn't go on.

"What, Sara?" he asked.

She could hardly believe the gentleness of his voice. He had always been so curt, so rough and mocking when he spoke to her. But now his eyes were calm and kind, and his voice held nothing but tenderness.

Sara gave him a despairing glance and tried again. "I guess you just did that so I'd know how it feels, right? It was kind of a...a public service gesture on your part."

"Oh, definitely not public service, Sara," he told her with a flash of his sardonic grin. "More like private service, wouldn't you say?"

"You know what I mean." She met his gaze directly. "It had nothing to do with..." She hesitated, dropping her eyes, then forced herself to look at him again. "It had nothing to do with love, or anything like that."

"Love is a luxury I can't afford, Sara. Love isn't meant for men like me."

"What do you mean, men like you? What kind of man are you anyway, Warren? What is it that makes you so different from everybody else?"

He shrugged and looked away, his face taking on the remote, shuttered look that she was coming to know so well. Desperate to understand him, emboldened by her fear and her new tumult of emotions, Sara moved toward him and grasped his arm.

"What's in the barn, Warren?" she asked him. "What are you really doing here in Crystal Creek?"

He stared at her coldly and shook his jacket free of her grasp. "Look, Sara, don't make this mistake."

"What mistake?"

"Don't assume that just because of what happened here a few minutes ago, you've got some right to intrude on my privacy. Nobody's had that right for twenty years, and you don't have it now."

"And is that the way you like it, Warren? You like being all solitary and untouched, apart from other people and the ordinary way they live their lives? It seems awfully lonely to me."

"That's the way I like it," he said curtly.

"Are you doing something illegal?" Sara went on with growing recklessness. "Everybody says you're doing something terrible in that barn, and the law will probably catch you soon."

"I guess that's what they say. They should know, Sara. After all, the people in this town have known me a long time."

Sara looked at him, angered by his stubborn refusal to let his guard slip even a little. She thought about what she'd seen the other night, the old barn with its covered windows and the key nestling in its hiding place. Suddenly, she had to clench her fists tightly to keep her hands from shaking.

Warren turned toward the door, then paused and looked back at her. " Sara," he said.

"Yes?"

"Don't do this again, girl. What you just did was a really careless, foolhardy thing."

She gazed at him in hurt astonishment. "I don't...I don't know what you mean. I certainly didn't do it all by myself, Warren."

"I mean..." He paused awkwardly, drew a deep breath and continued. "You don't know me, Sara. You don't know anything about me, and these are dangerous times. Sex is a dangerous business."

Sara's face drained of color and her eyes widened. She put a hand over her mouth and stared at him, thinking wildly about her parents, her children, all the conventional responsibilities of her life and the kind of dark, terrible hazards he was talking about.

Not to mention the oldest fear of all for a woman, the fear of pregnancy. She hadn't thought of any of that when she fell into bed with Warren Trent. It had never been Sara's habit to be so careless about her life, but the man drove her completely out of her mind with passion....

Gradually his warning registered. "What are you telling me?" she whispered hoarsely. "Are you saying that you're..."

"I'm not telling you anything. As it happens, you made a pretty good choice. I'm not promiscuous. In fact, I haven't been with a woman for almost two years. And I had some blood tests a couple of months ago when I did a little traveling overseas, so I guess I'm about as safe a man as you could find."

Sara's knees buckled, and she leaned briefly against the wall, almost dizzy with relief. "Then what are you saying?"

"I'm saying," he repeated patiently, "that having unprotected sex with strangers isn't a wise thing to do, Sara. What you just did here with me this morning, it was a reckless way to behave. Make sure you never do it again. Next time you experiment sexually, buy yourself some protection and see that it's used."

Sara felt a welling of outrage. "So what do you think, Warren? Are you afraid that I'm going to go around seducing every man who crosses my path from now on? Is that what you think of me?"

"I think you're a beautiful, sexy woman who's just learned what sex feels like. I'm real sure you're going to want that feeling again," he told her quietly. "And I think you're obviously so innocent about the ways of the world, even though you're thirty-four years old, that you need to be warned to be careful."

Sara watched him, searching for some kind of response as he turned the door handle and started outside. Again, he paused and looked back at her.

"Sara?"

"What?"

"Don't go back to him, even if he begs you. Find yourself a better man. Find someone who can love you properly, and hold on to him."

Then he was gone. Sara moved over to the window and drew the curtain aside a few inches to watch as he strode across the motel square toward the parking lot.

"I don't want another man," she whispered at his retreating figure, blinking back hot tears of misery. "I want you. And I don't even know who you are."

When he finally disappeared from sight, she let the curtain drop and moved back into the room, aimlessly gathering her supplies and trying to get herself organized and go on with her work.

But all she could think about was Warren Trent, his hands and eyes and mouth and the marvelous way he'd made her feel. Random bits of their conversation kept drifting back to her, troubling her like elusive scraps of some tantalizing mystery.

I haven't been with a woman for almost two years, his voice echoed within her mind as she ran the vacuum cleaner over the stained carpet. *I had some blood tests when I did a little traveling overseas. The people in this town have known me a long time....*

"Why were you traveling overseas, Warren?" she murmured aloud, gathering her cleaning supplies onto the cart and going into the bathroom to wring out the scrubbing cloths. "Who are you? What's in the barn?"

She looked down at his pile of suitcases, all neatly stacked and secured with padlocks, as they had been ever since the day she'd done her bit of amateur sleuthing. And again she saw the image of the shuttered gray barn, silent and unrevealing in the twilight, and the strange little man with the ponytail watching as Warren hid the key behind the window covering.

CHAPTER EIGHT

MARY GIBSON DROVE through the electronic gates and into the visitors' parking lot, realizing, with a little shock of surprise, that this was the last time she would ever have to make this arduous journey to see her husband.

One more month, she thought.

The words sang in her mind as she submitted to a brief search at the door, then followed the female guard into a small visiting room already half-filled with anxious women and quiet men in prison garb.

"He'll be right with you, Mrs. Gibson," the guard said. "He knows you're coming."

"Are you sure he knows?" Mary gripped her handbag and seated herself at one of the tables.

The guard smiled and looked suddenly matronly and pleasant, even in her harsh uniform. "When you're coming to visit, that's pretty much all he talks about for a week beforehand, Mrs. Gibson."

Mary nodded. A door opened across the room and her husband entered, starting toward Mary, his face alight with eagerness.

"Hi, Al," Mary said shyly as he approached. "How've you been?"

"Just fine, Mary. Just fine." Bubba Gibson stood with his gnarled hands on the back of a chair, gazing hungrily at his wife. "Don't you look fine," he murmured, then turned to the guard, who was approaching them with a confiding grin.

"All set?" she whispered.

Bubba nodded and reached for Mary's elbow. She got to her feet, staring at him in surprise.

"A little treat today, for your last visit," the guard said. "You can walk outside and sit on a bench to talk."

"Oh," Mary said with startled pleasure, smiling at the woman. "That's real nice."

"Well, he's been a pretty nice guy, this man of yours," the guard said. "He's done us a lot of good, helping out and talking with the younger fellows here, and we appreciate it."

Bubba smiled at the woman. Mary glanced at him, taken aback by yet another difference in her husband. Bubba Gibson had never been able to interact with any woman, regardless of her age or status, without a kind of jovial, heavy-handed flirting that seemed to be second nature to him.

But all that was apparently gone now. Bubba's attitude to the female prison guard was quietly courteous, calm and friendly, without any trace of familiarity. Again, Mary felt a surge of optimism, and a tremulous happiness that was different from anything she'd ever known.

The guard led them through a heavy side door opening onto a small fenced garden with a stretch of dusty grass and ragged pecan trees shading a few functional metal benches.

"Gawd." Bubba sighed, raising his pale face to the sunlight. "Don't that feel good, Mary? I never thought a man could get high on something as simple as the way the sun feels shining in his eyes."

Mary gripped his hand and walked beside him to one of the benches. "Wait'll you get home, Al. You're likely going to be out in the sun eighteen hours a day. There's so much work to do."

Bubba sighed again and sank onto the bench, drawing her down beside him. "It seems too good to be true," he said. "How's Sara and the kids?"

"Oh, they're all fine," Mary said automatically. "Just fine."

"Sara's still working over at the Lonely Bull?"

Mary nodded. "It's been real hard, but in a way I think it's good for her, too. She won't consider quitting, no matter what I say. I think it's something she wants to do just to prove she can do it."

"I never figured Sara to be that tough, did you? Reckon she's surprised a lot of people."

Mary grinned suddenly. "Reckon she has."

Bubba put his arm around Mary's shoulders and drew her close, hugging her shyly. "First time I've been alone with my wife in a long time," he whispered against her hair.

Mary shivered in his arms. "Oh, Al, I feel like a girl again," she confessed. "I'm all shaky."

He laughed and kissed her, a gentle, tentative kiss. They drew apart in flustered nervousness, conscious of a guard beyond the front gates and another standing unobtrusively at the edge of the open space near the door.

"How's my boy, Davey? Still getting into all kinds of trouble?"

Mary laughed. "He's waiting so hard for you to come home. He has a calendar up in his room and he crosses the days off every morning before school, just like he's waiting for Christmas."

Bubba flushed with pleasure. "I didn't know the boy liked me so much."

"Oh, he likes you a lot, but that's only part of it," Mary said dryly. "He wants a pellet gun in the worst way, and I told him he couldn't have it until Grandpa came home."

Bubba chuckled. "Well, we'll have to see about that. Maybe not till next year," he added firmly. "Davey's only seven, and that's pretty young for guns."

Mary sighed and leaned against her husband, thinking how wonderful it would be to have him back, to have someone sharing the decisions and problems.

"How about Laurie? Is she settling in pretty good?"

"She's amazing, Al. She's into everything in school, has friends in and out all the time, the phone ringing all day long. You'd think she'd lived in Crystal Creek since she was born."

"Well, that's real good," Bubba said with warm satisfaction. "It's a tough thing to uproot kids at that age. Sara's done well, bringing them home and getting them settled so easy."

Mary hesitated, frowning as she thought about Sara's tense, preoccupied look these days.

"Mary?" Bubba asked in concern.

Mary shook herself and turned to him reluctantly. "Well...I was just wondering if those kids are maybe going to be uprooted another time, Al."

"Why? What do you mean?"

Mary told him about Steven's visit the previous weekend, and her suspicion that Sara was considering going back to Connecticut.

Bubba gazed at the wire mesh bordering the dusty yard, his face troubled. "What do you think about that, Mary?"

"I don't know what to think," Mary said. "I know there's always this feeling that it's good for families to get back together and work out their problems. But I looked at him real close, Al, and there's just... something about him. Something I don't like. I think he was pretty hard on Sara while they were married, even though we never suspected a thing."

Bubba's big hands tensed. "Did he hit her?"

"Not that. But he..." Mary flushed. "He had a girlfriend, and he even brought her right to their house when Sara was away. She came home with the kids one day and caught them. And," Mary added hastily, "I told you how he was awful about the money...."

Bubba put his arms around her awkwardly, his big body quivering with the shame and remorse he felt. "Men change, Mary," he whispered. "Sometimes men can change."

She looked up at him, blinking furiously to keep from crying. "I know that, Al," she murmured. "Do you think I don't know that? But I'm still not sure about Steven Milne."

"Well," Bubba said finally, "I guess we'll just have to wait and see, won't we?"

"I don't know what else we can do. She's a grown woman. We sure can't be forcing our opinions on her anymore."

Bubba was silent for a moment, brooding as he stared at the rolling land beyond the fence. Finally, he shook his shoulders and forced his voice to sound light and carefree. "So, is there any more news?"

"Well, they had the wedding at the Double C last month just after I was here. A double wedding," Mary added, mildly tickled by the play on words.

"Cal and Lynn and their sweethearts?"

Mary nodded. "It was a real nice ceremony. Quiet, not too many people there, and the girls both looked so pretty. You'd have loved it, Al. I missed you so much."

Again, Bubba was silent, gazing beyond the fenced enclosure. "How's J.T. these days?" he asked finally.

Mary laughed. "Al, you won't believe it. We were over there last Sunday for a barbecue, and you should see him with that baby. It's the most amazing thing."

Bubba grinned. "Yeah? How?"

"Well, you remember how J.T. was with his kids when they were babies? Pauline would bring them to him after dinner, all clean and scrubbed, and he'd sit there as proud as anything, and hold them on his knee like they were made of glass and might break. Remember?"

"I remember," Bubba said with a wistful smile. "It seems like yesterday, Mary, when we were all young together and raising our babies."

Mary squeezed his hand fondly. "Well, with this new baby, J.T.'s a totally different man. He acts like he invented little Jennifer and built her himself out of spare parts. He carries her all over the place, sings to her, brags about her... I swear, Al, I wouldn't be surprised if he even changes diapers!"

Bubba gaped at her. "J. T. McKinney?" he asked in disbelief. "Mary, you're joshin' me."

"I'm sure not. Last weekend he was showing me her new tooth, and bragging that she can sit up already and she has superior reflexes because she reaches for the feeding spoon when he holds it up in front of her."

Bubba chuckled. "I'm glad I'll be comin' home soon," he said. "That's gonna be too much fun to miss, J.T. with a baby."

"I wouldn't be surprised if there's another baby around the Double C pretty soon," Mary said.

"Ruth and Tyler?"

Mary nodded. "They're both working so hard these days, planning the winery and building that new house of theirs, but Cynthia says they want to start a family right away. And I noticed Ruth was looking a little peaked on the weekend. I wouldn't be surprised."

"How does Tyler feel about that?"

Mary laughed. "Poor Tyler. He's still so much in love with that girl he can't even see straight. I'd never have thought Tyler McKinney could love somebody so much. I always reckoned he was a little cold, but I guess he just needed the right woman."

"We all need the right woman, Mary," Bubba said with quiet sincerity. "And it's sure a lucky man who finds her."

Mary smiled and nestled against him, marveling at the way her new happiness seemed to have sprung so magically out of dust and ashes. A year ago at this time, there was nothing in Mary Gibson's life that was really worth living for, just pain and humiliation and regret. Now the sky was full of rainbows, and she didn't really know what had happened to make the difference. So many things...

"Speaking of finding the right woman," she said at last, "you should see Brock and Amanda. That boy is just plumb foolish, Al. He's crazy in love."

Bubba frowned briefly. "I never met this girl, but you said she's a classy New York type, didn't you? It's hard to figure, Brock with a woman like that."

Mary chuckled. "Amanda used to be a classy New York type, but not anymore. That was just a thin veneer over a girl who's pure Texas. You should see her now. She and Alvin walked over yesterday for coffee, and both of them had cactus in their feet when they arrived. I had to do emergency surgery on them in the kitchen. Alvin howled like a baby."

Bubba threw back his shaggy head and laughed aloud, almost like his old booming laugh. "That Alvin, he's the most chickenhearted dog in the world. Is he still scared of your big black tomcat?"

"Hannibal? Alvin's terrified of him. Davey gets a kick out of teasing the pitiful thing, hiding around a corner with Hannibal and then jumping out when Alvin isn't expecting it. I think he's going to give that poor fat dog a heart condition."

Bubba shook with laughter and wiped tears from his eyes. "Are they livin' together at Brock's ranch these days?"

"Not officially. Amanda's still got her apartment in Austin and she's running her business there, too. In fact, she says it's doing pretty well, and that's going to be a help to Brock until he gets the ranch back in shape."

"Hard to see Brock Monroe takin' help from a woman," Bubba muttered.

Mary chuckled. "Oh, Al, don't be silly. It's a whole new world. These days marriages are partnerships, don't you understand? There's no hard-and-fast rules like when we were young. Everybody gives and takes and shares, and it's just wonderful."

Bubba cocked a bushy eyebrow at his wife. "And that's what my wife wants? A modern marriage, fifty-fifty and all that?"

Mary nodded, suddenly grave. "Yes, Al. That's exactly what I want."

"Well," Bubba said, nodding agreement, "who am I to argue? You're the girl with all the ostriches."

Mary giggled and cuddled up beside him again, still thinking about their young neighbors. "She's out there every weekend. Amanda, I mean. And you should see what they're doing to that old ranch house. It's going to be a real showplace, Al."

"I hope they don't repair the kitchen lintel that old Caspar Monroe blasted away with his shotgun. I always liked that story."

"They did replace it, but Brock's just like you. He mounted the old one in his study. Amanda thought it was barbaric."

Bubba nodded in satisfaction. "How's Vern and Carolyn?" he asked after a brief silence. "Still gettin' along good?"

"They sure are. They're just as settled as if they'd been married thirty years."

"Well, he's loved her more'n thirty years. Nice to see Vern gettin' what he wants, because he sure waited long enough."

Mary smiled, thinking about the contented look in Carolyn's eyes these days. Vernon Trent certainly wasn't the only one getting what he wanted from that marriage. . . .

"How about little Warren? Somebody told me last month that he'd just turned up in town, actin' real strange. Is he still around?"

"Oh, my, yes," Mary said dryly. "He sure is. The whole town is just on its ear, Al, watching that boy and trying to figure out what he's up to."

"What's the big mystery?"

Mary told her husband all about Warren Trent, about his strange meetings with sinister outsiders, his daily occupation within the shuttered barn, his cold, taciturn avoidance of townspeople and the wild speculations surrounding his activities.

Bubba listened, gazing with narrowed eyes at the springtime world beyond the fence, and gave a low, thoughtful whistle. "Sounds like maybe little Warren is fixin' to spend a few months out here as a guest at the Crowbar Hotel, don't it?"

"Folks think he's already spent more than a few months here in his life. And by the way," Mary added, "he's not 'little Warren' anymore, Al. He's more than six feet tall, almost forty years old and built like a steer wrestler."

Bubba shook his head. "Hard to figure. Warren Trent was always such a wiry little kid, like tryin' to catch quicksilver. Remember when Sara was little and I coached kids' softball for a few years, Mary?"

"It was so much fun," Mary said wistfully. "I'd take her toys and a blanket and a picnic lunch, and she'd play under the trees while you tried to teach all those wild boys to hit and catch balls.''

Bubba chuckled fondly at the memory. "Frustrating as hell. But Warren Trent was one of my stars, did you remember that?''

Mary stared at her husband. "He was?''

"He sure was. Ten times the talent of any other kid on the field, but I could hardly ever get him to play. The boy always had a chip on his shoulder the size of a two-by-four, and he was a real scrawny little kid. At game time I had to coax him down out of the trees, go to his daddy's drugstore and haul him out from under the back steps, find him down by the swimming hole . . . he was sure a tough case.''

"Didn't he like to play?''

Bubba frowned thoughtfully. "I think he loved to play. He had more natural ability than anybody I've ever seen. He could have gone all the way to the big leagues, Mary. But he didn't believe he was good, and I couldn't tell him because he was always so full of anger and hurtin'.''

Mary watched in silence as Bubba bent to pick a stalk of dusty bunchgrass and leaned back to chew on it thoughtfully.

"One day,'' Bubba went on, "when Warren was a couple years older than Davey, he didn't turn up for our championship game against Mason County. I found the kid down by the river catching snakes and hauled him back up to the ball diamond, put his shirt on and made him play. He hit a double and a home run and caught three balls in the field that nobody should ever have been able to catch, and we won."

"Then what happened?"

"When Warren came in from the field, I hugged the kid and told him I loved him. He threw off his shirt and tossed his ball glove down in the dirt and ran off."

"Did you run after him?"

"Well, sure I did. I found him hiding in the trees, crying his heart out. I sat for a long time and cuddled him."

Mary stared at her husband, wide-eyed and silent. "You never told me this, Al."

Bubba smiled awkwardly. "I had the impression that the kid never wanted me to tell anybody. It was just our secret, that time when he cried in my arms. I've never mentioned it to a living soul until right now, Mary."

There was a moment of awkward silence, then Mary turned back to her husband. "Do you think he might be dangerous?" she asked abruptly.

"Dangerous? How?"

"Like, would he...hurt somebody? Could Warren Trent be violent, do you think?"

Bubba frowned. "Mary, what are you talking about?"

"Well..." Mary began reluctantly, hating to burden her husband with situations at home that he was still helpless to do anything about.

"Mary?"

"Warren's shown a lot of... of interest in Sara and the kids," she murmured finally, looking down at her hands.

"Interest? Like what?"

"He was at the bus depot when they arrived, and helped her carry their bags. He got to know Davey then, and he talks to him from time to time. And he's staying at the motel where Sara works, so she sees him there, too."

"And?" Bubba asked tensely.

"I don't know," Mary said, letting her hands fall open on her lap in a little gesture of helplessness. "At first I think she was kind of scared of him, and then she just seemed annoyed by the fact that the man even existed, and now it's so complicated that I don't know what she's feeling."

"And nobody's got any idea what he's doing back in town? Not even Vern?"

"Not even Vern," Mary echoed soberly.

"Goddammit," Bubba muttered, clenching his fists and pounding them on the knees of his khaki prison trousers. "Mary, I don't know if I can wait a whole month to get out of here!"

"Of course you can," Mary said, leaning over to kiss him, and then nodding at the guard who approached, swinging her ring of keys with a discreet little tinkling sound.

"One more month," Bubba repeated, getting to his feet and turning to give his wife a sudden, fierce hug. "Hold on, girl. Wait for me."

"I'm waiting," Mary said when she could breathe again. "I'd wait forever if I had to, Al. A month, that's nothing."

Bubba passed the female guard with a trace of his old teasing sparkle. "This here wife of mine," he said solemnly, giving Mary another warm hug, "is one hell of a woman. I hope y'all know that."

Mary buried her face against his rough shirtfront for a moment, then followed him back through the door and waited as it was locked securely behind them.

WHILE MARY GIBSON WAS across the state visiting her husband, Sara was rushing through her workday at the motel so she could get home and relieve Maria of her baby-sitting duties.

Laden with cups and trays, she hurried among the noisy Friday lunch crowd, both hoping and dreading the prospect that Warren Trent might come into the restaurant for lunch, as he frequently did. But there was no sign of his broad shoulders and dark head among the laughing patrons.

Sara took orders and dealt with complaints, careful not to look into anyone's eyes. She felt that the events of the morning must somehow be branded on her face, and that anyone who looked at her carefully would know where she'd been, what had happened between her and Warren Trent in that shadowy little motel room.

Even her body felt unfamiliar to her, as if she'd somehow stepped outside herself and taken up resi-

dence in another person. There was a wondrous met-
amorphosis taking place within Sara Gibson, a series
of changes so sweeping and awesome that they frightened her. She dreaded the night to come, the quiet
lonely time in her own bed when she would be forced
to look at herself and recognize what she'd become.

What could have possessed her, to let him do what
he'd done? But, Sara admitted to herself, scrubbing a
table and laying out fresh silverware, it wasn't accurate to say that she'd let him. The truth was, she'd encouraged him. She'd craved Warren's touch, his hard
body and seeking hands, and she must have transmit-
ted a message to him somehow.

What did he think about her now?

Sara remembered his calm warning to be careful in
the future about her sexual behavior, his cryptic
statement that love was a luxury not meant for men
like him. Clearly he'd looked on their lovemaking as
an isolated episode. He had no intention of allowing
it to happen again.

But he'd enjoyed it, too. Sara knew that he had. She
recalled some of the things he'd whispered to her, the
way his mouth and hands had caressed her, and shivered at the memory.

"Double club an' fries, two Bull Burgers!" June
shouted from her place at the smoky grill. "Hey,
Princess, you working here today or just paying us a
royal visit?"

Sara gathered herself together, muttered an apology and moved hastily to pick up the loaded plates of food that crowded the high counter.

At last the rush began to subside and the restaurant emptied. Sara cleaned the littered tables, carried an armload of plates back to the kitchen and paused to pour herself a cup of coffee. She sighed with relief, lowering herself wearily into a chair at a small table wedged behind the fridge, and watched June scrape grease from the surface of the grill. The tall woman's body was taut and strong, her movements graceful in their spare efficiency as she worked. Sara fixed on June's big capable hands, then on the calm planes of her face, and felt a surge of wistfulness.

Maybe if she asked, June would go with her to the bar tonight. Jessica Reynolds was going to be making a rare singing appearance, and it was quite a treat for the Lonely Bull to host an artist of Jessica's talent. Then Sara wouldn't have to be alone with her troubled thoughts. She could have a few drinks, dance a bit, get so tired that when she went home, she'd fall into bed and go right to sleep, instead of lying awake thinking about Warren's face, his hands, the way his body felt, moving in hers....

Besides, Sara realized, helpless in the wake of this surging emotion, there was always a chance that Warren might be in the bar tonight, might even ask her to dance again. Then she'd get to be in his arms, hold his strong body close to her in the smoky darkness.

Help, me, Lord, she thought in despair. *Help me to deal with this. I just don't know what to do about the way I feel.*

"June, would you like to—" she said aloud, then fell abruptly silent.

June glanced up sharply, her face wary. "What? Would I like to what?"

Sara gazed at the other woman, her resolve crumbling. She couldn't bear another tongue-lashing from June right now. In fact, Sara's emotions were so turbulent and confused that a single unkind remark would probably have made her burst into tears.

"I was just wondering," she said, grasping at straws, "if... if you'd let Carlie go with us to Austin tomorrow afternoon. I'm taking my kids to see the ice show, and it's supposed to be really good. They're skating an adaptation of 'Beauty and the Beast.' I thought Carlie might like to go."

"No," June said coldly. "She wouldn't."

"But I think she'd really enjoy it. And Laurie, that's my daughter, she's just a couple of—"

June slapped the spatula angrily on the grill and faced Sara, her blue eyes blazing. "You think this trip would be real nice for Carlie, don't you? Give her a chance to see a whole different world, right? Well, there's no point in Carlie getting to see a whole different world, because she damn well has to live in the one she's stuck with!"

June subsided, her chest heaving angrily, and turned her attention back to the grill.

Sara looked on silently, uncertain what to say.

"Carlie dreams about ice skating," June muttered in a low, tight voice. "She watches it on TV every chance she gets, and pesters me to let her learn how."

"But can't she—"

"How can Carlie ice-skate?" June said bitterly, her eyes glittering with tears. "Can she get a special built-up skate, maybe? Some nice black custom job with a four-inch sole? That'd look real nice with them little skating dresses."

Sara put her cup down and searched helplessly for something to say. "But isn't there...I mean, couldn't another operation..."

"Oh, sure," June said wearily. "Another operation is all she needs. Just one or two more, and she'll have practically a normal foot, the doctor says. But where do I get the money for a couple more operations? You know how much it costs? You got any idea how much I've spent already?"

"I know it's expensive," Sara said quietly. "But why won't you let her go to watch the show if she likes skating? It won't cost a thing. I'm driving in anyway, and Amanda Walker got a bunch of free tickets for helping to supply the costumes. She can give me as many as we need."

"That's not the point," June said coldly, turning her back on Sara. "The point is, I don't want Carlie seeing a kind of life that can't be hers, and getting notions about things. It'll only bring her hurt."

"Parents have no right to make decisions about what kind of life their children should lead," Sara said firmly, surprising herself. "It's a bad mistake. Children are people, too, and their parents should remember that."

June whirled angrily to face the other woman, spatula in hand, her face twisted with fury. "Yeah? And where do you get off, telling me how to raise my kid? Are you such a terrific mother?"

"No," Sara said calmly. "Lots of times I make mistakes, really terrible ones. But that's not what I was thinking about. Actually I was remembering my father, and how he treated me."

"Bubba?" June said in surprise. "He thought you hung the moon, didn't he?" Her face was still pale with anger, but her voice had modulated a little. She moved closer to the table, looking down at Sara.

"Oh, sure. Daddy thought I was wonderful. But he also made all the decisions about me, what kind of person I was and how I should be treated. He called me his princess and demanded that I live up to the name, and I couldn't. It almost ruined my life."

June poured herself a cup of coffee and sank into the other chair, her eyes still fixed on Sara's face.

"It's really hard," Sara went on, "having everyone expect you to be a princess when you know in your heart that you're just an absolutely ordinary person. I always felt like such a fraud. But I couldn't tell my father that I wasn't a princess. I just crept through life all anxious and terrified of disappointing him, and then I grew up afraid of disappointing anybody else, either.''

She listened to her own voice, amazed by the things she was saying. Some of them, she hadn't even been aware of thinking, but as she spoke the words aloud, Sara recognized that they were true. What was more, the relief of saying them aloud, even to someone as unsympathetic as June Pollock, was intensely comforting.

"I turned into a woman so insecure and anxious to please that I was almost pitiful," Sara said, looking out at the square of sky beyond the dirty restaurant windows. "And I haven't changed. A while ago, I refused to go to the bar with you because I was afraid, I guess, that it wasn't the princess-type thing to do, although I knew I'd likely enjoy myself if I went. And you know what, June? Up until this morning, I was actually considering going back to my ex-husband, even though he shamed me and humiliated me every chance he got, and I don't love him at all. I was just so damned grateful to him for wanting me!''

June stirred sugar into her coffee and sipped it in tense silence.

"So don't take it on yourself to decide what Carlie needs, or how she should live her life," Sara concluded recklessly. "Ask her how she feels about it, and then listen to what she says. We owe our kids that much consideration, at least, just because we brought them into the world."

"Okay," June said abruptly, getting up from the table and moving across the room to stack dishes into the sink. "Carlie can go with you to Austin. What time will you come to get her?"

"About eleven o'clock, is that all right? We're having lunch in town, and the show starts at—"

"She'll be ready," June said, running jets of streaming water into the sink and turning her back deliberately.

Sara stared at the other woman for a moment, started to speak and thought better of it. At last, she hung up her apron and trudged outside into the glittering sunlight.

CHAPTER NINE

NEXT DAY, Sara drove with her children and Carlie Pollock through the rich, spring countryside between Crystal Creek and Austin. She smiled as she listened to the happy chatter of the young people in the car, pleased at how well they were getting along.

Laurie and Carlie were in the back seat, leafing though Laurie's neat albums of stickers. Carlie, too, was apparently a sticker fancier, and was awed by Laurie's impressive collection.

And Laurie's strong protective instincts were clearly stirred by this fragile little girl with her shining smile and the ungainly black boot on her thin leg. Anybody who was unfortunate or afflicted in any way tended to bring out this side of Laurie, a tender, fiercely sheltering quality that made Sara feel a warm pride in her daughter.

She glanced at David, who was beside her in the front seat. He chafed restlessly within the confines of his seat belt, obviously longing to join the chatter of the girls.

"Tired of being in the car, Davey?" Sara asked him with a smile.

"When will we get there?"

"Not long now. We'll be getting to the city in fifteen minutes or so."

"It's nice here," David said, looking out the window. "Isn't it?"

"Yes, it is." Sara glanced at her son's profile. "Do you still get homesick for Connecticut, Davey?"

He shrugged. "Not much. It's more fun here. I miss Dad sometimes, though."

Sara gripped the wheel and gazed straight ahead at the winding highway. "Lots of times," she ventured, "after a divorce, kids keep on wishing for a long time that their parents would get back together again. Do you ever feel that way, Davey?"

He looked at her quickly. "Why? Are you and Dad going to get back together? He said we might be going home. He told me last week on the phone."

"No, dear," Sara told him in a gentle voice. "We're not. In fact, I told your Dad last night that it was never going to happen. I just wanted to be certain you weren't hoping for that."

"I used to," David muttered, after glancing quickly over his shoulder to make sure the girls were deeply engrossed in their conversation. "I used to wish all the time that you and Dad would live together again. I even said it in my prayers every night for a long time," he added shyly.

Sara bit her lip. "Did you, sweetie?"

"Yeah. But now I don't anymore."

"Why not, Davey?"

"Well..." David frowned thoughtfully, fingering the buckle on his seat belt. "I like it here," he said finally. "I like Grandma and the ranch, and Bobby and stuff, and I like it that you don't cry anymore. I wish Dad would come visit us more," he added, "but I don't want to go back home."

Sara felt a quick flood of relief, and such a warm glow of love for her small son that she didn't reprimand him immediately when he unfastened the belt buckle and turned to kneel on the seat, gazing over at the two girls in the back. "Hey, does that thing hurt?" he asked, indicating the heavy boot on Carlie's foot.

"Shut up, stupid!" Laurie told him in a furious undertone. "It's none of your business. Mom, Davey undid his seat belt."

"I don't mind if he asks about my foot," Carlie said cheerfully. "The kids at school talk about it, too. They tease me all the time. The boys call me Lurch."

Sara gripped the wheel in silence, outraged by the casual cruelty of children, and surprised by Carlie's sunny resilience. June was certainly doing a wonderful job of raising this little girl.

"Does it?" David asked again.

"What?"

"Does it hurt?"

"Sometimes," Carlie said. "If I walk for a long time, or stand up at the blackboard or something, my foot starts to ache, and then Mama has to rub it with alcohol. Mama says I just need one or two more operations and it won't hurt anymore, and I can wear shoes like other kids."

"Is it scary, having an operation?" David asked, fascinated.

"You don't know anything about it," Carlie told him. "You're asleep the whole time."

"Asleep like in your bed at night, or asleep like in a coma?"

"I guess like in a coma," Carlie said, after thoughtful consideration, "because it's daytime and everything, but you don't wake up until they're finished, even though they're cutting you and stuff."

"You had an operation, Davey," Sara told him. "You had your tonsils out when you were five."

David glanced at his mother in surprise. "Was that an operation?"

"Certainly it was."

"I ate ice cream all the time, for three whole days," David told the girls importantly. "And I was real sick, wasn't I, Mom?"

"Yes, you were. Do up your seat belt, David," his mother added automatically. "We're almost there."

David sighed and strapped himself in again, while the two girls in the back seat returned to their animated, giggling conversation.

A COUPLE OF HOURS LATER, Sara glanced down with a smile at Carlie's rapt face. All the childish giggles had vanished long ago. June's little daughter was caught up in the spectacle she was watching, pale and taut with excitement.

Sara put an arm around the child and leaned over to cuddle her. "Having a good time, Carlie? Do you like the skating?"

"Oh, it's beautiful," Carlie said with a sigh of bliss, watching a pair of butterflies as they skimmed by on the ice, shimmering wings outspread. "It's so beautiful. I never saw anything as wonderful as this, never in all my life."

The butterflies danced and pirouetted across the silvery ice, and the spotlights dimmed and faded as they vanished into a forest of rustling green "trees." The trees closed solemnly around the butterflies, wrapping them in protective branches. Gradually, all the skaters drifted off the ice while darkness fell in the crowded arena.

There was a long, long moment of awed silence. At last the lights came up for intermission, amid a deafening burst of applause.

Carlie pounded her small hands together and shouted, transported with joy, while Laurie and her mother exchanged a smile over the little girl's golden head.

"Hey, Mom, guess who's here," said David, peering into the shifting crowds of people.

"Everybody in Crystal Creek, I think," Sara told him. "Laurie's already said hello to about fifty kids, I'll bet."

"This isn't a kid," David said, gazing into the crowd again. "It's that man."

"What man?"

"That man who works in the old barn. Mr. Trent. He's sitting with some weird little guy with a pony-tail."

Sara stared at her son, appalled. "Here?" she whispered. "Warren Trent is *here?* David, you must be imagining things. You're always making up stories like this."

"I am not!" David shouted in outrage. "He's right over there, see?" He pointed down to his left with a grubby finger. Sara leaned past the little boy to peer into the crowd below them.

She saw Warren almost at once, and her heart be-gan to pound at the sight of those broad shoulders, the dark graying hair and familiar tanned profile.

Warren Trent sat with his disreputable-looking friend in one of the most expensive seats, front and center down close to the ice surface. He wore his cus-tomary jeans and shirt, battered leather jacket and boots, while the little man beside him looked like a ragpicker in baggy pants and an old green sweater that was badly frayed at cuffs and collar. The two men were chatting amiably, sharing a big tub of buttered popcorn.

"What on earth are they doing here?" Sara whis-pered, barely aware that she was speaking the words aloud. "David, have they seen us, do you think? Does he know we're up here?"

"I don't know," David said, looking at the crowds passing on the steps. "Mom, can I have a hot dog? I want one of those big ones with the..."

But Sara didn't hear the rest of her son's demand. Warren Trent had just risen from his seat and was climbing the stairs next to them, taking the steps two at a time.

He stopped abruptly when he saw David and the girls, then shifted his glance to Sara.

"Hello, Sara," he said with a quiet smile. "Nice to see you."

Sara gaped at him, too stunned by his unexpected appearance to find anything to say. He looked so wonderful, she thought, with a painful twist of emotion. Those brilliant dark eyes, and his tanned face, his big powerful body that made every other man in the place seem small and insignificant...

"Do you like skating?" David was asking him, bouncing happily on the hard wooden seat.

"Not usually," Warren said, grinning down at the boy. "But Hans is crazy about it, so we decided to drive in and watch the show."

"Hans? That's the little guy with the ponytail?" David asked.

"David," Sara began helplessly, "dear, you shouldn't..."

"That's Hans," Warren said solemnly.

"Is he a friend of yours?"

Warren hesitated, his gaze shifting briefly to Sara again. "I guess you might say that," he told David.

"Hans and I work together, but we've gotten to be pretty good friends, too."

"Are you going out where the food is? Can I go with you to get a hot dog?" David asked the man.

"Sure," Warren said cheerfully. "If it's okay with your mother."

Again, his eyes moved to rest on Sara's face, with a warm thoughtful look that told her he was remembering their intimacy, those breathless moments when their naked bodies had lain together, wrapped in sweetness and passion....

"David," she said in confusion, "look, Mr. Trent doesn't want to bother with you out there. Laurie can take you."

"Mom!" Laurie protested. "Carlie and I want to go down right away and try to get some autographs on our programs."

"It's okay, Sara," Warren said with another of his rare, boyish smiles. "I don't mind taking David with me. Come on, kid," he told the boy with mock gruffness. "Get a move on, if you're coming."

Sara hesitated, still feeling helpless and distressed by this unexpected turn of events. But David was already on his feet, bouncing joyously next to Warren in the aisle.

"Do you have any money, David?" she asked.

"Grandma gave me five dollars. I want a big hot dog and some ice cream."

"How about you girls?" Warren asked. "Anybody else want anything? I've got this big strapping fella to help me carry supplies," he added, squeezing David's thin shoulder.

Laurie and Carlie placed their orders for soft drinks and food, then vanished with a flurry of excited giggles. Sara watched them make their way into the crowd of people heading for the gate, where a few of the skaters had reappeared and were signing autographs.

"Sara?" Warren asked gently, resisting David, who was tugging at his hand in an agony of impatience. "Anything you'd like?"

Again, she felt his dark eyes resting on her face, and heard the meaningful undertone in his words.

Sara looked up at him, mesmerized, longing to reach out and touch him. She felt an almost unbearable desire simply to make some kind of contact with him, to touch his leg or his wrist or stroke back the lock of dark hair that fell across his forehead.

"Just . . . just a cup of black coffee, please," she whispered finally, taking a couple of bills from her purse and holding them out toward him. "If you've got room to carry it. Here," she added, "this should be enough for what the girls ordered."

Warren waved the money aside and gave her a rueful grin over his shoulder as David hauled him off up the steps.

Alone in the stands, Sara tried to analyze her whirl of contradictory emotions.

She realized that she was no longer afraid of David being alone with Warren Trent. Those moments of rich intimacy had taught her, on some deep, instinctive level, that she had been wrong in her first impressions. Warren Trent was not a man to be feared. He might be complex and unpredictable, but there was too much tenderness hidden at the core of the man for him to be dangerous, especially to a child. Still, Sara firmly believed that he was involved in shady dealings, some kind of criminal activity that would no doubt get him into deep trouble when he was caught.

She moved tensely in her seat and looked down at the ragged little man with the ponytail, the stranger who had come here with Warren.

Warren's friend turned his head at that moment, glancing over at the skaters near the entry gate, and Sara caught a glimpse of his face. She'd encountered him several times at the motel, but today she gaped at him in startled recognition. This little stranger, she realized suddenly, was somebody she'd seen before, when she lived up North.

Hans. That was the name Warren had used, wasn't it?

Sara frowned, thinking about the name, which also seemed familiar in some distant way. She searched her memory, struggling to capture the vague impressions at the back of her mind.

Sara was positive that she'd never met the man personally. She'd seen his name and picture somewhere, probably in a newspaper.

Maybe he really was some kind of notorious criminal. He'd have to be, wouldn't he, to have appeared in a newspaper as far away as Connecticut? But Sara didn't have a sense of anything particularly negative associated with his face and name. There was just a remote, tantalizing feeling that she'd heard of this little man before, seen his picture and his name in print at some time in the past.

She was still straining to recover the memory when the girls returned, breathless with excitement, clutching programs covered with autographs. Warren and David followed soon after, laden with food and drinks, which David distributed with solemn importance.

Sara watched over the passage of the brimming cups and plates, then glanced up to thank Warren. But he was already gone, settling himself in his seat below them next to the little man in the ponytail.

The lights dimmed and the show started again, but this time the beauty of the pageant was lost on Sara. All she could see was a blur of color and motion, a swirling ocean of costumes beyond a pair of broad shoulders and a strong, quiet profile.

"I LIKED THE TEAPOT the best," Carlie said from the back seat, with a satisfied sigh.

"I liked the Beast," David announced. "He was really neat. Warren liked him, too."

"Did he? Is that what he said?" Sara asked, her hands relaxed on the wheel and her eyes on the sunset sky ahead as they drove toward Crystal Creek.

She felt an irrational urge to talk about the man, to speak his name and hear everything he'd said to David. But her son, with the annoying capriciousness of childhood, had apparently chosen this moment to be closemouthed instead of confiding.

"David?" Sara urged gently, as the girls in the back seat resumed their intense, whispered conversation.

"Yeah?"

"What did Mr. Trent say to you when the two of you were getting hot dogs?"

David looked mysterious and glanced out the window. "Oh, nothing much." Sara quelled an urge to grip the little boy's shoulder and shake some information out of him.

"Probably," she said casually, "he didn't want to say much of anything. He never talks much, folks say. I guess he doesn't talk to anybody."

"He talked to me!" David said indignantly, contradicting his earlier words. "He told me lots of stuff."

Sara shot him a skeptical smile, then turned her eyes back to the road ahead.

"He said I should call him Warren instead of Mr. Trent. He told me he knew my grandpa when he was just a little boy like me."

"Did he?" Sara said, trying not to show much interest for fear of drying up this trickle of information.

"Yeah. He said he really liked my grandpa."

Did he say anything about me? Sara longed to ask her son.

But she resisted, knowing how ridiculous she was being. Just about at the same level as Laurie and Carlie, who were both giggling over one of the handsome boys who'd skated as a young cavalier.

"He said he and Hans are staying in Austin tonight," David volunteered. "They have business to do in the city tomorrow, he said."

"Do they, now," Sara commented grimly.

What kind of business did Warren Trent have in Austin? And who was the mysterious little man in the ragged clothes? She was almost going crazy, trying to remember where she'd seen that face.

"Yeah. Warren said they're staying in a big hotel where there's a swimming pool and an exercise room and a jogging track to run on, all inside the roof."

Sara thought about the grimy little second-rate motel rooms currently occupied by Warren and his friend. Still, she mused, recalling the bundles of bills in his suitcase, there was no doubt that Warren Trent could afford to pay for a nicer place. But where did he get all the money? And why, if he had it, did he choose to dress so carelessly and live in such shabby conditions?

Sara sighed as they drove through Crystal Creek and pulled up in front of the old Pollock house. Forcing herself to put all thoughts of Warren Trent out of her mind, she looked over the seat at the little girls.

"Well, Carlie," she said with a smile, "here you are."

Carlie smiled back. "Thank you so much. I can hardly wait to tell Mama and Granny what it was like."

Sara got out to hold the door for the child, then looked up as June came down the front steps of the house.

"Oh, Mama, it was beautiful!" Carlie shouted, limping rapidly toward her mother and hugging her. "It was so awesome. There was a teapot that sang songs, and butterflies and trees and all kinds of things. It was wonderful, Mama, and I got all these autographs on my program...."

June looked down at the child's golden head so tenderly that Sara felt a lump in her throat.

"You can tell me all about it later, baby," she murmured. "Come on inside now. It's time for your bath. Say thanks to Laurie's mother."

"It was a pleasure to have her," Sara said with quiet sincerity. "Really it was, June. Carlie's such a sweet girl."

June glanced up quickly, giving Sara a long, measuring look. She appeared almost on the verge of softening, of actually saying something friendly.

Sara waited hopefully, holding her breath.

Finally, June's eyes hardened and her expression grew cautious and remote once more.

"Thank you, Sara," she said politely. "It was real nice of you all to take her."

"You're welcome," Sara murmured, feeling hollow with disappointment.

She watched with a sad smile as the little girls exchanged farewells and solemn promises to call each other the next day. Sara got back into the car as June and Carlie started back up the weed-strewn sidewalk to the house.

June walked slowly, adjusting her long stride to the child's limping gait, and bent her blond head solemnly to listen as Carlie chattered. Sara watched a moment longer, her eyes stinging briefly with tears, then shifted the car into gear and drove toward her mother's ranch.

MARY GIBSON PARKED her truck in the garage and trudged up the walk toward the ranch house, almost light-headed with fatigue. It was past dusk, gray and murmuring, and a band of faint gold was darkening to violet in the western sky. She began to mount the steps, and was almost at the top before she noticed her daughter sitting in the shadows on the veranda with a pile of mending in her lap.

"Hi, Mama," Sara greeted her with affection. "You look tired. I was starting to worry about you when it got to be nine o'clock. I thought the church meeting would be over a lot earlier."

"Oh, Lord," Mary said, dropping wearily into a rocking chair beside the younger woman. "They do go on sometimes. And I'm still worn out from that long trip to see your daddy yesterday. You know what, Sara? I never have to make that drive again in all my life. I can hardly believe it's over."

"Won't you have to drive out there to bring Daddy home?"

"No, thank God. Wayne Jackson has some kind of business to do over there next month, and he's going to bring Al back with him."

"How is he?" Sara asked. "I never got a chance to ask you."

"Your daddy? He's just fine. He's sure looking forward to coming home. When I tell him about all the work there is to do back here, he looks like he's flying off to heaven. Funny how a man could be looking forward that much to doing a ton of work, isn't it?"

"It's going to be so nice to have him back," Sara murmured.

Mary glanced over at her daughter's delicate profile. "Truly, dear? I wondered sometimes if you weren't angry with him for what he did, because of the way he smeared the family name and all. I know those things have always mattered to you."

"Not anymore, Mama. I guess it used to matter a lot—social status, public opinion and that sort of thing, but nowadays it's just not important. I'm so different, Mama. It's like I've hatched out of a cocoon and turned into an altogether different creature. It's a little scary," Sara added thoughtfully. "I'm not even sure what I am anymore."

Mary nodded and reached over to squeeze her daughter's work-scarred hand. "Well, if you've hatched out of a cocoon, sweetie, then you must be a butterfly now."

Sara gave a small, rueful chuckle. She squinted into the darkening sky, trying to thread her needle by the fading sunset glow. "I sure don't feel like a butterfly, Mama. I don't know what I feel like. But," she added, "I know that I'm not upset with Daddy anymore. I love him. I can hardly wait to see him again."

Mary smiled into the gathering darkness and rocked placidly. "So, how was the ice show?" she asked after a comfortable silence.

She listened while her daughter told her all about the pageant, about the children's behavior and little Carlie's blissful enjoyment of the day.

"That's real good to hear," Mary said. "Poor little thing, it's nice to give her some pleasure. She's always chipper, even though her life's been so hard and she must have a lot of pain with that foot."

"I know."

Sara fell silent as she stitched carefully at a small pair of blue jeans in her lap. Mary glanced at her daughter, sensing some kind of tension in Sara. "Anything else?" she asked gently.

Sara frowned and bit off the end of the thread. "Pardon, Mama?"

"Did anything else happen today?"

"Well," Sara began, with an elaborately casual tone that didn't fool her mother for a second, "one thing was a little surprising."

"Yes? What's that?"

"Warren Trent was there."

"At the ice show?" Mary asked.

"Yes. Isn't that strange? He was with that funny little man with the ponytail that I told you about. They were sitting just below us, eating popcorn and clapping like a pair of kids."

Mary shook her head thoughtfully. "He's certainly a mystery, this Warren Trent, isn't he?"

"Oh, yes, he certainly is," Sara said, with considerable strain in her voice.

Mary rocked and chatted, telling Sara about her husband's recollections of Warren as a little boy, about the child's prowess on the baseball diamond and his sensitive feelings.

"Your daddy had a real soft spot for the boy," she concluded. "I never heard that story until he told me yesterday."

"Seems everybody's got a story about Warren Trent," Sara said quietly. "Isn't it strange, Mama? Everybody talks about the man, and nobody knows a single thing about him."

Mary noted her daughter's withdrawn expression again, feeling cautious and troubled. "Sara," she ventured, "are you...afraid of him for some reason? Warren Trent, I mean? Sometimes when you talk about him, I get the impression that there's something going on and it's making you nervous."

Sara shook her head. "I used to be afraid of him, Mama," she confessed. "At first he scared me to death, he was so harsh and...and rude, almost threatening. But I don't think he's scary anymore. I'm just going crazy trying to figure out exactly *what* he is, that's all."

Mary chuckled. "So is Carolyn, the poor girl. I think she's going to die if she doesn't get her curiosity satisfied pretty soon."

Sara gave her mother a wan smile and then stood with sudden decision, tucking the basket of mending away under the porch swing. "I'm going for a drive, Mama, all right?" she said. "Maybe driving for an hour or so will help me sleep."

"Sure," Mary said comfortably. "Take the truck," she added, holding up the keys. "I'll go in and have a long hot bath. I don't think I'll have any trouble sleeping tonight."

Sara paused at the top of the steps, her face hidden in the shadows. "Davey's asleep already," she told her mother, "and Laurie's up in her room reading."

"Good. Be careful, dear," Mary said automatically, still disturbed by something in Sara's posture as her daughter turned and hurried down the steps into the gathering dusk.

SARA DROVE UP the side road next to the old barn and parked in the leafy grove where she'd hidden her vehicle once before. For a long time, she sat behind the wheel in the darkness, staring out the window into the murmuring shadows.

At last, her face grim with purpose, she took a flashlight from the glove compartment, got out of the truck and slipped on her jacket. She made her way cautiously though the tangled undergrowth in the direction of the old barn.

The moon was up by the time she reached the clearing, spilling over the derelict building and washing it with cold silver. Sara hesitated in the screen of brush at the meadow's edge, focusing tensely on the locked door, the empty trail leading to the barn, the silent highway beyond.

Finally, battling a wave of sudden, heart-stopping terror, she sprinted across the moonlit opening and flattened herself in the shadows beside the barn.

Holding her breath, Sara edged her way along the rough wall of the building, felt inside the window covering and moved her fingers cautiously until they brushed against a key hanging from a length of twisted wire. She gripped the key, withdrew it slowly and edged back along the wall to the door of the barn.

With a last frantic glance over her shoulder, she inserted the key in the padlock and turned it, then sighed in relief as the lock fell open. She removed the padlock, opened the door and slipped into the building, closing the door silently behind her.

Sara stood panting in the deep velvet blackness, still gripped with cold terror. She sniffed the air, frightened by an indefinable mixture of scents that were strange and menacing. Little sounds rustled around her, probably bat wings and the scurrying feet of small rodents. She felt an urge, almost unbearable in its intensity, to bolt from the place without turning on the light, return the padlock and key and run as fast as she could back to the warm safety of her truck.

"I've come this far," Sara whispered aloud, to give herself courage. "I can't back out now. I just can't. And this may be the only chance I'll ever have, because I know that Warren's in Austin tonight...."

She drew a long, ragged breath, then another, trying desperately to calm herself. At last, she moved her hands along the wall next to the door, searching for the light switch. Her fingers closed over it and she flipped the light on, then turned slowly to look at the interior of the barn.

Her mouth dropped open and she stood thunderstruck, staring at the incredible, fantastic sight that greeted her eyes.

Nothing in all the world, no amount of gossip or questions or speculation, could ever have prepared Sara Gibson for the shock of what was concealed within that old barn.

CHAPTER TEN

SARA HAD NO IDEA how long she stood there, transfixed, staring into the musty depths of the barn in wondering silence.

At last she stumbled forward, gazing with childlike, breathless enchantment at the marvelous objects all around her. She saw flying manes and tails, flashing hooves, a sea of brilliant saddles and trappings, shining mirrors, gold leaf and glittering jewels that caught and reflected the overhead lights.

"It's the old carousel," she whispered, pausing to finger the jeweled inlay on a red bridle, gazing up at the straining neck and bared teeth of the noble white steed beside her. "How on earth did anybody ever find it? Where did it come from?"

The antique carousel had been removed from the town square in Crystal Creek almost sixty years earlier, broken up and sold piecemeal to dealers around the country. Nobody from Sara's generation had ever seen the original structure. But Sara had often pored over photographs and histories of the magical ride, and listened by the hour to her grandmother and the other old-timers as they described its wonders.

She could tell now that the original pieces of the carousel, though still only partially assembled, were almost all there inside the old barn. Sections of newly constructed hardwood decking lay everywhere, pulled aside to expose the complex systems of gears and shafts that made the carousel rotate and the horses ride up and down. Some of the horses, already fully restored, were attached to the deck, while others stood about on little platforms in various stages of repair.

Sara moved around in breathless awe, studying the restoration work. The horses, originally hand-carved from fine hardwoods, were all different and rendered with exquisite detail, right down to the nails in their horseshoes and the condition of their teeth, carved to indicate their varying ages. They ranged in color from dapple gray to pinto to fierce black. Dainty white horses and handsome sorrels stood frozen in the silence of the barn, their long horsehair tails lifting in the soft currents of air that drifted through the ventilation ports high above.

All the black horses wore body armor, while many of the white ponies carried special adornments behind the cantles of their saddles. Sara saw carved grape and ivy leaves, gilded cherubim, pheasants, brilliant parrots, brassbound magic boxes fastened with tiny golden locks. The leather bridles, saddle blankets and painted breast collars were intricately set with gold leaf and glittering bits of cut glass that shone like tiny rainbows in the dusky interior of the old building.

"Oh," Sara breathed aloud, forgetting herself once again in her enchantment. "Oh, it's magnificent! It's so incredibly beautiful...."

She paused beside a sorrel steed that was faded almost to white, apparently damaged by years of exposure to the elements. The horse was being painted and restored with loving care and exquisite attention to detail. The head, forequarters and breast collar were completed, so the horse seemed to be celebrating a rebirth, leaping out from a cloud of obscurity into a new world of brilliance and beauty.

"What wonderful work," Sara whispered, examining the restoration with an artist's appreciation for the complex processes involved. Whoever was doing this, the work was absolutely first-class.

She heard a noise and whirled around, raising a hand to her mouth and gazing in alarm at the door.

Warren Trent stood there in the moonlit opening, staring at her with piercing eyes. Even through her dreamlike cloud of wonder, Sara could tell that he was coldly, bitterly angry.

She watched as he closed the door behind him and crossed the floor swiftly, his face tight with fury. "How the hell did you get in here?" he asked, grasping her arm.

Sara trembled, barely taking in his words, still dazzled by the beauty all around her. "Warren," she murmured, waving her hand helplessly, "where did all this come from? Who brought it here?"

"None of your damned business," he said tightly. "I asked how you got in here."

"I...I was watching you one day and I saw where you hid the key, and I wanted to know what was inside," Sara told him with childlike simplicity, still too overwhelmed to make any attempt at protecting herself. "Warren, it's the old carousel that used to be in the town square, isn't it? Who's doing this? I thought it was taken apart years and years ago, sold to dozens of different collectors."

He released her arm and watched her in wary silence.

Sara touched the sorrel horse beside her, the one that was only partially restored. "This work," she whispered. "It's marvelous, Warren. Please, won't you tell me who's doing all this?"

She fell silent momentarily, but then her eyes widened as her memory finally registered the name she'd been searching for all day. "Hans Keller," she murmured in awe. "My God, that little man is Hans Keller! Isn't he?"

Warren didn't answer, just continued to stare at her with that same implacable expression.

"I learned about Hans Keller in one of my college art restoration classes," Sara went on, talking mostly to herself. "He's one of the best in the world. He must be... Warren, it must cost a fortune to pay him for this work."

"Yeah," Warren said curtly, turning away from her to look at the partially finished horse. "It costs a fortune, all right. But Hans is worth every penny. Six of the horses were in this kind of shape when we got them last year. We shipped the others to Germany for him to work on, but this one just arrived here last week.''

''Where was it before that?''

''In somebody's backyard, in a little town down in Florida. I guess they were using it for a garden ornament.''

''Have they... do they have all the horses here now?'' Sara asked hesitantly, gazing at him in fascination.

''Fifty-two of them are here. There's two still missing, a gray and a sorrel, but my people think they've finally located them in a museum up in Boston. We're negotiating right now to have them released from the collection.''

''But Warren... who's doing this? Where's the money coming from? It must cost... I can't imagine how much it costs to do all this,'' Sara murmured helplessly. ''These horses were hand-carved by Franz Koning. Every one of them is worth a small fortune.''

''It costs a hell of a lot to buy them from private collectors,'' Warren said. ''But most of them are in museums by now, and public collections are usually willing to release them for a nominal cost if you can prove that you're doing an authentic restoration of the original carousel.''

Sara looked up at him, still dazed and uncertain.

''Besides, there are a lot of government grants available for projects like this. I only had to spend my own money on about half of it," Warren told her, his dark face softening a little as he looked proprietarily at the sea of flashing hooves and tossing manes.

"You? *You're* paying for all this?"

"Look, Sara, I didn't want anybody to know about this until after I was gone. God, I wish you hadn't come in here."

"Well, I'm here," Sara told him simply. "Warren," she added, grasping his arm and gazing up at him earnestly, "I'm not going to give anything away. I promise I won't tell a soul. I think it's absolutely wonderful, the most wonderful thing I've ever seen. Please, just tell me who you are, and why you're doing it."

Warren looked at her in silence for a long, tense moment, then shook her hand away and crossed the floor to sit on a portion of the hardwood deck, surveying the array of bright ponies. At last he shrugged in a gesture of resignation and looked up at her.

"You know who I am, Sara," he said. "I'm Warren Trent, the druggist's son who caused so much trouble back in the old days. And as for how I did it, well, that wasn't hard. Things like this are pretty easy if you have enough money."

"And you do?" Sara asked, moving over to sit next to him and staring up at him in disbelief. "You have this kind of money?"

"I have more money than I could ever think of spending," Warren told her simply.

"How? Where did you get that kind of money?"

He turned to her with a brief, humorless smile. "After that last escapade of mine, they sent me away for a while, just like your poor daddy. You remember that, Sara?"

"I remember," Sara said gently.

"Well, I ran away from there and drifted around for a few years, working at odd jobs. Finally I got work in construction as a heavy laborer. That was when I was about eighteen."

Sara watched his face and waited.

"I wasn't a very good worker," Warren went on, touching a gold tassel on a little saddle nearby. "I was lazy, I guess. I kept thinking up easier ways of doing things, inventing methods to make my job simpler. After a while, the foreman got interested and encouraged me to patent a couple of my ideas, and since then it's been all gravy."

"What kind of ideas?"

"Well, for instance, have you ever walked past a construction site where they're pouring concrete?"

Sara nodded.

"They build wooden forms to shape the cement while it dries. It used to be a hell of a chore to pry those forms away afterward, real tedious and messy. I invented a metal clip that holds the forms in place, then breaks away when the job is done. The clips are sold all over the world now. I get royalties every time they're used, and that adds up to thousands of dollars every day, just for that one patent. Sara, it takes two accountants back in Houston just to keep track of my money.''

"You live in Houston?"

"I guess so. I have other places here and there, but I guess I spend more time in Houston than anywhere else. I travel around a lot."

"Why?"

"Because there's nothing to hold me in any one place."

"No wife? No family or people you care about?"

Warren's face hardened. "I told you once before, Sara. Home and babies, love and apple pie, that's not for men like me."

Sara was silent a moment, studying his grim, tanned profile. "Did you think it would bring you some peace, Warren?" she asked softly, looking around at the jeweled splendor of the old carousel. "Did you hope that a gesture like this would somehow make amends for the past?"

"I didn't hope for anything," he said coldly. "I just wanted to do it because it was a debt I owed. I wrecked their town, and they hate me for it. I decided to give back something that's going to be a huge tourist draw and an economic boost to the whole county. I don't care what the hell they think of me. I just wanted to settle an old account, that's all."

Sara was silent a moment as she struggled to make sense of all the incredible things she'd seen and heard in the past hour. She took note of the dancing ponies, recognizing all the work that had been done and calculating how much still remained to finish the restoration.

"How did you find all the pieces?"

"They were scattered all over the country, mostly in museums and a few private collections, as I said. They're all dated and hand-signed by Koning, so they weren't hard to identify. I hired a couple of private investigators, gave them the details and turned them loose to hunt down the ponies. The decking and gears and everything, of course, has had to be manufactured, and we'll install a modern electronic organ instead of the old pipes."

"When will it be ready?"

"We're aiming for July fourth," Warren said. "The plan is to have it set up on the town square in time for the picnic."

"Are you going to present it? Have some kind of ceremony?"

He gave her a brief, wintry smile. "Come on, Sara. Can you really see me standing up in front of all those people and giving a little speech?"

"No," Sara murmured reluctantly. "I guess I can't."

"Not too damn likely. Hans and I plan to get those last two horses down here, finish the restoration and then bring in a crew to do the rest."

"How are you going to keep it a secret at that stage?"

"No problem," Warren told her, "if you'll just keep your mouth shut."

"Warren, I told you . . ."

"All right," he said, waving his hand in a curt gesture. "We plan to do it all the night before. We'll prefabricate the building to house the carousel, then haul it in there and erect it on the grounds, take the carousel to town in pieces and get it all set up, mount everything at night under spotlights. When the people arrive for the picnic, it'll be standing there as if it never left."

Sara regarded him in shocked disbelief. "But, Warren, that's just . . . it's impossible!"

"Why?"

"Well, it's such a massive undertaking. It would take so many people to set this whole thing up in one night. It's just . . . impossible," Sara repeated helplessly.

"I told you before, Sara, nothing's impossible if you're willing to spend enough money."

She looked at him, wide-eyed and silent, trying to imagine the townspeople arriving at the square for the annual picnic and finding the old carousel there, bright and shining in the morning sun as if it had dropped magically from the heavens overnight.

"And you won't be there to present it, or even to see their reactions," she murmured slowly.

"I sure won't. I'll be far away by that time, and I'll never be coming back."

"Warren, that's just not right! If you're going to do something like this, you should stay and do it properly. You should make a presentation and give the people a chance to thank you.''

Warren got up and moved restlessly away from her to examine the half-painted sorrel horse. "Nobody in this town wants to thank me for anything," he said.

"That's the way you feel, but it's not the truth. You may be a smart man, and you may even have gotten incredibly rich, Warren Trent, but there's a great big blind spot right in the center of you that keeps you from seeing how people really feel about you."

He turned to her, his eyes somber. "Is that so? How come you know so much about me, Sara?"

"Because I love you," she told him quietly.

When she spoke the words, Sara finally understood what they meant. She met his eyes in calm stillness, awed by the enormous depth and power of a love that filled her whole being.

Sara realized that she'd never known what love really was. The anxious girlish feelings she'd had for Steven, the troubled insecurities of her marriage, the times she'd sobbed in bitter anguish over the things her husband did...none of those emotions had anything to do with love. They were just messy, complicated, elusive feelings.

This love was a simple, shining warmth, as solid and massive as the sun, and it lighted Sara's whole universe. There was nothing complicated about her love for Warren Trent. It was basic and elemental, pure and real and immensely strong, and she knew beyond doubt that it would last forever.

He had turned away quickly when she spoke, his face shadowed with angry pain. "Why?" he asked in a cold voice, keeping his face hidden from her as he bent to examine one of the sorrel's broken rear hooves. "Why do you think you love me, Sara? Because you just found out I'm rich, or because I was the first man to make you feel good in bed?"

Sara felt a quick stab of impatience, and the urge to make an indignant denial, but it didn't last. Anger and hurt feelings couldn't survive in the shining reality of this kind of love. Her only concern was for him, for the bitter pain he felt and all the buried childhood injuries that kept him from ever yielding and trusting anybody.

"No, Warren," she said gently. "Not because of your money, and not because of your sexual prowess, either. I love you because of who you are, and because of this," she told him, waving her hand at the shimmering beauty all around her.

"Because of what?"

"This," Sara repeated, indicating the dancing horses, the mirrors and gleaming hardwood, the jewels and flowers and flowing horsehair tails. "Don't you understand, Warren? Any man who could think of doing something this wonderful, actually conceive of the idea and then bring it into existence . . . that's a man I couldn't help loving."

He turned to glare at her, with the same anguish in his eyes that Sarah had noticed the night she danced with him in the bar, before he broke away from her and vanished into the night. "Sara," he whispered, "don't hurt me like this. Please leave me alone. I'm not the man to be your husband and lover, or a father to your children. I'm just not that kind of man."

Sara watched his face quietly, her heart full. "I'm not making any demands on you, Warren," she told him gently. "I never will. I just want you to find some way to be at peace, because I truly believe that you deserve it."

For a moment his face lightened and kindled with emotion. Then he turned away again, the remote, cautious look back in his eyes. "As long as you don't make any demands on me," he told her coldly, "then we'll get along just fine."

As Sara watched his broad back and the set of his shoulders, she felt weak with yearning. "I guess I wasn't telling the whole truth," she said at last. "I want to make one demand, Warren. Just one."

He looked at her warily. "You do? What is it?"

"I want to help."

"Help?" he echoed blankly. "What do you mean?"

"Warren, you can do what you like about me, and about your own life. I'm just learning what love really is, but one of the things I know is that it's got to be absolutely free. I can't put any restrictions on you, or try to change you. If you want to mount this carousel in the town square and then vanish without a trace, that's your decision. Even if I never see you again, I'll always love you. But I still want to help."

"How can you help?"

Sara gave him a sad smile. "I've had college training in this kind of work, remember? I'll admit," she added, "that it's a little intimidating to think of working next to Hans Keller, but I could do a lot of the preparation work for him, and some of the broad, basic stuff. You two are never going to be finished on time unless you get some help. You've only got about six weeks, and a lot of these horses still need detailing and restoration. You know how tedious it is."

Warren looked at her. "You'd do that for me? No strings attached?"

"No strings attached," Sara told him. She tried once more to give him a reassuring smile, even though her heart was aching. "And the fewer people who know about this, the safer your secret is likely to be. So you'd be smart to take me up on my offer, wouldn't you?"

"I'd have to pay you."

"I wouldn't dream of it. Working with Hans Keller and being involved in something as wonderful as this...that's payment enough."

"Twenty-two dollars an hour," Warren said, as if she hadn't spoken. "That's what we were paying our restoration assistants back in Houston. I won't pay you less."

He paused, quietly surveying the welter of bright ponies.

"Will you quit your other job?" he asked her abruptly. "Can you come here and work all day?"

Sara shook her head. "That wouldn't be too smart of me, would it? I need a regular income. How can I quit my job when all this will be gone in a few weeks? I'll come every afternoon as soon as I get off work," she added, "and give you as many hours as I can."

"Sara, you're worn out all the time as it is. I can't have you working more hours."

"That's not your concern, is it?" Sara stood up and faced him. "You don't care about anybody, remember, Warren? You're just an ice-cold, selfish man. You should jump at my offer, not waste time worrying about whether I'm going to find it hard."

For a long moment their eyes met in silence. At last, he shrugged and turned away. "All right," he muttered. "Come whenever you can. I'll give you a key."

"Warren, why are you here?" she asked suddenly.

He grinned with a flash of his mocking humor and got to his feet, leaning casually on one of the horses. "Funny, that's the same thing everybody in this town's been asking for months."

Sara shook her head. "I mean, why are you back here at the barn? Didn't you tell Davey that you and Hans were staying in Austin tonight?"

"We needed another measurement on one of the horses to verify those two up in Boston, and Hans forgot to bring it. So I just ran back out to check."

"And caught me in the act," Sara murmured.

"Well, I knew from the start you had criminal tendencies," Warren told her with a ghost of a smile.

"Wouldn't doubt that my luggage was tampered with, too, once or twice," he added.

"Just once," Sara said, drawing a deep breath.

Warren's smile faded as he stared at her. "No kidding? You really opened my suitcases?"

Sara nodded timidly, relieved by the chance to confess. "One day early on, when we'd just had a real row, I started wondering if you might be...dangerous to my kids, or my family. One of the suitcases was open and I peeked inside."

"Why?"

"I don't know. Looking for... clues, I guess."

"Just like those detective girls on television."

Sara nodded again, feeling foolish.

"And what did you find?"

"I found a ton of money wrapped in bundles, a handgun and some wonderful old books on art restoration and antique toys."

Warren moved closer to her. "And what did our spunky little detective think of that?"

"I almost went crazy," Sara told him truthfully, gazing into his sober, dark eyes. "I just couldn't stand it, not knowing who you were and what you were doing back in town. Especially since David's always been so fascinated by you."

"And what have you decided about me?"

He moved still closer, so near that she could feel the warmth and strength of his body, and smell the clean scent of his soap and shaving cream that always affected her so profoundly.

"I don't think you're dangerous," she told him, trying desperately to stand her ground and meet his enigmatic look squarely. "Except maybe to yourself. And I don't think you're the desperado you make yourself out to be, either."

He reached out and touched her hot cheek, running his fingers gently over the golden dusting of freckles. "What *do* you think I am, Sara?"

"I think you're a man with a sensitive heart and a head full of dreams. I think you've been badly hurt, but you probably have a whole world of love to give, if you could ever bring yourself to trust anybody."

"And you want me to trust you?" he whispered, putting his hands on her shoulders and drawing her close to him. "A woman who pries into my luggage, breaks into locked buildings, calls me names . . ."

Sara held her breath and tried to still the thundering of her heart as he gathered her into his arms and bent to kiss her. This time he wasn't as gentle as he'd been before. Now his lips were hard and seeking, his arms almost painful in their crushing strength.

Sara could feel the hunger in his body, the savage, thrusting need. She responded to him with all of her being, kissing and whispering, biting his neck gently, grasping at his shoulders, sobbing with love and desire.

But after a few moments of frantic embrace, Warren pushed her aside and turned away deliberately, walking toward the door.

"Come on, Sara," he said in a muffled voice. "It's late. Let's get out of here so I can lock up."

"Warren..." Sara followed him, still aching with sexual arousal, stunned by his hasty departure.

"It's not going to happen, girl," he told her in a husky voice, not meeting her eyes. "It's just not going to happen."

"Why not?" Sara paused beside him and gripped his arm. "Why can't it happen? Don't you want me?"

He choked and moved away swiftly, shaking his arm with an abrupt gesture. "*Want* you? Oh, girl, I've wanted you since the first minute I saw you back there in the bus depot, fretting over that damned turtle! You looked so pale and brave, trying to struggle along with the weight of the world on your shoulders. My heart broke when I looked at you that day. And since then, with everything that's happened..."

He fell silent, studying the dusty floor with a haunted expression. Finally, he looked up again, meeting her eyes directly.

"Oh, yes, I want you, Sara. I've never wanted anyone the way I want you. You're the woman of my dreams. Not just for the sex, which was incredibly sweet, but for the weird combination of shyness and feistiness that's part of you. I love that so much. Is that what you want me to tell you, Sara? If I were to have a wife like other men, and she'd give me babies and a loving home, I'd want you to be that wife. Am I making myself clear?"

She stared at him, openmouthed, her head spinning.

"Warren . . ." she faltered.

"But it's not going to happen, Sara, and it's not your fault at all. Just look on me as damaged goods, or a real bad investment. I couldn't settle down and make one woman happy, not even you. I'm just a rolling stone and a loner, and I always will be. Save yourself the misery."

Sara wet her lips and tried to speak. "Please, can't we just . . ."

"We won't talk about this anymore, Sara," Warren told her with the gentleness that he'd exhibited to her on such rare occasions. "We'll just get busy and finish repairing our ponies, and give them to the town, and then we won't see each other anymore. And we won't touch each other again, either."

"Why not?" Sara asked with childlike misery. She could hardly absorb the things he'd said. All she wanted was to be in his arms, feel his mouth on hers, go to bed with him and hold him close all through the night until dawn washed over the hills, every night for the rest of her life.

"Because it hurts too damn much, that's why," he said coldly, the shuttered look back on his face. "Now come on, Sara, because you wouldn't be too happy if I locked you in here all night with the bats and the polecats, would you?"

Sara turned on dragging feet and followed him reluctantly to the door, thinking about the sad irony of the situation. They left behind a building full of wonder and enchantment, of beauty and happiness and children's laughter. But she took with her a heart like a desert, as dry and desolate as ashes.

"SARA!" Mary Gibson hailed her daughter, who had just parked the pickup truck in the ranch yard and was deep in conversation with David and Bobby. The boys were laden with an assortment of boards and woodworking tools, and were clearly anxious to be gone about their business.

Sara waved back at her mother, then mounted the steps wearily and sank onto the porch swing with a sigh. It was late in the afternoon, several weeks since her discovery of the old carousel. She had been working with Hans Keller every night, and her weariness by now was so bone-deep and numbing that she moved through life in a constant fog of exhaustion.

"Hi, Mama. The kids are building a clubhouse out in the mesquite behind the windmill."

Mary grinned. "I know. Wait'll you see the blueprints. They've moved up pretty fast from bug houses. This thing's going to have a curved staircase, an upper balcony and a games room."

Sara smiled faintly. "Is there any way they can hurt themselves, do you think?"

"Oh, I don't think so. Not unless it gets to be more than two stories high. I'll sure get concerned if they start turning out some kind of skyscraper."

"They're having so much fun," Sara said fondly, watching the two little shining heads, one dark and one fair, as the children bounced and shouted through the tangled mesquite. "I'm glad my kids are having the chance to enjoy the same kind of childhood I did. Growing up here was truly wonderful, Mama. And you and Daddy were the kindest parents in all the world."

Mary smiled and waved her hand in forced casualness, settling herself on the veranda rail opposite her daughter.

"Where's Laurie?" Sara asked.

"She went to Carlie Pollock's after school."

"Those two have gotten to be good friends, haven't they? I think it's so nice for them."

"It sure is," Mary agreed, squinting at one of her ostriches as it marched along the fenced paddock.

"I wish I could get to be friends with Carlie's mother," Sara commented wistfully. "But June still can't stand the sight of me."

"I'm sure she doesn't feel that way, dear," Mary said with a purposeful edge to her voice. "You're just so damned tired all the time, you probably tend to imagine things."

"Mama..." Sara began.

"Don't you Mama me, girl. I want to know what you think you're doing, wearing yourself to a frazzle like this. For three weeks now you've been coming home from work, grabbing a bite to eat and then going off again, dragging yourself home hours after dark and looking as pale as death all the time...."

"It's a secret, Mama," Sara pleaded. "I can't tell you."

"And locking yourself away in that barn with Warren Trent," Mary went on, as if her daughter hadn't spoken, "when his own family doesn't even know who he is anymore or why he's here in town! Sara, what do you expect me to do?"

"Just trust me, Mama," Sara said quietly. "I'm a grown-up woman. I know what I'm doing. And I couldn't be in better hands than Warren Trent's. In fact," she added with private sadness, "that man wouldn't lay a hand on me if you paid him, Mama. Believe me, I'm completely safe."

"But what are you *doing?*" Mary asked in despair. "You won't even let me tell anybody you're going to that barn every night. I'm sure Vern and Carolyn don't know a thing about it."

"I should hope not," Sara said. "I told you, Mama, it's a secret. Please just be patient, and please, please don't breathe a word to anybody about all this, because it's going to be such a wonderful surprise. You'll find out everything soon enough. Not long after Daddy comes home, in fact."

Mary's worried face softened and began to glow, as it always did when her husband's homecoming was mentioned. "Talk about wonderful," she murmured. "Al comes home the end of next week. It's going to feel so good to have him back, Sara."

Sara smiled and reached over to squeeze her mother's hand, then got reluctantly to her feet. "Well..." she began, moving toward the steps.

Mary's face creased with concern again. "Already? Can't you just stay for supper? I made barbecue, Sara. You know how much you love it."

Sara shook her head regretfully as she headed for the truck. "Sorry, Mama. I had a sandwich and a bowl of soup before I left work. Maybe I can heat up some of the meat when I get home, all right?"

Mary sighed and shook her head.

All the way down their drive and out onto the highway, Sara was uncomfortably conscious of her mother's disapproving frown.

But as she neared the old barn her guilty concern vanished in a wave of excitement. She parked behind the derelict building, ran to the door and knocked.

"Yah? Who's dere?" a voice called, brusque and heavily accented.

"It's me, Hans. Open up."

The door creaked open and a little leprechaun face peered out, streaked with brilliant turquoise paint. Hans Keller smiled in childlike pleasure when he saw Sara waiting in the afternoon light.

"Come in, Sara, come in," he said, bowing and holding the door for her, then latching it firmly behind them. "Come see what just arrived."

Sara followed the little man into the depths of the barn, gazing in awe at the two new horses, a sorrel and a dapple gray, that had just been shipped from the museum in Boston.

"Oh, Hans," she breathed, "look at them! They're almost perfect, aren't they? We don't have to do a thing to them."

He shook his head with critical approval. "A little here and there," he said. "Just touch-ups, so they match. You finish the black today, no?"

"I hope so. That armor's so damned tedious."

Hans grinned. "Lazy girl," he teased her gently, watching as she put on her painting smock and frowned at the array of brushes and paints.

"Messy man," she told him with an answering smile. "Paint all over your face, and you call me names."

He chuckled and returned to the careful work he was doing on a peacock blue breast collar.

Sara carried her palette over to the black horse on the other side of the carousel, pleased with the easy camaraderie of their relationship. Here she was, all alone in a derelict building with one of the most renowned figures in the world of art restoration, and they wrangled and joked together just like David and Bobby.

"Where's Warren?" she asked casually as she began to ply her brush around the intricate, jeweled inlay on the horse's trappings.

"He went to Austin to pick up the rest of the brass sleeves."

Sara looked up, touching the shining fluted shaft of polished brass that was attached to the black horse's withers. "Will the new ones match the others, do you think?"

Hans gave her a smile of calm sweetness. "Warren will make sure they match."

Sara nodded and went back to her work. "I guess he will."

She smiled dreamily, picturing all the warm little hands that would clutch these shining brass poles through the years ahead.

For a long time they painted in silence, pausing only to exchange brief questions or comments, each fully absorbed in the intricacy of the work.

Sara moved over to observe as Hans applied an edging of gold leaf to the breast collar. She watched in fascination while he worked. His hands were so sure and steady, so incredibly skillful as he handled the fragile tissues of gold.

"Hans..." she began.

"Yah?" he asked, without looking up.

"Hans, are we really going to be finished in time? It's less than three weeks now until the picnic. Does Warren truly believe he can have this whole thing mounted and ready by then?"

Hans glanced over his shoulder in surprise. "Of course," he said simply. "Are you very tired, Sara?" he added gently, changing the subject.

"It doesn't matter," Sara said. "I can rest when we're finished. But it'll be so sad if we can't get it done."

"We can get it done," Hans said, squatting back on his heels and looking up at her with a shrewd, kindly gaze. "Your help has been worth so much, Sara. Warren is very, very grateful to you."

"Is he?" she asked wistfully. "He certainly never mentions it to me."

In fact, since that momentous day when she'd discovered the carousel and declared her love for him, Warren had avoided any kind of intimate contact with her. Sara saw him almost every day as they labored over the carousel, but he was distant and carefully polite, keeping their relationship at all times on a formal employer-and-employee basis.

His attitude caused Sara deep pain, partly because she ached all the time for his smile and his touch, but mostly because he made it so clear that their association was only temporary. When the carousel was finished and mounted, Warren would be gone and Hans would return to his studio in Germany. None of them would ever meet again.

It was all that Sara could do not to burst into tears just thinking about it. She choked and wiped her eyes on the sleeve of her painting smock.

Has glanced over at her quickly. "Sara?" he asked.

"Nothing," she muttered, returning to the body armor on the prancing black horse. "Just some dust in my nose, that's all."

AFTER AN HOUR OR SO there was a knock on the door. Hans hurried to open it and Sara's heart beat faster when she saw that it was Warren.

He carried a bag full of hamburgers, fries and chocolate bars, a case of cola and a thermos of coffee. "Suppertime," he announced.

Sara sighed with relief, stood up and rubbed a hand into the small of her back.

Warren sat on a portion of the hardwood deck, spreading out the food. "Tired, Sara?" he asked politely, as if she were a stranger he'd just met in an airport.

"I'm all right," she said briefly. "It's been a pretty long day, that's all."

He looked at her for a moment, then turned to Hans. "Did you check the new ponies?"

The little man nodded. "They're good, Warren. Just a touch-up here and there. Sara can do them all by herself in less than three days, probably."

Warren nodded in relief. "Good. Then we're going to make it. Except..." His face darkened briefly.

The other two paused with their hands full of food and looked at him in concern. "Warren?" Hans asked, setting his hamburger on the deck and reaching for the coffee. "Is something the matter?"

"They can't find the tiger," Warren said abruptly.

Sara and Hans both stared at him. "But, Warren..." Sara began hesitantly. "Isn't the tiger in the Smithsonian? I thought you said it was one of the first things your people located."

Warren shook his head grimly. "That's what everybody thought. Seems somebody made a bad mistake. The tiger in the Smithsonian was carved by Koning, all right, but it doesn't belong to our carousel. It's dated eleven years later. Nobody has any idea where our tiger is."

Sara and Hans both stopped eating to gape at him in shocked silence. The absence of their tiger was catastrophic news, especially at this late date.

Each of the antique carousels had been highlighted by two stationary animal figures, usually camels, tigers, giraffes or elephants, that flanked the two benches, or "dragon seats," as they were called. The individual carvers vied with one another to produce the most beautiful and lifelike of these animal carvings, and Koning was world-renowned for his tigers.

Sara remembered pictures of the Crystal Creek dragon seats. One of the animal figures was a stately giraffe, which was already here in the old barn, fully restored to its original splendor. The other animal was the tiger.

Both giraffe and tiger had been carved larger than the horses, with exquisite coloring. The tiger paced lightly next to the dragon seat, head lowered in predatory fashion, jaws bared, eyes glittering. On his back was a saddle of splendid gold and royal purple, and Sara often savored thoughts of the lucky small children who got to ride on such a deliciously scary creature. She looked at the empty spot on the decking where the tiger was to be installed, right beside the spreading peacocks that adorned the dragon seat.

"Warren..." she suggested hesitantly, "couldn't you make some kind of deal with the Smithsonian? If the tiger in their collection is a verified Koning, wouldn't they release it for this carousel, if you bring them down and show them what we're doing?"

He shook his head. "Their policy is simple and ironclad. They'll only release a valuable artifact to a genuine restoration. That tiger stays in their collection until someone sets out to restore the actual carousel it belongs with. We can't possibly get it for ours."

Hans, too, regarded in bleak silence the empty space on the deck, then Warren's unhappy face. "Perhaps a substitute of some kind..." he ventured.

"Dammit, I don't want substitutes!" Warren said angrily. "I've spent a fortune and several years of my life trying to do this thing right. I want the tiger that belongs here, the one Koning carved to go with this carousel."

"Don't your investigators have any idea where it might be?" Sara asked, aching with his pain and disappointment.

Warren looked directly at her for a moment, his eyes sober and thoughtful. "They say it's a real cold trail. They were so sure the tiger in the Smithsonian was ours, and there's no record of another one in any collection in the country. One of the collectors says he's heard rumors in the business that it's possible the tiger never left this area."

"What?" Sara asked, astonished. "What do you mean?"

"I mean," Warren said patiently, "that when they broke up the carousel, somebody local bought the tiger for an ornament or a kid's toy or something."

"I've never heard of it," Sara said.

"It was sixty years ago," Warren told her. "Anything could have happened to it."

Sara shook her head. "If somebody from around here had bought the tiger and displayed it in their home, everybody would know about it forever. It's just that kind of town. Unless..."

She stopped short, one hand over her mouth, her eyes wide.

"Sara?"

Sara looked down, shaking her head, and took a sip of coffee from a cup that trembled in her fingers. She was almost overwhelmed by the sudden wild hope that filled her mind. But there was no sense in saying anything until she could do some research, go through the piles of old letters in her mother's attic....

"Nothing," she whispered. "Nothing at all. Let's just eat our supper, all right?"

CHAPTER ELEVEN

BRIGHT JUNE SUNSHINE washed over the green hills of oak and rustling cedar, spilled onto the lush valleys and the sparkling gravel of the creek beds. The world seemed silent and expectant in the midday hush, rich and fresh and gently welcoming.

Bubba Gibson gazed quietly out the window of the police cruiser, his throat so tight with emotion that he didn't dare to speak.

Beside him at the wheel, Sheriff Wayne Jackson maintained a tactful silence, drumming his fingers on the steering wheel and whistling through his teeth in time to the country tune on the radio.

"Well, almost home, Bubba," he said heartily at last, turning off the highway and pulling up to the gates of the Flying Horse ranch. "Feels good, doesn't it?"

Bubba nodded and brushed a hand across his eyes. "I can...I can walk from here," he muttered. "Thanks, Wayne."

"You sure?"

"Yeah. If you'd just pass me that sack..."

Wayne reached into the back seat for a canvas knapsack containing Bubba's few books and personal supplies, and handed it to the quiet man.

"Look, Bubba," he said awkwardly, "I never wanted it to end like it did."

Bubba cleared his throat and clapped the younger man on the shoulder. "No hard feelin's, Wayne. You did your job, that's all, an' I paid my dues. We'll put it behind us now."

"Sure," Wayne said gratefully, as his passenger opened the door and stepped out onto the pale crushed rock of the drive. "Keep well, now, Bubba. We'll be seein' you real soon. In fact, drop by the coffee shop in the morning, okay?"

Bubba waved and nodded, then stood quietly in the sun, watching as the police cruiser vanished in the distance. He hefted the canvas sack onto the grass and hesitated, looking at the front gates of his ranch.

Everything felt so strange to him, even the crisp jeans and shirt that Mary had sent for him to wear when he came home, and the well-cut boots that had always been his favorite pair.

Funny, Bubba thought, how clothes defined a man. In that prison suit he was just a sad number, another wrecked life. But in his jeans and boots and carved leather belt, he felt like somebody again, a man with a family and property.

"Thanks to Mary," he murmured humbly, looking again at the gates that fronted his beloved land. "Thanks to Mary."

He watched the shining expanse of highway where
the police car had disappeared, wondering how long
it would be until he had enough courage to go back
into the Longhorn with the crowd he'd always enjoyed so much. It was a different world now, and
Bubba Gibson wasn't at all sure where he fit in. To tell
the truth, he wasn't even sure of the welcome that
awaited him beyond these arched gates, but he
couldn't postpone it any longer. With a nervous sigh,
he tipped his hat lower over his eyes, hitched the
knapsack onto his shoulder and trudged through the
gates, heading up the curving drive toward the house.

But Bubba hadn't progressed more than a few paces
when a small body exploded from the tangle of mesquite behind the windmill and came thudding down
the drive toward him.

"Grandpa!" David shouted, beside himself with
joy. "Here's Grandpa! Hey, my Grandpa came
home!"

The little boy threw himself against Bubba's legs,
clutching him frantically. Bubba bent to gather the
small body into his arms, racked with deep sobs that
he couldn't control.

"Grandpa," David whispered, drawing away to
gaze at the pale, tearstained face above him.
"Grandpa, you're crying."

"I'm so glad to see you, boy," Bubba choked out,
gathering the wiry little body tight in his arms again
and burying his face in his grandson's golden hair.
"Just so glad..."

Another little boy appeared and stood solemnly nearby with two fingers in his mouth.

"You must be Bobby," Bubba said, smiling through his tears at the child. "I hear you're a pretty good builder."

The boy's dark eyes brightened and he edged closer, gazing shyly at the big man who was hugging David.

A girl approached them along the path, carrying a pail and a small sack of ostrich feed. She was thin and leggy in shorts and T-shirt, her hair flaming bright red in the sunlight.

"Laurie?" Bubba asked in wonder, standing slowly erect to gaze at her.

"Hi, Grandpa," she murmured shyly. "Welcome home."

"Well, if you ain't just the picture of your mama," Bubba marveled. "All grown-up already, and what a beauty."

Laurie flushed with pleasure and shifted awkwardly in the dust of the road.

Suddenly, they all turned to watch as a figure came flying down the steps of the house and ran wildly toward them.

"Al!" Mary called, her voice choking with emotion. "Allan Gibson, why on earth didn't you let us know when you were coming? Of all the..."

But she couldn't say any more because she was in his arms, laughing and crying, kissing him, whispering and hugging him in wondering joy, while the children

stood around them in a warm sunlit circle and the tall
ostriches paced quietly along the fence.

SARA STOOD uncertainly on the wide, sagging veranda of June Pollock's house, contemplating the
broken doorbell. It was early twilight, soft and mellow, and the air was fragrant with the scent of lilacs
and early roses.

Finally, drawing a deep breath to steady herself,
Sara raised her hand and knocked loudly on the
weathered door.

It opened almost at once and June stood there,
looking down coldly at her visitor.

"Laurie isn't here," she announced, before Sara
had a chance to speak. "The girls walked uptown to
get a soda and fool around in the square. They'll be
back before dark, I reckon, or they'll be in big trouble."

Sara held out a small canvas bag. "I brought her a
sweater and some extra socks," she said. "I thought
she might need them for the trip tomorrow."

June nodded and took the bag in silence. Several
school classes were going on a bus trip to the museum
in Austin the next day, and Laurie had been allowed
to sleep over at Carlie's house to celebrate the occasion.

"Anything else?" June asked, pausing in the act of
closing the door. Sara looked at her and shifted her
feet nervously on the worn planks of the veranda.

"June, could I . . . could I come inside for a minute? Please?"

June shrugged and held the door open, standing aside to allow Sara to enter. "You can sit in the parlor with Granny if you like," she said curtly. "I was just making a pot of ice tea."

"Thank you," Sara murmured, watching as the tall woman vanished down the hall in the waning light. Then she went into the parlor, where old Ellen Pollock sat just as Sara remembered her, drowsing in the rocker by the window with the fluffy white cat in her lap.

The old woman looked up as Sara entered, and her sunken eyes brightened. "Well, for heaven's sake, it's Elvira Gibson," she said happily. "Hello, Elvira. How are you?"

Sara hesitated. "I'm fine, Ellen," she murmured, seating herself in a faded pink velvet chair opposite the old woman.

Ellen Pollock nodded and stroked the cat dreamily. But when she glanced up again, her eyes were bright with anger at some ancient quarrel. "You stole that peppermint stick, Elvira Gibson," she said accusingly. "I know it was you. That was *my* peppermint, and you stole it."

"I'm sorry," Sara said humbly.

She smiled with relief when June came back, carrying a tray and three brimming glasses of ice tea.

"This is delicious, June," Sara murmured gratefully. "Just delicious."

She sipped the tea greedily, hoping with growing anxiety that her stomach wouldn't start to rumble. Sara had already worked five hours in the old barn after getting off her shift at the motel, and she hadn't yet found time to eat anything. In fact, she was becoming uncomfortably aware of a delicious aroma drifting down the hall from the kitchen. Sara stifled an overwhelming urge to ask June what she was baking.

"How's Bubba?" June asked after an awkward silence. "Nobody's seen him in town since he got home."

Sara shook her head, thinking about her father. "He's just been home a week," she said at last. "I think Daddy's kind of shy about going to town. He doesn't know how folks are going to treat him. And he's working so hard at the ranch. Seems he just can't get enough of work."

June nodded, then looked closely at Sara. "Why are you here?" she asked abruptly. "Do you want something, or what?"

Sara drew another deep breath and set her glass carefully on a graceful old fluted table next to her chair.

"June," she began, "I know you don't like me, and I don't blame you at all. When I look back at the way I treated you, and the way I've behaved to other people, I don't like myself much either. But I need to ask a huge favor of you and I'm begging you to say yes, because I don't know what I'll do if you refuse. I just don't know what I'll do."

Sara paused, out of breath and flushed with emotion after this impassioned speech.

June appraised her visitor with level blue eyes. "What do you want?" she asked again.

Sara clasped her hands tightly in her lap to stop them from shaking and looked at June with desperate pleading. "I want to look in your cellar."

THE CELLAR beneath the old Pollock house was not a pleasant sight. The old concrete walls were white and flaky, worn almost to powder in some places, and cobwebs hung from the exposed beams in huge drifts of dusty lace. Junk was piled everywhere, all the sad mess accumulated by June's lazy, drunken father, who'd spent a lifetime starting projects that he never finished. The two women labored in the musty stillness, hauling aside old motors, ancient wringer washing machines, parts of cars and broken furniture.

"It would help," June muttered in exasperation, brushing a dirty hand across her forehead, "if you'd tell me what we're looking for."

Sara glanced at the other woman, feeling hot and foolish. "I can't, June," she said reluctantly. "It's a secret, and it's not mine to tell."

"So what makes you think your damn secret is going to be in my cellar?"

"Just . . . just something your grandmother said the last time I was here. Please, June," Sara added humbly. "Please, just help me move these old doors so we can see what's behind them."

June shone her flashlight into the cavern behind the ancient boiler. "Nothing in there but some piles of old sacks," she said.

"Please, can we just move the doors and look?"

June sighed, and lifted one of the heavy oak doors that Sara was straining to move, carrying it easily across the uneven cement floor and leaning it against the wall.

"See?" she said, turning with a dismissive wave of her hand. "It's just a pile of old sacks, like I told you."

But Sara was no longer aware of June. She knelt by the pile of sacking, peeling away the layers of moldy burlap to expose a heavy covering of oilcloth. She could feel something that was concealed beneath the oilcloth, something lumpy and unyielding. "Oh, my," Sara whispered, her hands shaking with excitement. "Oh, June, if this is what I think it might be . . ."

June stared at Sara for a moment, then knelt beside her to peel away the oilcloth wrappings. Suddenly she gasped and leaped to her feet, her face white with terror.

A pair of wild red eyes glittered in the darkness of the cellar, and a snarling mouth filled with sharp white teeth gleamed cruelly at them from within the dusty shrouds.

Sara forgot herself completely and hugged June in delight. Tears streamed down her face. She was almost incoherent with joy, half laughing and half crying.

June pushed the smaller woman aside gently, moving closer to stare in awe at the snarling face, the glossy striped body and threatening front paw that emerged from the folds of oilcloth.

"What the hell is it?" she breathed. "Where did it come from?"

"It's been here for sixty years," Sara whispered, brushing her eyes with the dusty sleeve of her jacket. "It's from the old carousel that used to be in the town square, June."

June stared at her. "It is? How did you know about it?"

"From something your grandmother said," Sara repeated. "She told me about going into the depths and seeing a tiger. When I . . . after I remembered her saying that," Sara went on, stumbling over the words in her excitement, "I looked through our attic and found some old letters that my grandmother wrote to her sister. Apparently your grandfather bought the tiger thinking it would be a good investment. He wanted to keep it in the front hall, but your grandmother was terrified of it. She made him hide it away in the cellar, and I guess everybody forgot about it after a few years. Oh, June, I was so scared that maybe your father had found it and sold it, or even thrown it away! I haven't slept for days, worrying about it."

June looked down pensively at the snarling striped head. "A good investment, my grandpa thought?"

"Yes. He was right. June, I know somebody who wants very much to buy this tiger. And you know what? It's worth enough money to pay for Carlie's surgery, and anything else you might want besides.''

June looked at Sara's dusty, tear-streaked face, then turned to gaze down at the tiger in stunned silence. She reached out a callused hand to touch the tiger's ear, and ran her fingers thoughtfully down the line of the snowy ruff beneath his snarling jaw.

''Well, well,'' she murmured at last, with characteristic calm. ''I'll be damned.''

Sara laughed and hugged her elbows, afraid she might fly apart with happiness and excitement. It was a long time before she could trust herself to speak.

''June?'' she ventured finally, in a timid voice. ''May I ask you something?''

June smiled down at her, the first smile of genuine warmth that Sara had ever seen on the tall woman's face. ''Now what?'' she asked in mock exasperation, but her voice was gentle.

''June, do you think...could I have something to eat? I'm just about starved.''

In fact, when she spoke the words, Sara began to sway on her feet, and would have fallen if June hadn't put a strong arm around her shoulders and half carried her up the stairs to the kitchen.

IT WAS LATE and the moon was climbing above the hills by the time Sara left the old Pollock house, having sworn June to secrecy and confided most of the details of Warren's plan.

She knew that his secret was safe, despite the necessity of telling June what he was doing. June had given her word not to tell, and nothing would make her betray a confidence. Sara smiled, remembering June's cordiality, the animation on her face when she sat opposite Sara at the old kitchen table, planning for Carlie's final surgery.

Sara drove along the winding road until the old barn came into view, and her smile faded as she drew abreast of the derelict building. Some problems in life were so easily solved, she thought wearily. But others, it seemed, were as impossible as trying to draw down the moon. Cold silver light spilled over the weathered barn. Sara's heart beat faster when she saw Warren's truck parked at the rear of the building, its chrome bumper gleaming dully in the moonlight.

She pulled off the road and parked by the barn, nerving herself to walk through the darkness and tap at the door.

"Yeah?" he called sharply from within. "Who's out there?"

"It's me, Warren," Sara called back. "Let me in, please. I need to talk to you."

He opened the door and peered at her, then stepped aside quietly to admit her to the barn.

"Where's Hans?" Sara asked, passing him and moving over to look at the bright rows of prancing horses, now almost completely restored.

"He went into town earlier. He's getting a real bad cold, poor guy. Lucky we're almost finished."

Warren seated himself on a packing crate, his face dark and brooding, and Sara watched him quietly.

After a moment, he glanced up at her. "Why are you here, Sara? I thought you were going home early to get some sleep."

"I had...I had an errand to do," Sara faltered, avoiding his eyes. In spite of herself, she glanced at the empty space on the hardwood deck where the tiger belonged, next to the dragon seat.

For the past couple of weeks she'd been painfully conscious of Warren's bitter disappointment at their failure to find the missing animal. Sara was beginning to understand something of the man's hard-driving force, his relentless stubbornness and the quiet, dogged determination that had helped him make such a success of his life.

At least financially, she amended privately. Nobody could say that Warren Trent had made a success of his life in any emotional sense.

She looked at the hard sculpted planes of his face, and felt almost faint with love and sorrow.

"Warren," she said gently, sitting opposite him on the deck of the carousel.

"Yeah?" He looked over at her with an inquiring glance.

"I found your tiger."

"*What?* Sara, what did you say?"

Warren leaped to his feet and rushed across the dusty floor to seize her arm, staring down at her with burning eyes.

"I said," she repeated in that same calm voice, "that I've found your tiger. I know where it is."

He peered at her cautiously, clearly suspecting her of teasing. "You did? Where is it?"

"Not far from here," Sara told him. "You were right, Warren. The tiger never left Crystal Creek."

"And you know where it is? Sara . . ."

"Sit down, Warren," she told him. "Sit down here beside me for a minute. I want to tell you something."

He lowered his long body to sit next to her, still gazing at her with piercing intensity.

Sara was almost overcome by his nearness and her longing to touch him, but she forced herself to keep her hands folded tightly in her lap. She bit her lip and stared at the gray pony next to her, struggling to organize her thoughts before she began to speak.

"Warren," she said at last, "I've told you that I love you. I'm not ashamed to say it, even though I know that you don't want me in your life."

She glanced up at him with a brief, sad smile, then looked away quickly. "I guess I just have no pride anymore," Sara went on, looking at the rough, weathered boards on the opposite wall. "All that pride that used to be such a big part of my life, it's gone now, Warren. I've realized that pride is such a useless thing. It just gets in the way of life and relationships. So I don't mind telling you that I love you, even if you'll never love me back."

"Sara . . ."

She waved her hand in an abrupt gesture. "Don't talk to me, please, Warren. I really need to say all this."

He nodded and watched her face in silence.

"I told you I wouldn't ever make any demands on you," Sara went on, "but then when I was sure I'd found the tiger, I decided to break that promise. I convinced myself it was for your own good, because I love you so much."

"What do you mean, Sara?"

"I was going to use the tiger to strike a bargain with you, Warren. I decided that I'd tell you where it was if you'd promise to stay and present the carousel to the town, be here in person to let the people know exactly what you've done."

He opened his mouth to speak, but Sara silenced him again, putting her hand gently on his arm. "I've changed my mind again, Warren," she told him. "I looked at the moon when I was driving out here, and thought how much it's seen and how long the world's been spinning around, and I realized that you can't fix things by bargaining. People have to make their own choices, and loving them isn't enough to heal them."

Sara was afraid to look at him, terrified that she would start crying if she met his eyes.

"The tiger is in June Pollock's cellar, Warren. It's in perfect condition. It's been there ever since the carousel was dismantled."

"My God," he breathed, staring down at her. "How did you find that out, Sara?"

"That's not important." Sara got to her feet and started toward the door. "June knows what you're doing here, but she won't tell anybody. Just be sure," Sara added with sudden fierceness, "that you pay her what that tiger's worth, Warren Trent. She really needs the money, a lot more than some of those rich collectors who sold you the horses."

Warren nodded and got to his feet, walking beside her to the door. "Of course I'll pay her," he said quietly.

Sara paused by the door and gazed up at his face in the shadows of the old barn. She was almost breathless with pain, as if her heart were actually breaking apart inside her. "Goodbye, Warren," she whispered.

"Don't you mean good-night?"

"No," she said, meeting his eyes steadily. "I mean goodbye. I'm not coming back."

"Sara, look . . ."

"This job is practically finished," Sara told him. "You and Hans don't need me anymore, and the picnic is in just a few days. We won't be seeing each other again, Warren. But I'll always love you."

Her throat tightened and tears stung behind her eyes. She turned, unable to look at him any longer, and plunged through the door and out into the moonlit stillness.

Sara fled across the dusty grass to her truck, trying to hold back her sobs, while Warren stood framed in the brightly lit doorway of the barn and watched her in silence.

CHAPTER TWELVE

LATER IN THE WEEK, Sara walked slowly next to June along the path curving by the creek bed. She sighed and lifted her face to the gentle glow of the waning sun, drawing her sweater closer around her shoulders.

"Are you getting a chill?" June asked quickly. "I knew we shouldn't walk so far. You're not nearly strong enough yet."

Sara smiled at the taller woman. "June, I'm not an invalid," she protested mildly. "There's nothing actually wrong with me, you know."

"Like hell there isn't," June said, her voice rough with concern. "When I found out what you been doing all this time, working full time at the motel and then spending hours and hours on that damned carousel besides, not eating proper for days on end...no wonder you look like the first stiff breeze is gonna carry you off. The man should be shot, making you work that hard."

"He didn't *make* me, June. Actually, he had no choice in the matter."

"Well, *I* have a choice," June said firmly. "And I say it's time for you to get back home, have a bite to eat and go straight to bed."

"It's barely nine o'clock," Sara said. But when June spoke, she realized that she was still not quite as strong as she pretended to be, and the idea of going to bed was really very tempting.

She'd come near to breaking down that night she left the barn for the last time, so weak with exhaustion that she couldn't possibly drag herself out of bed the next day. When Mary Gibson called the motel to report that Sara wouldn't be in to work, June had left Louie cooking breakfast eggs in the kitchen and driven straight out to the ranch, blowing into their lives like a warm, golden hurricane or some other overpowering force of nature.

She instructed Mary to keep her daughter in bed, to carry her meals on a tray and not on any account to let Sara exert herself. She took the children off to stay with her in town a few days so the house would be quiet, and worked double time at the motel to cover most of Sara's shifts as well as her own.

And every evening without fail, June paid a visit to the Gibson ranch to see how the patient was faring, and to issue dire threats if she even suspected that her instructions weren't being followed to the letter.

Sara laughed at June's fussing, but she had to admit that it was pleasant being babied and coddled, and having her friend's vigorous presence safely between her and the world. Only now was she beginning to realize how close she'd come to physical and emotional breakdown. Even now, her body was recovering, but her emotions were still fragile....

"Louie's interviewing some new girls," June said, adjusting her long stride to Sara's faltering pace.

Sara glanced up in surprise. "He is? What for?"

"My job, for one thing," June said casually. "I dunno if you want to keep working in that dump, but I sure don't."

"What are you going to do?"

"Well," June said, bending to pull up a stalk of grass and chewing it thoughtfully, "first I'm going with Carlie to Dallas to have her surgery done, and staying with her as long as it takes. Then I think I'm going to the community college in Austin to take a course as a licensed practical nurse. That's something I always wanted to do."

Sara grinned at her. "Oh, I see. So *that's* why you're fussing over me so much. You're just practicing. You're learning how to deal with sick people and push them around."

June chuckled. "I've always known how to push people around," she said cheerfully. "Sick or not. It's easier when they're off their feed a bit, that's all. They can't fight back."

Sara laughed with her, then sobered. "That's wonderful news, June. Truly wonderful. I'm so glad to hear it. You must be feeling prosperous," she added, with a cautious, sidelong glance. "Making all these plans, I mean."

"Yeah," June agreed calmly. "I'm feeling prosperous, all right."

"So he . . . he paid you for the tiger?" Sara asked, finally throwing caution to the wind. "Did he come and get it?"

June stared ahead at the curving path, her face impassive. "What's the deal, Sara? Are we talking about him, or not?"

"I just wondered if . . ."

"You told me you never wanted to hear his name mentioned again. Are you changing your mind?"

"I'm . . . I'm stronger now," Sara said, feeling her cheeks grow warm. "Besides, I don't really care anymore. I don't care what he does."

"Yeah, *right*," June said, jeering softly. "Like Davey doesn't give a damn about whether his ball team is in the tournament on the weekend. Just couldn't care less."

"All I asked," Sara persisted, with a feeble attempt at dignity, "is whether he came to get the tiger. I don't see why you have to make a federal case out of it."

June cast the other woman a keen, speculative glance, then nodded. "He did," she said. "He came to pick it up this morning, just after he checked out of the motel."

"He . . . he checked out?"

"I think he's gone back to Houston. So is the other guy, the little dude with the ponytail. You know, I liked that man," June added with a private smile. "He was a real little gentleman, that ponytail guy. He asked me to dance the other night in the bar."

Normally Sara would have been enchanted by the picture of June, so statuesque, whirling around the dance floor in the arms of little Hans. But she was still stunned at the news that Warren was already gone. She'd always known he would be leaving, but the reality of it, the dreadful finality, was almost too much for her to bear.

A couple of tears trembled on her cheeks, damp and icy in the evening breeze. June glanced over at her quickly, then turned away with gruff tact. "Warren asked about you," she said quietly, gazing down the path again. "He seemed real concerned when he heard you were sick."

Sara, too, looked straight ahead, trying to control the trembling of her lips, and refused to answer.

"He left a number in Houston," June went on. "He said you could call him anytime, that he'd like to hear from you."

"Well, I won't be calling him," Sara said in a small, tight voice, dashing her hand across her eyes. "You can burn that number, June."

"Look, kid, I know you don't like talking about this, but I still think you're making a big mistake. I think you're going to keep on eating your heart out over this guy. You look stronger, but you're dying from the inside out, Sara. You need to go and talk to him. If you don't, I think I will. I think there's a few things he needs to know."

"Like what?"

"Like how much you love him. How you can't even hear his name without getting all shaky and trembly, the way you are right now. How you have that tatty blue T-shirt of his that you stole from the motel room, and you sleep with it under your pillow...."

"You *wouldn't!*" Sara gasped, staring at the other woman in horror. "I thought you were my friend, June."

"Damn right," June said placidly. "I'm the best friend you'll ever have. And I think you need to talk to this guy."

"I...I can't, June. Besides, he doesn't want me."

"Well, he's sure got a funny way of showing it, doesn't he?"

Sara's heart gave a sudden wild little leap of hope, then began to hammer nervously in her chest. "What do you mean?"

"I mean," June said patiently, "that the man looks about as bad as you do. I think he's crazy for you. You'd think," she added with cheerful sarcasm, "that a couple of so-called adults would be able to figure out that they should be together, especially when they're nuts about each other."

"But he's different, June. He doesn't want a relationship with anybody. I just fell into his life by accident and he spent most of the time holding me at arm's length. Now that he's safely gone, he'd never let me back in."

"He would if you didn't give him a choice. Do it the way you did with the carousel. Force your way in there and tell him this is how things are gonna be, and let him learn to deal with it. He loves you, Sara. He's just got to find it out for himself, that's all."

Sara's chin lifted. "I don't want any man on those terms, June. If it's not what he wants, I won't force myself on him. Besides, it hurts too much," she added piteously, her face crumpling. "Oh, June, it hurts so much!"

"Poor kid," June said, her voice softening with tenderness. She dropped an arm around Sara's shoulders and hugged her gently. "I guess things are all set for the Fourth," she said finally, in a more casual tone. "Warren said he's got it all organized."

"They're still going to set it all up secretly the night before? Do you think they can do it, June?"

"Well, it's a tough town to keep a secret in, but I'm pretty certain it hasn't leaked out yet. If word was around, I'd have heard something. Besides, knowing how that man is, I reckon he'll finish this job the way he started."

"I wonder what people are going to think when they go to the town square on the Fourth and see the carousel there," Sara asked wistfully.

"They're gonna think Warren Trent's crazy not to be around, after all the trouble he went to. And," June added with a scowl, "they'll be right, dammit. The man should be there."

Sara thought about him, suddenly overwhelmed by burning physical memories of his hands and mouth, his dark eyes and the rare flashing sweetness of his smile. "June..." she whispered. "June, please don't talk about him anymore. I don't think I can bear it."

June nodded, her face impassive, and glanced into the sunset sky in the direction of the ranch house. "Look, Sara. Your daddy's seen us coming and he's heading for the barn, just like always. He's sure shy of people, isn't he?"

Sara nodded, grateful for the change of subject. "Mama's getting worried about him, I think. He won't go to town for coffee or talk to neighbors on the phone, or anything."

"Poor Bubba," June said with sympathy. "It can't be easy, what he's gone through. But he's got to face up to things sooner or later."

"I guess we all do," Sara said with a wan smile at her friend. "Don't we, June? Life's real hard, and we all have to face up to it sooner or later."

SARA WOKE in the bright summer morning and lay drowsily in her bed, wondering what was different about the day. She felt so good, fresh and rested for the first time in weeks.

Then, gradually, reality crept in and she moaned aloud with unhappiness, turning over and burying her face in her pillow.

She felt rested because she'd had a few days off, with lots of sleep and regular meals, and her body had responded to the change even though her soul was wounded beyond repair.

They'd taken over her life, Mary and Bubba and June. They'd tucked her into bed like a child for long, healing sleeps, brought her trays of food while she sat quietly on the veranda, let her take slow, careful walks along the creek bed. And they'd kept the world away, surrounding her with love and protection while they waited for her strength to return. But her heart was broken, and no amount of pampering was going to change that.

Sara rolled onto her back again, gazing at the square of blue Texas sky beyond her ruffled curtains. It was going to be such a beautiful day, she thought sadly. It was the Fourth of July, the day of the town's annual picnic, but the people of Crystal Creek still had no knowledge of the wondrous sight that awaited them when they gathered for their celebration.

Sara hadn't been back to the barn since her last conversation with Warren, and didn't know how he had managed the final installation of the carousel. But she hadn't the slightest doubt that he had succeeded in his plans by now. Warren Trent was not a man who failed when he set out to do something.

Sara would have staked her life on the belief that the carousel was standing quietly in the town square this very moment, the painted ponies gleaming in the morning light, the gilded mirrors catching fire from the sunrise, the organ poised to spill its lively music into the summer calm.

And Warren was gone. He was finished with his symbolic act of contrition, and by now he had vanished back into the solitary world where he lived alone with his memories and his suffering.

Sara felt tears gather in her eyes again, and bit her lip hard enough to cause pain. The tears came very readily these days, because of her exhaustion and vulnerability. But she was impatient with her weakness. There was no point in crying over Warren Trent, because he was as inaccessible as the clouds that drifted across the calm, sapphire sky. Sara had to learn somehow to live with the memory of his eyes and mouth and his sweet lovemaking, to find happiness and fulfillment in a world where she would never see him again.

She heaved herself out of bed, dressed listlessly in shorts, T-shirt and sandals and went downstairs to find the kitchen already humming with activity.

David and Laurie were both wild with excitement over the picnic, the parade, the baseball tournament and the evening fireworks. Even little Carlie Pollock, who had spent the night with Laurie, glowed with unaccustomed animation. Her pale face was shining as she perched on a high stool by the counter and helped Mary mix pancake batter.

Sara smiled at the children, moved almost unbearably by the sight of Carlie's thin leg in the clumsy black boot. All the pain of the past months had been worthwhile, she told herself, just knowing that Carlie would soon be free of that encumbrance, able to run and play, to dance and skip and whirl across the ice on flashing skates.

The door opened and Bubba Gibson came in from outside, broad and hearty in his work clothes.

He crossed the room to kiss Mary, ruffled Carlie's bright hair with a big gentle hand, then looked down at David, who was dragging at his arm, shouting for attention.

"Grandpa! Grandpa! Can I wear my baseball uniform to the picnic? Laurie says I can't. She says I have to take it in the car and change before we play."

Bubba considered, smiling over the boy's head at Mary while she spooned pancake batter onto the griddle.

"Well now," he said cautiously, "when's your first game, Davey?"

"Right after lunch."

Bubba rubbed his chin with a thoughtful hand, gazing down at his grandson.

Sara poured herself a cup of coffee and smiled at her father. He looked so much better now than when he'd first come home. He was already getting back the weathered, sun-browned look that she remembered from childhood, and he moved with more confidence, filled the room with his presence, just as he always had.

"Well," Bubba said, "if you play right after lunch, Davey, then I think you could probably wear your uniform to the picnic. Just be sure you don't spill soda pop or potato salad on it, though," he added sternly. "Nobody likes a sloppy ball player."

David shouted with happiness and raced out of the room, while Laurie watched him in scorn.

"Stupid kid," she muttered.

Bubba grinned at his granddaughter and seated himself at the table, smiling his thanks as Mary brought him a heaping plate of food. "A man likes to wear his baseball uniform on the Fourth of July, Laurie," he said mildly. "It just makes him feel more like a man, somehow."

Laurie passed by his chair and kissed the top of his graying head. "Are you wearing your baseball uniform, Grandpa?" she teased him.

"You know, I probably could," Bubba said thoughtfully. "I haven't played baseball for a good many years. But since I lost that big fat belly of mine, I reckon I could fit into my old uniform again."

"Don't be silly. Your grandpa's not wearing his baseball uniform to the picnic," Mary said calmly, giving Carlie a hug as the little girl pulled a chair up to the table. "He's wearing the new shirt I bought him, and some nice dress jeans and his best riding boots."

Bubba cleared his throat awkwardly, looking down at his plate. "Mary..." he began.

"What, Al? Here, you girls have some more pancakes before David comes back and takes them all."

"Mary, I'm not going to the picnic."

Mary looked up at her husband in astonishment. "Not going? Al Gibson, what on earth are you talking about? You've gone to that picnic every year of your whole life since you were a baby in diapers. Of course you're going."

Bubba shook his head. "There's a lot to do here, Mary. I want to finish that stretch of fence in the south pasture, and one of the ostrich sheds needs a window replaced. . . ."

"But Al," Mary protested, still looking at him in helpless concern. "It's the Fourth of July! We never work on the Fourth."

Sara held her breath, studying her father's troubled face. She knew just how he was feeling, understood his panicky dread of meeting the townspeople again, mingling with his old friends and neighbors and trying to pretend that nothing bad had happened in his life.

"Daddy," she said with sudden fierce emotion, "you have to come to the picnic. You just *have* to. I'll be so disappointed if you don't, I won't be able to stand it."

Bubba looked up at her in surprise. "Why, Sara? How come it matters so much?"

Sara looked down at her plate, uncomfortably conscious of the startled silence in the kitchen, and the way the two girls and her parents were gazing at her in concern.

"There's . . . there's going to be a surprise at the picnic," she muttered finally, her cheeks flaming. "The most wonderful surprise, Daddy. I can't stand it if you aren't there to see."

"A surprise?" David asked, hurrying back into the room in his baseball uniform. "What kind of surprise, Mom?"

"I can't tell you," Sara murmured. "I can't tell any of you just yet. But I don't want you to miss it," she added earnestly to her father, the ready tears starting to form in her eyes again. "Please, Daddy. Please, just say you'll come to the picnic with us."

Bubba stared at this beloved daughter of his, whom he'd never been able to deny anything since the day she was born. Sara could see him wavering, see the misery in his blue eyes as he struggled with what she was asking of him.

At last he nodded and gave her a bleak smile. "Sure, honey," he said. "If it means that much to you, I'll come to the picnic."

SARA WONDERED if her father was regretting his decision when they parked the car down the street from the Longhorn Motel and Coffee Shop, and he moved around to lift the picnic basket from the trunk. His tension was so evident in the awkward movements of his big body, the cautious way he glanced around at the noisy, sunlit throngs on the street.

The children spilled from the car and vanished into the crowd, shouting with excitement, barely taking time to receive final instructions on where to meet for the parade. Mary and Bubba and their daughter were left alone on the busy street. They paused in the sunlight, wrangling automatically over the very same things that Sara remembered from all those long-ago picnics at the town square.

Her father wanted to spread their blanket over in the corner by the baseball diamond, while Mary preferred the shade of the big pecan tree, handy to the washrooms inside the courthouse.

"Come on, you two," Sara said abruptly, almost wild with impatience and anticipation. "You always fight about the exact same thing, and you always wind up doing it Mama's way, so let's just head over to the pecan tree right now. Hurry up!"

They began to make their way through the crowds of people who lined the street for the parade and massed at the edge of the square. Sara could sense a strange tension gripping some of those in the crowd, an awed silence and excitement. She realized that a number of people must already have seen the carousel, and word was beginning to spread throughout the town. Mary and Bubba, though, had no such knowledge as yet. Sara was conscious of their puzzled looks as they glanced around at friends and neighbors, many of whom seemed to be behaving so strangely.

You could almost tell, Sara thought with interest, who knew about the carousel by now and who didn't. Some of the community, like Sara and her family, were just arriving, making their way in blithe holiday spirits to their accustomed places in the square. Others wore that same look of stunned astonishment, of shock and wonder, as they stood in little groups whispering together.

Sara and her parents passed Brock Munroe and Amanda Walker, who were among the newer arrivals and clearly hadn't heard about anything unusual. Mary gave a little cry of pleasure and hugged Amanda, who looked as fresh and dainty as a flower in her yellow shorts, white cotton shirt and sandals. Brock stood nearby, his eyes shining with love and pride as he gazed down at the small dark-haired woman beside him.

"Hello, Bubba," he said awkwardly, smiling over at his neighbor.

"Good mornin', Brock," Bubba said, then bent hastily to pat Alvin, who cowered at Amanda's feet and surveyed the noisy crowd with dark, frightened eyes.

Alvin was also in holiday dress, looking festive and almost handsome in a new red collar decorated with a huge bow striped in red, white and blue. He licked Bubba's hand and rolled onto his back, waving his paws in the air and exposing his fat belly.

"Oh, Alvin," Amanda said to him with a brief tug of the red leather leash. "Get up, for goodness' sake. You're messing up your pretty bow, after I went to all that trouble."

Bubba grinned faintly as he knelt beside the ragged little dog. "I've never seen Alvin lookin' so good," he told Amanda. "I think he's even lost a little weight, like me."

Amanda gave him an answering smile. "Not much, I'm afraid," she said ruefully. "I've tried to put him on a diet, but Alvin could find a meal in the middle of the Sahara Desert. He's such a greedy dog."

Alvin sat erect to gnaw on one of his back paws and cast her a reproachful glance, his bow quivering.

Bubba reached for Mary's arm, avoiding Brock's look of awkward concern. "We'd better be goin', Mary," he said. "We need to find the kids and get our blanket spread out before the parade starts."

Sara glanced back at the younger couple, who stood watching them leave. They wanted to be friendly, she realized. If her father had extended any kind of invitation, Brock and Amanda would have been happy to join them for the picnic.

But Bubba Gibson was a lot like Warren Trent. He was so painfully conscious of his own wrongdoing, and so sensitive to the reaction of his neighbors, that he wouldn't give anybody a chance to be friendly. He plowed through the crowds with stolid determination, barely looking up to acknowledge the greetings of passersby, intent only on getting to the pecan tree and hiding himself in its leafy shade.

J.T. and Cynthia passed near them, laden with pieces of baby equipment. Jennifer Travis McKinney rode proudly in her father's arms in romper suit and sunbonnet, crowing with delight as she took in the colorful throngs of people. J.T. called happily to Bubba when he caught sight of his old friend and Mary made a move to join the other couple, but again, her husband propelled her forward, drawing her hastily into the crowd.

Oh, Daddy, Sara thought in sorrow. *Won't you even give them a chance to show you how they feel?*

Once more she was struck by the similarity between her father's situation and Warren's. Hopelessness washed over her in a dark wave as she wondered if Bubba, like Warren, was going to spend the rest of his life avoiding his neighbors just to protect himself from hurt.

All at once Mary stiffened. Sara looked up to see Billie Jo Dumont approaching them through the crowd. The young woman looked lush and beautiful, her long strawberry blond hair glistening in the sunlight, her ample, curving body richly displayed in brief denim cutoffs and a halter top.

Bubba, too, tensed at her approach. Then, with quiet deliberation, he paused to put one arm around his wife and the other around Sara. He stood between them, holding them close.

"Good mornin', Billie Jo," he said courteously when she paused to glance at them. "It's a real nice day, isn't it?"

Billie Jo's eyes flickered and turned dark with pain when she saw Bubba's solid family unit. For the first time, Sara felt a reluctant twinge of sympathy for this young woman, who'd caused her mother such unhappiness.

There were two sides to every story, she realized. Billie Jo had yearnings, too, and reasons for what she'd done. What was more, it was obvious that she could feel pain just like anybody else. Sara was intensely proud of her mother when Mary nodded and smiled at Billie Jo, murmured a quiet greeting, then moved on beside her husband.

They'd all been so impatient with her mother, Sara thought, following her parents into the town square. People had wanted Mary to rage and shout, to show her fury and punish her husband publicly for what he'd done, as if that was somehow the proper way to behave in this situation.

But Mary had been right all the time. Anger and vindictiveness accomplished nothing. Healing only began when people could forgive, put the pain behind them and move on with life. And Mary had been wise enough to understand that....

Sara was so deep in her thoughts that she was startled when her parents stopped abruptly in front of her and stood gaping at the grassy expanse by the courthouse.

Sara moved up beside them, smiling at their stunned faces, at Bubba's slack-jawed astonishment and Mary's look of childlike wonder.

The old carousel stood where it had once been, all those years ago, on a slight rise of ground near the courthouse. It was housed in a new building with folding wooden panels that had been drawn aside to expose all the marvels of the ride, its gleaming hardwood deck and gilded mirrors and brilliant lights, its dancing ponies with their flashing heels and brass posts glistening in the morning light. People were massed all around, murmuring and shifting on their feet, admiring the silent ponies in awe and whispering among themselves.

Sara's children appeared out of the crowd and pressed close to her, their eyes wide as they looked up at the bright circle of horses.

"Where's Carlie?" Sara whispered.

"June came and got her," David whispered back. "Mom, where did it come from? Who brought it here? June said you'd tell us."

Sara's parents turned to look at her.

"Sara," her mother murmured, "sweetheart, did you know about this?"

Sara nodded, hugging her children while tears trembled on her eyelashes and ran down her cheeks. "Isn't it beautiful?" she whispered, indicating the bright, gilded ponies. "Isn't it the loveliest thing you ever saw?"

The tiger paced silently next to the dragon seat, his big striped body glistening in the sunlight, his fierce jaws snarling at the onlookers who crowded nearby. Sara blinked back her tears, conscious of her family's urgent, questioning looks.

"Sara?" Bubba muttered. "Sara, girl, how did you ever..."

A stir ran suddenly through the crowd. Sara tensed, then glanced again at the carousel in stunned amazement.

A man had just mounted the hardwood deck and stood next to one of the prancing black horses.

The man was Warren Trent.

CHAPTER THIRTEEN

FOR WHAT SEEMED like hours, the world was frozen in time and the sun stopped climbing the morning sky. Sara swayed on her feet and would have fallen if her father hadn't reached out quickly with a supporting arm. She stared up at Warren, her mind whirling in confusion. It was such a shock to see him here in front of the holiday crowd, after she'd accepted so completely the fact that he was gone and would never be back.

Sara gazed hungrily at his tall body, and the clean planes of his handsome face.

Oh, I love you, she told him silently through the hushed murmur of the crowd. *Warren, my darling, I love you so much....*

Gradually the significance of his presence began to dawn on her. She tensed and stared at him in awe, waiting for him to speak.

The rustle and stir of the crowd, too, died down after a moment. People drifted quietly nearer the carousel, drawn from all over the square and up and down the crowded streets of the town. Soon most of the population was massed in a semicircle around the glittering carousel looking expectantly at the man who stood leaning against one of the jewelled black horses.

Warren cleared his throat, fingered the horse's bridle for a reluctant moment and then started to speak.

"I reckon all you folks know who I am," he began. "And I know a lot of you have been upset to have me around the past couple of months, because you didn't know what I was up to."

The tall man shifted on his deck of hardwood while the people watched him, wide-eyed and silent, too startled to make any reaction.

"I know you had a right to be suspicious," Warren went on, clearing his throat again. "I was a real hell-raiser back in the days when I lived in this town. I caused a lot of people a whole lot of pain, and ever since I've been looking for a way to say..."

His voice faltered and he paused for a moment, surveying the crowd with a look of tense unhappiness. Then he squared his shoulders and went on.

"I've been wanting to tell you all how sorry I am," Warren finished simply. "But it's a real hard thing to do."

Another ripple of surprise ran through the crowd. The faces that looked up at him now were less suspicious, more quietly interested. Sara could even sense a subtle growing warmth in the crowd, and she held her breath as he began to speak again.

"Life's been real good to me," Warren told the people massed below him. "I invented a few little gadgets that brought me a whole lot of money, and the idea's been growing in my mind that someday I'd like to give something back to the town to make up for all those things I did wrong. After a while I thought about the old carousel, and then I started hunting for it.''

He went on quietly, telling them the history of their carousel. He told of Franz Koning, the brilliant German artist who'd carved all the horses on a commission from the Hill Country counties, and the glorious history of the carousel, then its sad demise and long slide into disrepair and obscurity.

Finally, in a calm, unassuming voice, he told how he'd hired detectives to track down the missing horses, engineers to design the shafts and levers, experts to simulate the organ music in a modern electronic instrument, and how he'd brought it all together out in the old abandoned barn, with the expert help of Hans Keller.

"It was fun," he concluded wistfully, looking down at the assembled townspeople with a shy smile, "and I hope you all have as much fun with it through the years as I did putting it together. And now I'll go and leave you to it," he concluded abruptly, his face turning remote and cautious once more.

But they wouldn't let him go. A roar came swelling out of the crowd, a solid wave of warmth and affection that wrapped around him and drew him back onto the hardwood deck where everybody could see him. Warren Trent stood there in awkward silence, looking amazed as thunderous waves of applause broke over him, rising and falling in an endless rhythm.

He dashed at his eyes and tried to smile.

"Well, thanks, folks," he muttered. "Thanks so much. You're real nice."

Sara, like many others, was brushing at her tears as she watched the astonishing scene at the old carousel. Warren Trent wasn't a threatening, sardonic mystery any longer. He was just a shy, lonely child, the boy her father had hugged after that long-ago baseball game, and he was clearly overwhelmed by the loving acceptance of his neighbors. Still, he was controlled enough that his descent into visible emotion was short-lived. Sara could see the way he pulled himself back under control, then indicated that there was something more he wanted to say.

She could see as well, looking up at him with eyes softened and made clearer by love, just how remarkably he'd changed since the last time she spoke to him. His face was calm and peaceful now, and his eyes had a gentle clarity and a deep settled look of contentment that she'd never seen in him before.

After all those lost and wandering years, he'd found a way to make peace with his past. Warren Trent, Sara realized with a warm flood of happiness, had finally come home.

He moved close to the edge of the deck and gazed into the crowd, then turned back to look at Hans Keller, who stood near the centre of the ride, poised to pull back the throttle and set the ponies in motion.

"All set, Hans?" Warren called.

The little man nodded, his ponytail bobbing, while the townspeople looked up at him with curiosity and new respect.

"Well," Warren went on, "this is the very first ride for this old carousel, and there are a few real special people I'd like to have up here for the occasion."

He paused, looking anxiously into the crowd, his eyes moving from face to face. Suddenly his dark features lighted with that rare boyish smile.

"Carlie Pollock," he said gently. "That's one little girl who deserves the first ride on one of these ponies, because Carlie and her mama were the ones who gave us this old tiger here, when nobody in the world knew where to find it."

The townspeople gazed in wonder at the snarling tiger in his royal purple saddle while Carlie limped forward, her face luminous with excitement. Warren bent to lift her with an easy motion and placed her on the jeweled black horse, kissing her cheek tenderly as he settled her in place.

Carlie gripped the fluted brass rod and smiled proudly at the people below, not even conscious of the heavy black boot that made her limp and struggle through life. Today, Carlie was a graceful queen on a royal charger, haughty and beautiful, riding in stately procession before legions of her adoring subjects.

June and Ellen Pollock slowly mounted the steps of the carousel, summoned by Warren. June helped her grandmother down into the dragon seat next to the tiger, then settled herself beside the old lady, resting one arm companionably across the tiger's broad striped back.

Sara watched them with a misty smile, thinking how much alike June and that tiger were. They were both beautiful and strong, fierce but soft, with hidden depths of riches and quality that you had to work so hard to discover.

June caught Sara's eye and grinned down at her with such gentle affection that Sara was once more in danger of dissolving into tears.

"And a couple of others," Warren went on. "First, there's my brother, Vernon Trent, who was the best brother any boy could have. Vern," he said simply, looking down at his brother's face in the crowd, "I always loved you. I'm sorry I was such a little bastard all those years. And I love your wife, too," he added. "She's the best thing that's ever happened to you. Come on, you two."

Vernon Trent's face reflected his deep emotion as he grasped his wife's hand and pushed through the crowd to the carousel. He and Carolyn both paused to embrace Warren, then turned with expressions of awe to look at the rows of exquisite carved ponies.

With the calm expertise of a lifetime of horsemanship, Carolyn Trent vaulted into a scarlet saddle inlaid with gold and jewels, then watched with a loving smile as her husband heaved himself cheerfully onto the gray pony beside her. Carolyn turned and waved happily to the crowd, her golden hair rich in the morning light, her face glowing with excitement, so that she looked as young as little Carlie while they waited for the music to begin.

Warren, though, was not yet finished. "There's somebody in this crowd," he said quietly, "who's always been real good to me. In fact, he went a long way to helping set me on the right track, even though he never knew it. But now I want to thank him for his kindness, and for being such a good, loving friend to a boy who was a whole world of trouble."

Warren paused awkwardly and the crowd glanced around in puzzled silence, waiting for him to continue.

"Bubba Gibson," Warren said softly, "would you come up, old friend, and bring your wife and grandkids?"

Bubba tensed in shock when his name was spoken, and his broad face turned pale with alarm. Sara saw how he glanced wildly around him, looking for an escape, longing to plunge into the obscurity of the crowd. Mary, it seemed, noticed as well, because she took her husband's arm firmly in her small hands and drew him forward.

Sara's heart swelled and ached with helpless sympathy when she saw how hesitant her father's steps were, how his big shoulders quivered with fear as he moved slowly to the front of the crowd. He mounted the steps of the carousel beside Mary, with David and Laurie at his side, and turned nervously to face the assembled citizens of Crystal Creek.

A profound silence fell, so still despite all the people that the chatter of birdsong was clearly audible in the rustling trees overhead.

"Hey, Bubba!" J. T. McKinney shouted suddenly from the depths of the silent crowd. "Welcome home, cowboy! We've all missed you."

Other voices joined in, rising together in a wave of warmth and welcome, a wall of love that left Bubba trembling with emotion just as Warren had been a few minutes earlier.

He gazed helplessly at his friends and neighbors, who were shouting and applauding, making the morning ring with happiness.

Mary looked up at her husband, her face shining with love and pride.

Bubba tried to speak, but the effort was too much for him. He turned aside with shaking hands to lift Laurie onto one of the horses, then David.

"You, too, Bubba," Brock Munroe called genially from the crowd. "We want to see you and Mary on those ponies, too."

Another roar went up. Bubba grinned down at the crowd with a flash of his old sparkle. "You do, hey? Think I forgot how to ride over the winter, do you? Well, watch this!"

He lifted Mary onto a white steed carrying a pheasant behind the saddle, then swung himself with easy grace onto the horse next to her, settling his big body in the saddle and waving his hat at the crowd.

They beamed and shouted again, overcome with delight.

Sara stood alone in the crowd, clapping and shouting along with them, so lost in happiness that she had a misty, floating sensation, strangely disconnected from the world around her.

Warren lifted a hand in warning as Hans moved over again to start the carousel. "One more person," he said, his eyes combing the throng of people with blazing intensity.

He found Sara's face in the crowd, and their eyes met and held for an endless moment that left her shaken and full of wonder.

"There's a woman here today who taught me what it means to love someone," Warren told the crowd quietly. "She showed me what forgiveness is, and hope and love and sacrifice. She said things to me that nobody else has ever said, and forced me to think about my life in a different way, and I owe her the whole world. I hope she'll give me a lifetime or two, and we'll see if that's long enough for me to pay her back."

His eyes remained fixed on Sara's, drawing her forward. She pressed through the crowd, her steps halting and uncertain, but the people moved aside to let her pass. The silence was profound, almost breathless, as she mounted the carousel and Warren gathered her into his arms. The onlookers didn't start to cheer and applaud until he lifted her onto a dainty sorrel horse. Then he stood close to her on the deck, his arms wrapped around her, and motioned Hans to start the carousel.

Music spilled into the bright morning air, lively polkas and marches and ragtime tunes. The horses began to circle, slowly at first, then with more speed until they were just a blur of color and motion, of gold and jewels and rainbow light.

Sara felt herself drowning in happiness, lost in a sweet, spinning world of gaiety and splendor, filled with a deep contentment that had no end. Warren rode beside her and held her close in the circle of his arms, kissing her face and neck. The strength and scent of him, that warm masculinity that she'd always loved, were somehow part of this wonderful day, of the music and flowers and dancing ponies, the happiness of the crowd and the excited laughter of the children.

"Come around to the other side," Sara murmured to Warren as the sorrel horse rode up and down in sprightly rhythm. "You're on the wrong side. You won't be able to catch the brass ring."

"Oh, Sara," he whispered huskily, his breath warm against her cheek. "Sara, darling, I've already caught the brass ring. And I'm never letting go, not as long as I live."

The ponies circled and leaped, then gradually slowed while the people clapped with delight, and children scampered onto the deck for the next ride.

The music started up again, drifting past the soft white clouds, past the blazing summer sun, through the sky and off among the remote stars, carrying with it a merry twinkle from a bright distant world.

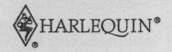

HARLEQUIN®

Harlequin proudly presents four stories about
convenient but not *conventional* reasons for marriage:

- To save your godchildren from a
  "wicked stepmother"

- To help out your eccentric aunt — and her sexy
  business partner

- To bring an old man happiness by making him
  a grandfather

- To escape from a ghostly existence and become a
  real woman

Marriage By Design — four brand-new stories by four
of Harlequin's most popular authors:

**CATHY GILLEN THACKER
JASMINE CRESSWELL
GLENDA SANDERS
MARGARET CHITTENDEN**

Don't miss this exciting collection of stories about
marriages of convenience. Available in April, wherever
Harlequin books are sold.

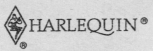

Where do you find hot Texas nights, smooth Texas charm and dangerously sexy cowboys?

If you missed any Crystal Creek titles here's your chance to order them:

Crystal Creek®

#82513	DEEP IN THE HEART by Barbara Kaye	$3.99
#82514	COWBOYS AND CABERNET by Margot Dalton	$3.99
#82515	AMARILLO BY MORNING by Bethany Campbell	$3.99
#82516	WHITE LIGHTNING by Sharon Brondos	$3.99
#82517	EVEN THE NIGHTS ARE BETTER by Margot Dalton	$3.99
#82518	AFTER THE LIGHTS GO OUT by Barbara Kaye	$3.99
#82519	HEARTS AGAINST THE WIND by Kathy Clark	$3.99
#82520	THE THUNDER ROLLS by Bethany Campbell	$3.99
#82521	GUITARS, CADILLACS by Cara West	$3.99
#82522	STAND BY YOUR MAN by Kathy Clark	$3.99
#82523	NEW WAY TO FLY by Margot Dalton	$3.99
#82524	EVERYBODY'S TALKIN' by Barbara Kaye	$3.99

(limited quantities available on certain titles)

TOTAL AMOUNT	$
POSTAGE & HANDLING	$
($1.00 for one book, 50¢ for each additional)	
APPLICABLE TAXES*	$ _____
TOTAL PAYABLE	$ _____
(check or money order—please do not send cash)	

To order, complete this form and send it, along with a check or money order for the total above, payable to Harlequin Books, to: *In the U.S.*: 3010 Walden Avenue, P.O. Box 9047, Buffalo, NY 14269-9047; *In Canada*: P.O. Box 613, Fort Erie, Ontario, L2A 5X3.

Name: _____

Address: _____ City: _____

State/Prov.: _____ Zip/Postal Code:_____

*New York residents remit applicable sales taxes.
 Canadian residents remit applicable GST and provincial taxes.

CCREEKB1

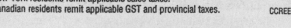
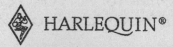

HARLEQUIN®

HARLEQUIN®

Don't miss these Harlequin favorites by some of our most distinguished authors!
And now, you can receive a discount by ordering two or more titles!